PRAISE FOR

Sun and Moon, Ice and Snow

A Book Sense Pick

"A vivid, well-crafted, poetic fantasy for readers who have enjoyed works by Robin McKinley and Esther Friesner or who are ready to move from Gail Carson Levine's fairy-tale adaptations to more sophisticated fare." —*Booklist*

"Perfectly delicious to read." —*Kirkus Reviews*

"*Sun and Moon, Ice and Snow* is one of those rare books that can be enjoyed by families, not just the children." —CurledUpKids.com

"George creates a visually stunning story that is part fantasy and part fairy tale." —*VOYA*

"George has a knack for storytelling, and she is at her best when describing her fully imagined world of ice bears, fauns, gargoyles, and selkies." —*BCCB*

"George demonstrates her mastery of both Norwegian folklore and storytelling by taking an old yet familiar story and making it captivating from start to finish." —*SLJ*

Also by Jessica Day George

Dragon Slippers
Dragon Flight
Dragon Spear

Princess of the Midnight Ball

Sun and Moon, Ice and Snow

Jessica Day George

BLOOMSBURY

NEW YORK BERLIN LONDON SYDNEY

Published by Bloomsbury U.S.A. Children's Books
175 Fifth Avenue, New York, New York 10010

The Library of Congress has cataloged the hardcover edition as follows:
George, Jessica Day.
Sun and moon, ice and snow/ Jessica Day George. — 1ˢᵗ U.S. ed.
p.   cm.
Summary: A girl travels east of the sun and west of the moon
to free her beloved prince from a magic spell.
ISBN-13: 978-1-59990-109-1 • ISBN-10: 1-59990-109-9 (hardcover)
[1. Fairy tales. 2. Folklore—Norway.]
I. East of the sun and west of the moon. English. II. Title.
PZ8.G3295Su 2008   [398.2]—dc22   2007030848

ISBN-13: 978-1-59990-328-6 • ISBN-10: 1-59990-328-8 (paperback)

Typeset by Westchester Book Composition
Printed in the U.S.A. by Quad/Graphics Fairfield
4 6 8 10 9 7 5

For my parents:
You gave me life, you gave me love,
you gave me a plane ticket to Norway.
Thank you.

Part 1

Woodcutter's Youngest Daughter

Chapter 1

Long ago and far away in the land of ice and snow, there came a time when it seemed that winter would never end. The months when summer should have given the land respite were cold and damp, and the winter months were snow filled and colder still. The people said the cold had lasted a hundred years, and feared that it would last a hundred more. It was not a natural winter, and no one knew what witch or troll had caused the winds to howl so fiercely.

There was nothing to do in the long nights when the sun never rose and the day never came but huddle together by the fire and dream of warmth. As a consequence, many children were born, and as food grew scarcer, the people grew even more desperate.

It seemed that there was no bleaker place than the house of the woodcutter Jarl Oskarson. Jarl himself was a kind man, and devoted to his family. But Jarl and his wife, Frida, had been blessed, or burdened, depending on one's outlook, with nine children. Five of them were boys, who were a help to their parents, but four were girls, which displeased Frida greatly. She had no use for girls, she would say with a sniff as she sat by the fire. They were empty-headed and would one day cost the poverty-stricken family the price of a dowry. No one dared point out to her that the four girls did all of the cooking, washing, and mending, leaving Frida with ample leisure time.

So disappointed was Frida at seeing that her ninth labor had resulted in yet another worthless girl that she thrust the screaming baby into the arms of her eldest daughter, Jorunn, and refused to give her a name. Because the naming of daughters was a task for mothers, and her mother had refused that task, the ninth child of Jarl Oskarson remained nameless. They simply called her *pika,* which meant "girl" in the language of the North.

The nameless state of their last child worried Jarl. Unnamed children could not be baptized, and the trolls had been known to steal unbaptized babies. Jarl loved his children despite the family's poverty, and so he set out gifts to appease the troll-folk. Cheeses, honey-sweetened milk, almond pastries, and other delicacies that they could barely afford. Frida called it a waste, for she did not believe in trolls, but Jarl spent most of his days deep in the forest, and he had seen troubling things there. When the food disappeared, he held it up as evidence that such creatures were real, but Frida just sniffed that it was more likely their neighbors' dogs were growing fat while she starved.

When the pika was nine, the eldest child, Hans Peter, came home from the sea. He was a tall young man, blue-eyed and handsome, or at least he had been handsome before he left. Now, after five years aboard the merchant ship *Sea Dragon*, he was stooped and tired, his hair more silver than gold, and his blue eyes had a haunted look. He had traveled far, he said, and seen some things more wonderful than he could describe and others too terrible to relate. He had been injured on a journey so far to the north that sun and moon seemed to touch in the sky as they passed, and now he was home to stay.

This vexed Frida greatly, because she had been very pleased to send her eldest son into the world. There had been one less mouth to feed and the promise of wages sent home. But now Hans Peter sat all day in their cottage, carving strange figures on the firewood before dropping it into the hearth. Hans Peter's injury must have been healed before he returned home, or perhaps, Jarl told the others, it had not been an injury of the body. Whatever it had been, there was no sign of it now, save for the young man's melancholy.

But the pika worshipped him. She thought that her brother was still the handsomest man in the district, even though everyone else said that title had surely passed to the next brother down, Torst (for all the woodcutter's children were fair). But Torst liked pulling the youngest girl's braids and teasing her, while Hans Peter was soft-spoken and kind.

He had learned some of the language of the Englanders on his travels, and he called the youngest girl "lass." It still meant nothing more than "girl," but it sounded prettier than "pika."

"Aye, lass," he would say, holding up a piece of wood he had been carving, to show her the strange, angular marks upon it. "This is 'bear.' And this here"—pointing to another—"is 'whale.'" And then he would cast the wood into the fire. And the lass would nod solemnly and snuggle close to listen to one of his rare stories about the life of men at sea.

Jorunn, who, as the eldest girl, had the charge of teaching the younger children their letters, scoffed at the lass when she insisted that Hans Peter's carvings were a sort of language. "It's not the language of England, that's for sure," she retorted, tossing another one of the carvings into the fire and using a bit of charred stick to write the alphabet on the scrubbed table. "For the priest says that every Christian land uses the same letters. And the priest went to school in Christiania." Her words carried a solemn weight: Christiania was the capital, and the priest was the only person for miles around who had been there.

But Hans Peter continued to show his little lass the carvings, and she continued to study them with big, solemn eyes. Of all the children, she alone had dark brown eyes, though her hair was more reddish than gold, which was not uncommon in that family. Before it went gray, Jarl had boasted the same color hair, and four of the nine children had inherited it.

When the lass was eleven, Jorunn married a farmer's son who was too poor himself to expect much in the way of dowry, and they moved into an extra room in his father's house. That same year, Hans Peter traded some of his more commonplace carvings to a tinker from the south, so the family got the flour and salt they would need to last another winter. He hadn't particularly enjoyed making wooden bowls and spoons, but the patterns of fish and birds he had carved around the edges of the bowls had made the lass clap her hands with pleasure.

Frida was marginally appeased, and a little of Jarl's burden was eased. And the lass grew, and Hans Peter carved. And the winter continued, without sign of spring.

Chapter 2

In the North, they say that the third son is the lucky son. He is the one who will travel far, and see magic done. The third son of King Olav Hawknose had ridden the north wind into battle and returned home victorious, weighted down with gold and married to a foreign princess. In tales the third son is called the ash lad, or Askeladden, and he is both clever and lucky.

Hoping to inspire her own third son to such heights, Frida had named the boy Askeladden. The woodcutter's wife dreamed of one day going to live in the palace her own ash lad would build for her with the gold he found in a hollow log. Then he would save an enchanted princess and bring her to the palace to live with him and his doting mother.

Askeladden Jarlson was not the hero of legend and tale, however, and everyone but his mother knew it. He preferred drinking the raw ale of the mountains and dodging work to living off the land or his wits. And, as he told the young lass with a wink and a nudge, he much preferred saucy farmers' daughters to icy princesses.

This particular afternoon, Hans Peter had moved over on the bench and given the lass the place closest to the fire. He usually sat there for the convenience of the light and so that he could throw his shavings into the fire with an easy toss, but he did not need the heat. The cold did not seem to bite into his bones as it did to the rest of the family. He said it was because he had been to a place that was colder than hell, and nothing after that would ever be as chill.

"Here, lass," her eldest brother said, holding up a bit of wood. "What's this then?"

By twelve she could recognize many of the strange symbols. "Reindeer," she replied promptly. "But don't show Mother; she'll be so angry."

Hans Peter winked at her, in a much friendlier way than Askel had. "Don't you worry. Before you can wrinkle your pretty nose, this will be a spoon with flowers 'round the handle."

The door of their small cottage burst open, and fifteen-year-old Einar came rushing in. He left the door open in his haste, letting in the wind and snow. He stood in the middle of the main room, hands on knees, and wheezed for a few minutes.

The rest of the family, those who were at home at any rate, stared at him. It was some moments before sixteen-year-old Katla ran to close the door. She wheeled around to continue staring at Einar as soon as the heavy door was safely latched.

"In—in—in the vill-village," he gasped. "Jens Pederson said he saw it."

"Saw what?" Askel looked up from the corner where he was polishing his worn boots.

"Saints preserve me from half-witted children," Frida murmured to herself, and pulled her tattered shawl tighter about her shoulders. She picked up her knitting, ignoring Einar.

"The—the—the—," Einar stammered.

"The—the—the," Askel mocked, and went back to his polishing.

"The white reindeer," Einar spit out, making his family freeze in astonishment.

Stories of the white reindeer were as plentiful as stories of lucky third sons. Everybody knew that if you found the white reindeer, it would give you one gift. And what wonderful gifts the reindeer had granted! Fabulous dowries for poor fishermen's daughters, sacks of gold, new houses, kettles that were always full to the brim with delectable foods, seven-league boots, golden ships . . . and many more wondrous things.

Everyone was on their feet now, jaws agape. Everyone except for Hans Peter, who shook his head and went back to carving. Askeladden crossed the room in two strides and grabbed Einar by the shoulders, shaking the younger boy.

"You are certain? The white reindeer was seen?"

Einar nodded, struck dumb once more.

"Where?"

"To—to the east, past Karl Henrykson's farm. By the three waterfalls."

Askel released his brother and grabbed up the boots he had been polishing. Thrusting his feet into them, he pulled on one of the patched parkas that hung by the door. Then he took down a pair of skis and poles.

"Don't wait up, Mother," he said gaily, and went out into the snow.

The other children, who until now had not said a word, all scrambled to follow. Frida made no remark as all her remaining children save Hans Peter and the lass divided up the warm clothes and skis and went out into the cold. When the last of them were gone, she turned to Hans Peter and the lass, displeased.

"Well, your brothers and sisters are determined to make this family's fortune, but I see that you are not," she snapped. She stalked over to the hearth and took up the spoon that Katla had been using to stir the soup.

"The little one is too young to be off in the forest chasing moonbeams," Hans Peter said. "And a nameless child should never wander in the woods."

"And what's your excuse, a great big man like you? Rather sit all day by the fire like an old woman warming your lazy bones?"

"The lass is too young, and I am too old," Hans Peter

said mildly. "I went chasing moonbeams aboard the *Sea Dragon*, and I have always regretted it."

The little lass looked from her grumbling mother to her sad-eyed brother and didn't know what to do. She could remain here, she supposed. As Hans Peter had said, she was too young to be out in the cold, and night was falling. But what a glorious thing it would be to catch the white reindeer, the lass thought, and to ask it to make Hans Peter happy again.

"I'm going too," she announced, and got up from her place by the fire. She felt a little thrill of fear, but thought that if any trolls confronted her, she would claim to be her sister Annifrid.

"What?" Hans Peter looked startled. He dropped the piece of wood he was carving and took one of her hands in his own. "My little lass, this is not a good thing to do."

"I'll be all right," she told him, mustering confidence she did not feel.

"There are no parkas left," Hans Peter pointed out.

"I'll use a blanket," the lass said after a moment's consideration. She had set her mind to finding that reindeer, for Hans Peter's sake, and nothing would deter her.

"You'll freeze to death," their mother said shrilly. "If you'd wanted a parka to wear, you should have moved faster. Come and stir this soup; I still have stockings to darn."

"No." The lass put her chin up. "I will find the white reindeer."

"Then wear mine," Hans Peter said. He climbed up to the loft and the lass heard him rummaging in his sea chest. He rarely opened it, and she could hear the hinges squeak in protest when the lid closed. Hans Peter descended the ladder and held out a parka and a pair of boots. "These will keep you warm. And safe."

"Oh, I couldn't!" Her hands rose to her cheeks, stunned by the beauty of the items he held before her.

The boots and parka were lined with the finest, whitest fur she had ever seen. On the outside they were of softly felted wool as white as new snow, embroidered with bands of bloodred and azure blue. The spiky patterns of the embroidery matched the style of the carvings that Hans Peter made, but none of these symbols were familiar to the lass.

"You can and you will," he said, holding them out. "The boots are too big for you, of course. But if you keep your old boots on underneath, they'll work well enough. Strap on some snowshoes and you'll be able to walk like a bear. And the parka will cover you from stem to stern, which is a good thing in this cold."

"Those things are too fine for her," their mother snapped, her gleaming eyes checking the seams and verifying the quality. "We could sell them to the next trader for a pretty penny, and no mistake." She crossed her arms under her bosom. "Why did you not say before that you had such things to trade? And here the family is going wanting!"

"I'll not sell these for love nor money," Hans Peter said. His eyes held the dead look that they'd had when he first arrived home, the look that was only now beginning to fade.

"But," Frida began.

"I'll not sell these for love nor money," her eldest son repeated. "I earned them with blood, and I'll part with them when death takes me, but not before. The lass shall have them tonight, and after that, back into the chest they go!"

Not wanting to argue with him in this strange, fierce mood, the lass took the proffered clothing and put it on. The parka extended well past her knees and the boots rose to meet it. With her own scuffed boots underneath, they were just snug enough, and she had to push the heavy sleeves of the parka back in order to use her hands.

"I've never been so warm," she said in wonder. She had never known what it was like to feel the glow over your whole body that you felt on your cheeks and hands when you sat close to the fire.

Her brother pulled the hood up, tucking in her hair, and pulled the ribbons to tighten it around her face. "God willing, one day you shall be this warm all the time," he told her, his voice gruff with emotion. Then he held back the sleeves while she tugged on her mittens, and she went off in search of the white reindeer.

Chapter 3

It did not take long for the young lass to find the trail of the other searchers. The snow had become so trampled and muddied that it was hard to see what they were following; any signs left by the white reindeer had long been obliterated. Even through the thick, fur-lined hood of Hans Peter's parka she could hear hounds baying and men shouting and cursing. She rolled her eyes at the foolishness of it. Any animal would bolt to hear such a din, and the white reindeer was a creature out of nature, a magical beast with the intelligence of a man. It would be long gone by now.

The searchers had gone straight up the side of the mountain, and the girl could see them now, struggling between the dense pine trees. So she went around the base instead, following a small stream that wound between the trees. The edges were iced over, but the middle still ran free where the flow was fast moving.

She was so enjoying the sensation of being warm, and making such good time walking along the bank, that she didn't realize what she was seeing when she rounded a boulder and came upon the white reindeer. The boulder had concealed a small, dense thicket. And caught in that thicket was the legendary creature itself.

It was as white, or whiter, than the snow around it. As white, or whiter, than the parka she wore. As white, or whiter, than anything she had ever seen. Its great rack of antlers was dark and burnished like polished wood, and its rolling eyes were blacker than soot.

"Oh, you poor thing!" The lass went forward to see if she could help. "You're trapped."

From the tracks in the snow, the reindeer had been coming down the side of the mountain and had slid down a small drop-off into the brambles. The animal snorted and tried to swipe at her with its entangled antlers as she approached, but the lass just clucked her tongue.

"I can help you get free, just hold still now," she said in a soothing voice.

All thought of holding the creature there until it granted her wish was gone. The lass had a tender heart and hated to see an animal suffer. The brambles had scratched the reindeer terribly, and dark red drops were staining the fine white pelt. Its breath made clouds in the air, and its hooves struck sparks on the stones beneath the churned snow.

"Sh, sh, sh," the girl soothed. "I'll get you free."

Moving slowly, she sidled up to the animal and took hold of a long bramble cane that had wound itself several times around the left branch of the reindeer's antlers. The canes were still green at their heart, which was bad for the reindeer because it meant that they couldn't be easily snapped off.

As soon as she let go of the first cane, it sprang back, pricking the back of her hand even through her thick woolen mitten. It struck the reindeer on the side of the head, making the animal bellow and twist.

"Stop that," the lass ordered. "You're making things worse!"

Realizing that there was no other way, she opened her parka to get the little belt-knife she wore. The rush of cold air that came in froze her ribs until she thought that taking a deep breath would crack them.

Seeing the knife out of the corner of one rolling eye, the white reindeer stamped and bellowed, but it couldn't move very far. It was now so securely wrapped with brambles that it would never get itself free.

"Hush now," the lass said, "this is for the brambles, not for you."

Sawing through the canes was tedious and snagged her mittens badly. She took them off, but her fingers quickly became too stiff to be much good, and she had to put the mittens back on and blow down into them until her fingertips regained feeling. All the while she softly sang the lullaby that Jorunn had sung to her when she was little. The singing soothed the reindeer, and it calmed under her hands, which made it much easier to untangle the creature's antlers. She tried to cut as few canes as possible, seeing each severed branch as a handful fewer cloudberries to find in the months to come. But it was more important to get the poor beast free.

When the last of the canes was loose and the reindeer could raise its head and rattle its great antlers at the sky, the lass gave a whoop of delight. The white reindeer stepped delicately from the circle of mangled brambles and turned to face her.

"Thank you," it said.

The young girl's jaw dropped. She had been so absorbed with freeing the reindeer, she had forgotten that this was not just any reindeer. This was a magical creature . . . one that could grant wishes.

"You're welcome," she said, feeling suddenly shy. She hadn't caught the animal, but maybe, if she asked nicely . . . ? She made a tentative motion with one hand. Perhaps she should grab hold of its antlers, while it still stood so close? But she couldn't bring herself to do it.

"I shall grant you a boon," the reindeer said. Its voice was throaty, yet musical, and it made the girl's heart ache to hear it, as if she were hearing beautiful music that she would never hear again.

"Oh, please, that would be wonderful," the lass said. She made as if to clap her mittened hands, remembered just in time that she was still holding the knife, and hastily dropped it into one of the parka's pockets.

"What do you wish?"

"I wish for my brother Hans Peter to be made whole," the girl said, breathless with hope.

"He is ill?"

"He went away to sea, and when he came back, he was . . . different. Faded. Sad. Gray." It was hard to describe the change: there was nothing specific, just a general sense of wrongness when you compared him now to how he had been.

"Hmm, a puzzle," said the white reindeer. It stamped and shifted its feet in the dusk. The girl moved too, for now that its head was unencumbered, the huge animal was taller than she and its antlers spread wider than her outstretched arms. "What is that?" The reindeer's voice was sharp. With its velvet muzzle, it pointed at the sleeve of Hans Peter's parka.

The lass looked down. The moon was rising, and in its milky light the embroidery on the parka stood out like the dried drops of blood on the reindeer's silky pelt. She frowned at the embroidery. Some of the symbols looked half-familiar, and she hazarded a guess at some that lay around the cuff. "A journey? Ice and snow?"

"That is the writing of the trolls," the reindeer trumpeted. It recoiled from her. "You have been cursed by the trolls!"

"No, no, *I* haven't," the girl protested. "It's my brother's parka, and his boots. He brought them back from his sea voyages. Please help him!" She held out her hands to the reindeer in appeal.

"There is nothing I can do," the reindeer said, shivering and flinging droplets of blood into the snow around them. "If the markings on this garment are true, then what has harmed him is well beyond my power."

The lass began to cry. Hans Peter, cursed? Then there was nothing anyone could do for him, and he would have to spend his life there, under the bitter eyes of their mother, haunted by this evil. She sagged to her knees.

"Tch, tch, little one," the reindeer said in a kind voice. It whuffled her shoulder with its soft lips. "Is there nothing you want for yourself? A pretty gown? A dowry? I am usually asked for such things by human girls. Would you like a handsome suitor?"

The girl gave a wobbly laugh and smeared the tears away from her eyes. "I don't think I'll need a dowry, and I doubt that any suitor would court me for long," she told the reindeer. "I'm an unwanted fourth daughter. I don't even have a name."

"Then I shall give you one," the white reindeer said. "A creature of such generous spirit should have a name of her own, or the trolls might steal her away and use that fine spirit to fuel their dark magic."

And then the reindeer leaned its velvet muzzle close to the girl's ear, and named her a name in the language of the great beasts of the forest and mountain, the sea and plain and desert hot, which is the true language of all creation.

The young lass, who now had a name to treasure in her heart, lifted shining eyes to the white reindeer. "Thank you, thank you, a thousand times thank you."

Higher up on the side of the mountain, the girl heard the sounds of shouting and the crash of dogs and men bullying their way through the underbrush.

"Go, hurry," she told the white reindeer.

The huge animal bent its head and pressed its black nose to the center of the lass's forehead, then turned and ran off into the night. The lass stayed where she was, on her knees beside the little stream, until the searchers found her.

"Pika, what are you doing out here?" Askeladden grabbed her arm and hauled her to her feet. "Did you see which way the reindeer went?"

She blinked at him, thinking fast. The others clustered around, holding their torches high. A few even carried spears, as though they thought it would be better to wound or possibly kill the reindeer than let it get away.

"What are you talking about?" The lass looked around innocently. "Askel? Why did you come this way?" She pointed at the tracks in the snow leading away from where they stood. "I thought you were looking for a *white* reindeer?"

"We are, you silly girl!" Askel shouted. "Did you see it?"

"That wasn't the white reindeer; it was a brown one.

It got caught in the brambles and I set it free." She pulled out of his grip. "I thought it might be one of ours, but it was wild and ran off."

"A *brown* reindeer?" Askel sagged, dismay writ large across his face. "I saw it from the top of the hill! I could have sworn it was white."

"It had snow caught in its fur," she said.

"Here, Askel, you've been leading us a merry chase, and to no purpose," one of the other men shouted, disgusted. The others were grumbling as well, and a few had started off in other directions, looking for signs of their quarry.

"Gah!" Askel ran his hands over his face in irritation. "We'll never find anything in this dark, even with the moon," he complained. He grunted and turned back to his sister. "You'd best be on home, pika. It's not safe for you out here, you know that." Then his eyes fixed on what she was wearing. They narrowed, and he sucked in his breath. "Where did you get that parka?" His own coat was a motley collection of old furs and bits of wool, more patches than whole cloth.

"It's Hans Peter's," she said, backing away from the greedy look on his face. "And he said I could borrow it, just for today."

"So that's what he's been hiding in that old chest," her brother mused, a hard look on his face. "I wonder what else he brought back from his journeying."

"Nothing for you," the girl retorted, but Askeladden

wasn't listening to her. He was staring across the stream, a calculating look on his face.

"I'm going home," she said, but her brother didn't answer. She didn't repeat herself, but simply turned and made her way back along the stream and down the lower slope of the mountain to her family's little cottage.

"Well?" Her mother was standing by the fire, looking angry.

"I found a brown reindeer," the girl said, taking off the beautiful parka and holding it out to Hans Peter.

"A *brown* reindeer does us little good," her mother snorted. "We have brown reindeer in plenty in the barn, or didn't you know?" She went back to the soup pot.

Hans Peter took the parka from the lass and knelt down to help pull off the boots. The girl tapped him on the shoulder and, when he looked up, jerked her head at the ladder to the loft.

He nodded, understanding. "Help me carry these back up, will you?" he said for their mother's benefit.

She picked up the right boot, he took the left, and she followed him up the ladder. He did not open his sea chest in front of her, but sat on it, and motioned for her to put the boot down by the foot of his cot. She set it on the floor beside its mate with reverence, then sat on the end of the cot so that she could speak low and still be heard.

"Askel saw me in these things," she said, feeling

ashamed, as though she had betrayed a secret. "He won-dered what else you had brought back from your journeys."

"He was after me before, when I first got back," Hans Peter said, shaking his head. "Ah, well, it looks as though I'm up for another round of pestering." He saw her stricken face and smiled. "Don't worry, my lass. Askel is persistent, but I'm stubborn. He won't find anything I don't want him to." He rubbed his hands to-gether briskly as though washing away the topic. "Now. I don't suppose you caught sight of the white reindeer, did you?"

The lass had thought to tell him the same lie she had told Askel and their mother, but her expression gave her away. She couldn't lie to Hans Peter, not when he was al-ways so kind to her, and had let her wear his special parka and boots.

"You did see it," Hans Peter breathed. His face bright-ened. "Was it magnificent?"

"It was," she agreed, bouncing a little on the cot at the memory.

"How close did you get?"

"Very close." She gave a muffled little laugh. "Very."

He marveled at her. "You caught the white reindeer?"

"Some brambles caught it for me," she whispered, leaning in even closer. "And I felt so badly for it that I freed it without a care for whether it was white or brown. And so it—" But then she stopped. It had granted her a boon, not the one she had first asked for, but a priceless gift nonetheless.

"It granted your wish?" Hans Peter waited for her nod. "I'm guessing that you didn't wish for a new cottage or dinner not to be burned ever again," he said with a soft laugh.

The girl closed her eyes, feeling foolish. Of course, she should have asked for a new house! Or a soup pot that never ran empty. Or a purse of gold.

"It did offer me a rich dowry," she mumbled.

"But you didn't take it, because you're too wise for that," he said, patting her hand. "Too wise to wish this lot of ingrates to have a golden palace."

"I should have—"

"You should *not* have," he assured her. "Please tell me that, just this once, you wanted something for yourself."

"I did," she blushed, lowering her head.

"What was it, if I may ask?"

"A name."

There was silence then. For a long time, brother and sister sat together, not moving. Then Hans Peter let go of her cold hand and put his arm around her, holding her tight to his warm side. "Ah, my little lass," he said finally. "What a treasure to give you, you who have not even a name to call your own."

"Would you . . . would you like to hear it?" she choked out. She had not thought of how awkward it was going to be, telling her parents that she had a name after all these years. And what if they asked where she had gotten it? It was a beautiful name, but anyone who heard it would know that it was not from these lands.

"No," Hans Peter said quietly. "You keep it safe; keep it close inside your heart. There are places in this world where not having a name is a lucky thing, a saving thing." His gaze was directed far beyond their cabin walls.

The girl shivered a little, seeing the bleakness of his expression. "But why have a name if no one knows it?" she whispered.

"One day there will be a time and place for your name," he told her. "But until then, perhaps you're better off being our pika."

"Your lass."

"My lass," he agreed, tweaking a strand of her hair.

They heard the cabin door bang open, and Askel's voice roaring below. Hans Peter rolled his eyes, and his youngest sister laughed, and they went down the ladder together to face their brother.

Chapter 4

It was a little while before the lass noticed that something about her had changed. Her family did not keep a cat, and the reindeer were tended by her brother Einar. They had a few chickens, but chickens were not great conversationalists, and if the lass noticed that she could understand their cackling, it didn't stick in her mind.

It wasn't until Jorunn and her husband, Nils, came for a visit, bringing with them their half-grown hunting dog, that the lass noticed it. The dog was a leggy animal with a sweet temperament that loved to sit by the fire while Hans Peter carved. When anyone came near, it would thump its tail on the floor and give him or her a look that was almost a smile.

The second night of Jorunn's visit, the lass was making *lefse*. As she lifted one off the hot griddle with the flat stick, she heard a voice say, "That looks tasty."

Thinking it was Hans Peter, she grinned over at him. "Thank you. Do you want a bit?"

"Hmm?" Hans Peter looked up from his carving. "What did you say?"

"I asked if you wanted a bit of *lefse*."

"Not really." He made a face. "I don't like them plain."

"Then why did you say it looked tasty?" She deftly transferred the flat disk of bread to the platter on the table.

"I didn't." He gave her a puzzled look.

The girl looked around. No one else was near.

There was a thump on the floor, and the lass looked down at the half-grown pup. It was gazing up at her, wagging its tail. "Can I have a bit, if he doesn't want it?"

She looked sharply at the puppy. "Did you hear that?" She pointed the *lefse* stick at the animal, but her question was directed at Hans Peter.

"Hear what?"

"The dog asked for a bit of *lefse*."

"No, it didn't."

"Yes, I did," said the dog. Its ears drooped. "But you don't have to give me any if you don't want to."

"Hans Peter," the lass said, lowering her voice so that the others wouldn't hear. "The dog is talking to me."

"I see." He put aside the bit of wood he'd been carving and carefully sheathed his knife. Standing, he went to his youngest sister and put a hand on her shoulder. "Do you have a headache?"

"No."

"Have you eaten today?"

"Yes." She shrugged off the hand in irritation. "He's

speaking to me. I'm not sick or mad or dreaming." She pointed the stick at the dog again. "Say something else!"

"Can I have a piece before it gets cold?"

"There!" She turned triumphantly to Hans Peter. "Did you hear that?"

"No." He shook his head, but he looked thoughtful. "But I did hear it make noise. Growls and yips, like dogs do."

"But I heard the words quite clearly." She slapped down the stick in frustration. Then, seeing that her mother was looking their way, she quickly spread more batter on the hot griddle and smoothed out another *lefse* with the edge of the stick. While it was cooking, she turned her attention to the dog again. "Did you know that my brother can't understand you?" she asked in a low voice.

"No one can," the dog said easily. "I talk all the time, but you're the first person to understand." He raised a hind leg and scratched at one ear. "Your sister is nice, but I beg all day long, and she never gives me anything good." His big brown eyes fastened on the stack of *lefse* cooling on the table. "Please? Just a bit?"

The lass tore a strip off the edge of a pancake, rolled it up, and tossed it to the young dog. He caught it with a snap of his teeth and lowered his head to eat. When he was done, he looked back up at her with a sigh. "That tasted as good as it looked," he told her.

"Thank you," she said, still stunned.

"Are you still talking to the dog?" Hans Peter's bewildered expression had passed and now he looked curious.

"Yes, and he's talking back," the girl said.

"Have you ever heard an animal talk before?"

"No, I . . . wait." She pursed her lips. "This morning I could have sworn that one of the chickens said, 'Here she comes again!' when I opened the coop. But Einar and Anni were in the yard too."

"Hmm." Hans Peter crouched down beside the dog. "Can you talk to me, boy?"

The dog studied him and finally said, "I can try."

Hans Peter looked up. "It just sounded like a whine."

"He said he'd try," she reported.

"What are you two whispering about over there?" Jorunn, jolly and rosy cheeked, came over to the fireside. "Are you teaching Nils's dog a trick?" Her long-fingered hands rested on her pregnant belly with pride.

Hans Peter and his youngest sister exchanged looks. He cleared his throat. "We were trying to teach the dog to talk, but it doesn't seem to have worked."

"Oh, well! Nils says he isn't very smart."

The lass bristled at this. The dog seemed quite intelligent to her. "I think he's smart. Let's try the trick again." She winked and pointed a finger at the dog. "Speak, boy!"

The dog sat up and barked.

"Good boy!" The lass tossed it a bit of *lefse*. "Now, lie down!"

It obediently lay down on the threadbare rug.

Another bit of *lefse*. "Roll over!"

The dog rolled onto its back.

"Hah!" The lass tossed it a last bit of *lefse,* amid the cheers of her other sisters, who had crowded around to watch.

"Kindly stop feeding that animal our dinner, pika," their mother sniffed, bringing an end to the merriment.

"Yes, ma'am." The girl straightened and went back to work. Jorunn and Hans Peter gave her sympathetic looks.

"Nils!" Jorunn greeted her husband merrily when he came in with the other boys from the barn. "Only see, my littlest sister has taught the dog some tricks."

Nils laughed and came forward, and the dog dutifully performed his new feats. When their mother was not looking Jorunn crumbled a bit of yellow reindeer cheese off the wedge on the table and gave it to the dog.

"I wish you were as good with the reindeer," Einar said wistfully as they sat down to dinner. "There's something wrong with our oldest doe."

"What's that?" Jarl looked down from the head of the table. "Is she not giving the usual amount of milk?"

"She's not giving *any*," Einar grumbled. "She just tries to bite me when I come near, and after I get her hobbled and tied so that I *can* milk her, nothing comes."

"That's a concern," Jarl said, rolling some dried fish in a

piece of *lefse* and chewing it thoughtfully. "That white-faced doe has always been our best."

"If she's too old to give milk, she's ready for the stew-pot," Frida said. "Butcher her tomorrow. Torst, you've a good hand with that."

Jarl shook his head, and Jorunn's husband, Nils, skillfully turned the topic to something more pleasant. The lass was eager to continue talking to the dog, but it had been banished to the barn while they ate. He was not brought in that night, and she was forced to lie awake in the big bed with her mother and sisters, wondering if she were going mad, or if God had simply found an odd way of blessing an otherwise overlooked girl.

The next morning the lass went to the barn to see how Einar was doing. She had listened to the chickens, but only briefly. They were talking, all right, but it wasn't very interesting, and they didn't notice when she talked back. She was more concerned over the reindeer, because, like her father, she did not want to see the white-faced doe butchered. She had never cared much for reindeer, but that particular doe was the prettiest of their small herd.

Thinking of reindeer gave her pause, and she stopped just inside the barn. She had spoken to the white reindeer. Had it done something to her, so that she could talk to animals now? She thought of the kiss it had given her, the way its soft nose had felt touching her forehead, and the warmth of its breath. A certainty grew in her breast: this was not a gift from God, but from the strange, ancient spirits of the earth.

"Are you going to help or not?" Einar was in the far corner of the barn. He was holding a pail in one hand and a stool in the other, using them as barriers to keep the doe backed into a corner. She was lowing piteously, and her brown eyes were rolling.

"It hurts, it hurts, it hurts," she moaned.

"Einar, stop that!" The lass went up to her brother and punched him lightly in the shoulder. "She's hurt."

"She's just stubborn," Einar grunted, waving the stool in the reindeer's face.

Giving a sort of bark, the normally gentle animal ducked its head and actually charged at Einar. The lass stepped up and caught hold of the frayed rope collar as the doe lunged. The large reindeer dragged her several feet before stopping, and Einar dove into a pile of sawdust and dry moss that they used for reindeer bedding.

"Hush, now; hush, now," the lass soothed the animal. "Ignore that silly boy, and tell me what's wrong."

"It hurts," the doe panted, leaning against her. The reindeer was shaking and there were damp patches of sweat on her thick brown coat.

"What hurts?" the girl cooed.

"My udder," the reindeer replied, and shuddered.

Einar was standing a few paces away, gaping at his youngest sister. "Is it really talking to you?"

"Yes," she said shortly, and knelt down by the reindeer. "Please let me look. I promise I won't hurt you," she said. The doe shuddered again, but nodded her head all the same.

The lass crouched lower and looked at the doe's swollen udder. It was hard to see with all the thick, shaggy hair, which was probably why Einar hadn't noticed the problem before. There was a bite mark near one teat, and it was infected.

"A fox bit her," the girl said to her brother. "Look here."

Einar crouched down to look and gave a low whistle. "Well, I'll be . . . I never even noticed!" He slapped the reindeer's side. "Sorry, girl. I'll get some cloths and clean it."

"Papa bought that medicine for the cut on Anni's hand last year," the lass said, straightening and giving the doe a much gentler pat. "There's some left in a brown jar in the dish cupboard."

Nodding, Einar dashed away to get the cloths and medicine. The lass stayed behind, stroking the reindeer's nose.

"I'm sorry that we didn't know," she said softly. "From now on, I'll make sure no more foxes bother you."

And she did, too. For how could the foxes fail to listen to her, when she listened to their woes in return?

It soon came to be known in that region that the youngest daughter of Jarl Oskarson had a way with animals. She could be trusted to calm a skittish horse or talk sense to the most wool-headed mutt, and foxes and wolves gave Jarl's barnyard wide berth. When such things were whispered within hearing of Frida, she would sniff and turn away. But Jarl would glow with pride over his youngest daughter, and think to himself that it was a pity his wife had never found a name for her, for she was turning into quite a likely young woman.

Chapter 5

When the lass was sixteen, there was only herself, Hans Peter, and Einar left at home. The others had all married, or in Torst and Askel's case, gone off to work in Christiania. It was a happy time, despite the weather. For though it was still cold and food was scarce, there were fewer mouths to feed.

In her practical way, the lass could appreciate her mother's coldness toward the children, and her grim joy at seeing them off into the world. It was nice to have more room in the bed, and more blankets to wrap around you. It was pleasant to have a full belly after dinner, and know that you could have a full belly at tomorrow's dinner as well.

The young girl's reputation as one who knew animals had continued to spread, and that brought the family some small reward as well. People would give half a dozen eggs from one hen for her to tell them what was wrong with another, and a brace of ducks for helping to train a new dog. The lass enjoyed listening to animals, though she never fully explained to anyone but Hans Peter how it was she got to the root of the problems.

At sixteen, the lass should have been walking out with one of the young men who lived nearby, but animals interested her much more than young men did. She did not want to end up like her mother: bitter and lonely, with nine children underfoot. The lass loved little children and thought that someday she might like one or two of her own, but first she wanted to see the world. She wanted to travel, and meet new people, and solve the mystery of Hans Peter's sad eyes. Then maybe she would come back to their valley and marry some farmer's son.

One summer day, or as summery as it ever was, she thought on this while she drew water from their well. She had already brought in the cheese Jarl had left as a troll-gift. Since the white reindeer had named her, she had taken to retrieving the gifts as soon as her father was off to cut wood. Then she would disguise them: cut the cheese into slices or churn the cream into butter so that he wouldn't notice. Frida took this as a sign of good sense in her youngest child, and Jarl continued to think the trolls were being appeased.

In order to draw the water, she had to drop the bucket, hard, and break the crust of ice on the surface. But it was warm enough that she needed only a couple of wool sweaters and her mittens, no parka, so she was considering going out to look for cloudberries in the afternoon.

She heard a strange crying noise and started. Half the water slopped out of the bucket and back into the well.

The lass let the rope slide through her mittens and wheeled around.

"Sorry, girl," growled a friendly voice. "Didn't know you were woolgathering."

The lass looked up, and up, to meet the smiling eyes and bearded face of Jorunn's father-in-law, Rolf Simonson. He was a huge, bearlike man with uncommonly dark hair and pale, merry eyes. In his arms he held a ragged blanket that squirmed and mewled. That was what had made the crying sound she had heard.

"Got something for you," he grunted, holding out the bundle. "Found it this morning, and I said to Nils: Jorunn's little sister would like this bit of a thing. I'll take it to her." He let out a hearty laugh.

The lass stared at him. Why in the name of all the saints would he bring her a *baby*? The squirming, crying bundle couldn't be anything else.

"Come here and take it, girl, it won't bite—well, it will, but the little nipper's teeth don't hurt all that much." He waved the bundle in her direction again.

"What is it?"

"It's an orphaned pup." Rolf Simonson laughed. "I would have thought you'd jump at the chance for a dog of your own!"

The young lass sagged back against the well. "I thought it was a baby," she said weakly.

Jorunn's father-in-law roared with laughter, causing

the puppy to cry and wiggle even more. "A baby? Did you think I'd stolen away your sister's latest? A baby!"

The laughter and the squeaking had drawn Frida and even Hans Peter out of the house, and now they stood in the yard and looked from the girl to Rolf Simonson. Hans Peter was smiling his faint half smile, and Frida had made her face as welcoming as it ever was.

"Neighbor Simonson," she said. "Will you come in and have a mug of ale?"

"That I shall, Mistress Frida," he replied. "But first your youngest must take this puppy from me, before I drop it."

Indeed, the little creature, though still obscured by the folds of the old blanket, was squirming ferociously. Another minute and it would writhe its way out of the farmer's massive hands and fall to the rocky mud of the yard. The lass took hold of the bundle just in time.

A little furry head poked out as she did, and the puppy cheeped at her. Its eyes were not yet open, and it was dark gray with black markings. It cheeped again, and then sank its needlelike milk teeth into her finger.

"Ouch, stop that!" She pulled her finger free and tapped the puppy's nose with it. Her gaze on the little creature, she followed Rolf Simonson and her mother into the house, with Hans Peter bringing up the rear.

"It's only a few days old," Hans Peter judged, as he and the lass crouched by the fire to have a good look at the puppy.

"Less than that, even," Rolf Simonson told them. "I found him this morning when I went to the barn. Mother must've crawled out of the woods and snuggled up in the long grass just behind my barn to have him. Wandered off to have the rest somewhere else and forgot this one."

"Thank Neighbor Simonson for the dog," Frida snapped at her youngest daughter. She dipped him a mug of ale from the barrel in the corner and set it down on the smooth-scrubbed table.

The lass leaped to her feet, blushing with embarrassment. "Thank you so much, Neighbor Simonson. It was very kind of you to think of me."

"You're welcome, girl," he said, waving away her thanks and then taking up the mug for a long swig. "A girl with your talent for animals should have one of her own!" He laughed and took another swig.

The lass could tell that her mother was not pleased to have a dog added to their household. But Jorunn's father-in-law would hear if they gave the animal away, so Frida would be forced to let her daughter keep it. The lass was ecstatic.

"Hem," Hans Peter coughed, bringing her attention back to the dog. "Lass?"

She sank back to the hearth and took the puppy in her hands. It began sucking noisily on her thumb.

"Lass?" Hans Peter was tugging at her sleeve.

"What is it?" She gave him an annoyed look. She had

been about to get up and get some reindeer milk for the puppy. She was thinking of using an old leather glove for it to suckle from.

Hans Peter waited until their mother and Rolf Simonson were busy gossiping to lean in close and whisper in her ear. "Take a good look at this . . . puppy."

She looked down at the little creature. Its soft fur stuck out at all angles, and it was still busily sucking at her thumb. The wisp of a tail was whirring in an almost circular motion. She looked up at Hans Peter, her brows quirked in a silent question.

He lowered his voice even further. "Can't you see it?"

She shook her head, still confused.

"Maybe its mother was a dog, though I doubt it, but if so, then its father certainly wasn't."

The puppy let go of the girl's thumb, turning its head, with its eyes still shut tight, toward Hans Peter. It growled, really more of a high-pitched squeak, and batted at his hand with a paw.

"Oh." The lass saw it now too. Hans Peter was right: maybe one of the little pup's parents had been a dog, but it was doubtful. By the look of things, it was a full-blooded wolf.

The girl looked at her brother, then over at the table where her mother and their neighbor were deep in conversation. She picked the wolf pup up and stood. Everyone turned to look at her. Her mother was annoyed at being disturbed. Rolf Simonson gave her a merry wink. Hans Peter made a concerned noise and rose to his feet as well.

She cleared her throat. "Neighbor Simonson, if you don't mind, I shall call the pup 'Rollo,' in your honor."

He raised his mug of ale in salute. "To young Rollo, my namesake!"

Frida snorted, and Hans Peter opened his mouth as though he would say something. The lass gave them both defiant looks and turned away.

"I'm going to cut up that old leather glove that doesn't have a mate," she announced. "He'll need to be fed right away."

Which is how the youngest daughter of Jarl Oskarson came to possess a wolf for a pet, and the stories of her way with animals grew as quickly as Rollo did.

Chapter 6

A s dearly as the young lass loved to talk to animals, she
had always felt, deep inside, that one day it would
bring her trouble. That that day didn't come until deep in
the harsh winter months of her seventeenth year was the
only consolation.

By then Rollo was a strapping young animal: deep
chested, long legged, and covered in soft thick fur. He
was mostly gray, with a white underbelly that he showed
only to the lass, and occasionally Hans Peter, if he was
desperate for a good scratch. Across the top of his head
and shoulders were striking black markings.

"Look at him," Hans Peter said, standing by the chop-
ping block to watch the wolf.

Rollo was casually lounging on the edge of the yard,
near a tuft of dry grass that stuck up out of the snow.
There was a family of mice living in the grass, as Rollo
knew quite well. Despite his mistress's scoldings, he was
determined to catch at least one of them. After all, they
were on his property.

"Rollo," the lass said warningly. She was sitting on the

woodpile, reading a letter from their sister Katla, who lived by the sea with her fisherman husband.

Clumsily refolding the letter with her mittened fingers, the lass pocketed it and shrugged deeper into her old patched parka. "Brr. I wish that Mother would finish with the candles."

"Why *do* you sneeze when she's making candles?"

"It's the *things* she puts in them." Her nose wrinkled. "The herbs and dried flowers. I wish she would just make plain ones."

She caught sight of Rollo and half rose. "Oh, he's going after one! Naughty!" She pointed at Rollo, whose lounging had acquired a certain tension. One black-tipped ear was pointing upward.

A plump gray mouse had emerged from the base of the tuft of grass and was testing the air with a quivering nose. Rollo maintained his position. The mouse skittered forward an inch. Rollo didn't blink. The mouse paused, sniffed the air, and then scuttled right over Rollo's left front paw. He didn't flinch.

When the fat little mouse was half a pace from Rollo, the wolf leaped into the air and came down with both front paws on the mouse. Tongue lolling, he dropped down and poked his paws with his black nose, sniffing his catch.

While Hans Peter laughed and slapped his thighs, the tenderhearted lass hurried over to her pet. "Now, Rollo, that's enough," she scolded. "You've scared the poor thing. Let it go."

Rollo gave his mistress a pleading look.

"Don't you try that with me, wolfling," she said in her most withering tones. "You get plenty to eat; you don't need to add mouse to your diet."

"But they're vermin," Rollo reminded her. "If they get in the house, they'll chew holes in things and eat *our* food."

"Well, this one isn't in the house. It's outside. And it belongs outside." The lass put her hands on her hips and tapped her booted foot. *"Rollo."*

Heaving a huge sigh, the wolf opened his paws and the little mouse staggered away. Its nose was twitching so fast that it was a blur, and it kept stopping every few steps to sway, as if faint. Taking pity on it, the girl bent over and gently scooped it up, then put it down just at the mouth of the little hole where it lived with its family.

Sighing again, Rollo stood up, shook out his thick pelt, and wandered nonchalantly over to the woodpile to sniff at the kindling that Hans Peter was stacking. "A lot of wood" was his comment.

"He says that it's a lot of wood," the lass reported.

Hans Peter brandished a stick at the wolf. "You're the one who told the lass a storm was coming."

Rollo made the little yipping noise that stood for yes. He and the lass had managed to work out some signals for Hans Peter, so that he could, to a certain extent, understand the wolf. Jarl thought it most clever of his daughter and her pet, and he himself would speak to the wolf often, and try to interpret his answers. Frida thought the situation unnatural, though, so Hans Peter and the lass made it a point to treat Rollo as they would any other dog whenever Frida was around. Rollo understood, and played the part of the goofy mutt for Frida. He would chew on old slippers and whine at the door whenever there was a noise outside, even though he didn't like the taste of slipper and knew full well that it was only the wind.

"It's an awful lot of wood, and outside," Rollo said, and the lass translated. "I don't think you'll need *this* much, but some of it should be inside, so that you can get to it."

"I see." Hans Peter looked at the pile. "Does he know how high the snow will be? Or how long the storm will last?"

"Deep and long," the lass translated. "But how deep or how long he isn't sure. But he thinks that it will not be as bad as the storm his first winter."

"Well, that's a blessing at least," Hans Peter said with a grunt. He was transferring the wood to a large canvas sling so that it could be carried into the house.

Sixth months after Rolf Simonson had brought the lass the pup, a blizzard had come down on their valley. For ten days the family huddled in their cottage, praying for the snow to stop. When it did, it was higher than the roof of their cottage, and it was another week before they could tunnel their way across the yard and check on the reindeer. Jarl made his living cutting down the large trees deep in the forest, but it had been over a month before it was safe enough to return to his work. They'd had to kill three reindeer to make up for the loss of income. No one living could remember a storm as terrible, and it had made even Frida cross herself and mutter about trolls as they dug their way to the barn.

Now the lass hurried to load a sling of firewood. Rather than flinging it around to her back as her brother did, though, she simply slid hers along the hard-packed snow to the front door. They both kicked their boots against the doorframe as they went in, to knock off the snow, and Rollo daintily shook his feet before stepping onto Frida's clean-swept floor.

They had timed their entrance right: the last of the candles was cooling on the table, and the herbs had been put away. The lass sneezed three times in quick succession and hurried to make dinner.

As the first snowflakes fell, they were sitting down to eat when the door to the cottage suddenly banged open to reveal a huge, white, furry creature. Frida shrieked, and the lass leaped backward off her bench. Rollo sprang from his position by the fire and stood between the people and the monster in the doorway, hackles raised, and snarled.

With a guffaw, the fur-clad figure pulled aside the high collar obscuring its face. It was Askeladden, up from the city. He laughed again at their expressions, and then shook himself so that the snow fell off his parka and hood and revealed the gray fur underneath.

"You're getting snow all over the floor," the lass told her brother, recovering quickly.

"Then get the broom and sweep it up before it melts, girl," her mother ordered. "Come in and sit down, son; have some stew. Einar is helping Nils patch their roof; we have plenty to spare." She fluttered around her favored third son. "How nice of you to visit. I've missed you."

"This isn't just a visit," Askeladden said, shrugging off his snow-clogged outer clothes and leaving them on the floor for the lass to care for. "I've come a-hunting."

"Hunting? Here?" Jarl shook his head. "There's naught worth hunting in these parts but snowfoxes, and I'll wager you have enough of those outside the city."

"Not snowfoxes," Askeladden said with his charming grin. "*Isbjørn*. Giant white *isbjørn*. A creature they say makes the white reindeer seem like poor game."

"*Isbjørn*? There's no ice bear in these parts," the lass said as she swept up the snow scattered over the floor. She rolled her eyes at Hans Peter, but he wasn't looking at her. His eyes were fixed on Askel, and his face was gray.

"There is *a* bear in these parts," Askel said. "A number of hunters have seen it. A massive beast, and whiter than the snow." Askel's hands described the proportions of the bear in the air over the table, and his eyes shone. "The royal furrier in Christiania is offering five hundred gold crowns to whoever brings him the pelt." His eyes shone even brighter at the mention of the money, and so did Frida's. "The king wants a bearskin parka," he added. "And I'm going to provide it for him. Imagine if I was the man who brought down this mighty bear . . . the king himself might want to meet me!"

"This is your chance, son," Frida said, laying her arm around Askel's broad shoulders and giving him a squeeze. "You'll make your fortune with this hunt. I can feel it in my bones." She kissed his cheek.

"Hans Peter, are you all right?" The lass had gone to her favorite brother and laid a hand on his shoulder. He looked as if he were going to be sick. He had let his spoon, with a piece of carrot still on it, fall to the table beside his bowl, and his hands were limp in his lap.

"Do not hunt this *isbjørn,*" Hans Peter said in a strange, hollow voice. "It is not a natural creature."

Askel's voice was thick with derision. "How could you possibly know *anything* about this animal? Why, none of you had even heard of it until I told you of it just now."

"Bears do not come here," Hans Peter said. "White or brown. For an *isbjørn* to wander this far south . . ." He trailed off. "Do not hunt this bear, Askeladden." A shudder passed through Hans Peter, and the lass tightened her fingers on his shoulder. "I know more of *isbjørn* than I ever care to. No good can come of this."

"What nonsense is this?" Frida shrilled. "What do you know about bears, shut away here by my hearth day after day, as though you weren't a man grown who should be off making his own way in the world?" She shook her finger at Hans Peter. "Askeladden is going to make his fortune, and I'll not have your jealousy ruining things for him."

"Now, wife," Jarl began. He reached across the table to pat her hand, but she shook him off; he grimaced. "Hans Peter does his part with the farmwork and his carvings. And let us not forget that he once sailed the northern seas on a trading ship."

Frida turned away from her husband and her eldest son to make her point clear: this was not enough for her. A slow anger boiled in the lass's stomach. She had been rejected by her mother when she was born, and was used to being dismissed as worthless. But Hans Peter . . . that was something else. It angered the girl to think that Frida could be so cold as to turn against her eldest son this way. True, Askeladden was the lucky third son, but what had he ever done in his life? Trapped a few foxes, shot a few wild deer, flirted with a few foolish farmgirls, and not much else.

"If you want to sit here by the fire like an old woman all your life, brother, that is your decision," Askeladden said in his haughty way. "But I have chosen a different road, one that will lead me to riches, and fame."

"The third son's birthright!" Frida said.

"It is a fine thing, to set your sights on crystal towers

and golden thrones," Hans Peter said quietly. "But first you had better see what lurks within those towers, and what sits on those thrones. Every palace needs a foundation, Askeladden. Make sure that yours isn't of human bones." And with that, Hans Peter got to his feet, his every movement as slow and jerky as an old, old man's. The rest of the family watched in stunned silence as he made his way up the ladder and into the darkness of the loft.

"He's mad," Askeladden said quietly after a moment.

"He's hurting," the lass said fiercely. "He's hurting, and none of you care." She was still standing, her fists clenched. Rollo stood beside her, pressed against her thigh, uncertain what to do to comfort his beloved mistress.

"Pika, pika," Jarl said softly. "*I* care. But there's naught we can do." He smiled sadly at his youngest child. Then, turning his gaze to Askel, his smile faded. "I have never known your brother to speak madness—"

"Until now!"

Jarl held up one hand in a sharp gesture to silence Askeladden. "I have *never* known Hans Peter to speak madness. His counsel has always been sound, and he knows far more of the world than I ever hope to. You should listen to his advice."

"Jarl, don't talk nonsense!" Frida pounded on the table with her bony fist. "Hans Peter is a good-for-nothing, and my Askeladden is a strong, brave man. He's a fine hunter, and if he says that he will bring down the *isbjørn,* he will!"

"Thank you, Mother," Askeladden said in a lofty tone. "I think I shall sleep here tonight, to rest up while this storm blows itself out, and then I shall be off after the bear."

"An excellent plan, my son," Frida said. "Here, have some more stew, and some bread and cheese. You need to keep up your strength. And before you leave tomorrow, I'll pack you a bag with plenty of dried meat and cheese and bread, for the hunt."

"You will regret this," the lass said.

She was speaking to Askel, but she never knew if he heard her. Her gaze was fixed on the little window beside the door. The shutter had flapped loose when Askel had come in, and she had not yet closed it. The greased reindeer hide pane barely let the light filter in when the sun was shining, but now she thought she could see the snow swirling outside. It seemed to make shapes: an *isbjørn* and the shambling form of a troll.

"You will regret this," she repeated, her voice no more than a whisper. "We all will."

Chapter 7

When Askeladden had been gone three days, even
Frida began to worry. The storm had been fierce,
but after the skies cleared, the pristine snow looked welcoming. Askel had tested his skis and found the chill tem-
perature had made the snow perfect for travel. He loaded
up his knapsack with food, his crossbow, bolts, and knives,
and waved a cheery farewell to his mother.

Hans Peter sat by the fire and said not a word to anyone, not even to the lass when she pressed him to eat
something. He ate reluctantly and didn't carve a single
piece of wood. Rollo sat beside him, his head on Hans Peter's knee. His silence affected the entire family, and
added to it was a strangeness in the air.

Jarl went out and about his work, as usual, skiing
through the trees and pulling back a great sledge of wood
at the end of each day. The lass and Frida milked the reindeer and made cheese, and the lass found a squirrel's cache
of nuts and ground them into meal. But all this was done
in silence. Though not a talkative woman, Frida had a
sharp tongue and enjoyed giving orders to her husband

and remaining children. But for three days she said almost nothing. The lass did not sing, Hans Peter did not tell stories, and Jarl did not share the details of his day.

And then another storm descended.

The wind raged around the little cottage, and there was not even time to secure the animals. Jarl tried, but the snow had turned into needles of ice, and he hardly made it two steps out the door before he was forced to come back in. The skin around his eyes, the only part of him exposed to the weather, was stung raw.

"There's no way to bring the chickens in," he panted as the lass helped him remove his ice-covered outer clothes. "We may lose them all. But the bigger animals should do all right: the barn is tight, and they had water and feed."

"I made sure of the chickens," the lass told him, trying to reassure her father, whose expression was as bleak as she had ever seen it. "They're safe enough."

"You're a good girl," he said, patting her head absently even though she was only a handspan shorter than he.

"And who is making sure that my Ash-lad is safe?" Frida demanded. "Where is he sheltering from the storm?"

"I don't know, wife," Jarl said, sagging down on a chair by the table. "All we can do is pray."

"Is he not the lucky third son?" Hans Peter spoke for the first time since making his pronouncement to Askeladden. "Is he not, as you call him, the Ash-lad? Surely he will ride out this storm in some fabulous palace, and will return triumphant tomorrow with a princess and a chest of gold." His words would have been insulting if his voice hadn't been so drained of emotion.

"And so he shall," Frida said, giving her eldest son a defiant look. "He is the best and brightest of all my children, my lucky third son, and he shall return in triumph, as you say."

The young lass didn't say anything. She wanted her mother to be right . . . not about the gold and the princess, although that might be nice. No, she wanted her brother to return in safety. She was not half so fond of him as she was of Hans Peter, but he was still her brother, and the lass could not bear to think of losing even one member of her family.

Lost in these dire thoughts, everyone jumped when Rollo lunged to his feet and streaked to the front door. He stood before it, hackles raised, his growl cutting through the silence in a most unpleasant way. Hans Peter also got to his feet, drawing his sharp whittling knife, and moved between the door and his youngest sister.

"Rollo? What is it?" The lass didn't care if her mother heard her talking to the wolf. She was covered in gooseflesh and thought that she could see a shape moving outside the little front window. A shape not made of wind and snow.

Rollo's growl rose in pitch, and he took a stiff step forward just as the door burst open. A great, white, fur-covered figure barely managed to squeeze through the door, shoving Rollo aside as though he were a puppy. Frida started to laugh, to say something, obviously thinking that it was her darling Askeladden come home.

But it was not Askeladden, wrapped in furs and coated with snow. It was not a human at all. It was an *isbjørn,* a great white ice bear of the North, and it was standing in the middle of their cottage and looking right at the lass.

"Rollo, don't you dare," she hissed.

The wolf, more stunned than hurt, had regained his feet and looked ready to pounce on the bear. Never mind that the creature outweighed him by more than a ton, where his mistress's safety was concerned, Rollo had no fear.

"Rollo, I mean it, come here," the lass insisted, slapping her thigh.

Snorting to show the bear that he was not afraid, Rollo backed his way over to the lass and took up his position beside her. None of the other humans moved. Frida was frozen in place, a ladle in one hand and the pot of stew in the other. Jarl stood beside the table, one hand on the bread knife and the other clenched in a fist. Hans Peter was still standing protectively in front of the lass and their mother, his short woodworking knife drawn. But his hand was shaking so badly that it looked as though he would drop the knife any moment, and his face was the blue-white of frozen cow's milk.

"What do you want?" The lass's voice was shrill. "Go away!"

The bear swayed from side to side, blinking its black eyes. The wind blew gusts of snow through the open door that drifted around its massive paws, and the lass could see that the bear was, indeed, whiter than the snow. The gleaming quality of its fur reminded her of starlight, and moonlight, and the pelt of the white reindeer, who had given her a name.

"Go away!" She made a shooing gesture.

"Can you understand me?" The *isbjørn*'s voice was deep and rumbling, and it caught a little, as though it was unaccustomed to talking. Frida gave a little squeak, and Jarl lifted the knife off the table at what sounded like a threatening growl.

"Yes," the lass replied shortly.

The bear's eyes closed, and it came a little farther into the cottage. It was crowded against the table now, within reach of both Jarl and Hans Peter and their knives, but it did not seem to care. The black eyes opened.

"Come with me," the bear rumbled.

"What?" The lass felt like her skin was shifting over her bones.

"You. Come with me."

"What's it saying?" Hans Peter's voice was barely a whisper.

"What's it *saying*?" Frida's voice was much sharper, but not much louder. "It's a *bear*! Kill it!"

"He wants me to go with him," the lass said. Her voice

shook, and she didn't bother to whisper. She knew from the bear's voice that he was male, and from his eyes that he did not mean to harm anyone. "Why?" This last she addressed to the bear.

The *isbjørn* swayed from side to side. A low moan issued from its throat. "Can't say." Its brow furrowed and it moaned again. "But. Need you. You come now."

"He says he needs me to come with him," the girl said in a bewildered voice.

"No." Hans Peter's face was white and strained. He waved his knife at the bear, not threatening it so much as urging it away. "No. Leave her be."

The bear shook its head. "Need you. Please. Come with me."

"Why do you need me?" the lass pressed. "Come where?"

"Live with me in a palace. For just one year." Every word seemed to drag out of the bear's broad muzzle with more and more effort.

"He wants me to live with him in a palace for one year," the lass reported to her shocked family.

"No." Hans Peter dropped the knife to the floor with a clatter. Whirling around, he caught hold of both of the lass's shoulders and shook her gently. "Don't do this. Please don't do this. You cannot know what evil there is in the world."

"You, live in a palace?" Frida's eyes were moving from

the bear to her youngest daughter, and she looked much more interested than frightened now. She licked her lips. "So, this is an enchanted bear? Like King Valdemon in the old legends?"

"Don't talk nonsense, woman," Jarl growled. He had not dropped his knife. "Get away from here," he said, brandishing his knife in a much more violent manner than Hans Peter had.

"You will not be . . . harmed," the bear said.

Jarl took another step forward, hearing only a growl.

"Husband, wait a moment," Frida said. "Perhaps this is the luck that Askeladden has brought."

"Having an *isbjørn* take my youngest child isn't 'luck,' " Jarl replied. "And I doubt Askel had anything to do with it."

"This is the bear he was hunting, I'm sure," Hans Peter said. "And as I thought, it will bring no good to any of us."

"It wants to take the pika to live in a palace." Frida's hands were on her hips: she was about to get stubborn.

"Mother," Hans Peter said in that strained voice, "you cannot know what you are saying. This is not a natural thing—you said yourself that this was an enchanted bear. You cannot want the lass to enter into this enchantment."

The lass gently moved out of her brother's grip and stood so that she could look the bear in the eyes again. The bear gazed back, its black eyes holding the same hurt and pain that she saw in Hans Peter's. "You will not harm me?"

"No!" Hans Peter grabbed one of her hands in both of his. "No!"

"Oh, act like a man," Frida snarled at him. "Your sister has an opportunity most people could only dream of, to—"

"To enter into such horror that you cannot imagine," Hans Peter said in anguish.

"To live in a palace," Frida finished.

Even the *isbjørn* froze at this pronouncement, and all eyes were now on the lass's mother. She was staring through the open door beyond the white bear, looking beyond even the snow that swirled and lightened the darkness. "A palace," she repeated.

"My lord *isbjørn*," the lass said, breaking into the silence. "It is all well and good that I shall live in a palace for a year, but what of my family? If you have such wealth, can you not give a little to them?"

"Daughter." Jarl's voice was anguished. "No."

"Little sister, please," said Hans Peter desperately. "Do not do this." He turned to the bear. "Why have you come here? Did *she* send you?"

The bear rocked back and forth, looking at each member of the family in turn. "This Askeladden? He hunts me?"

"Yes."

"Lucky third brother?" The bear's words had an edge to them.

"I suppose," the lass said, cautious. "But so far he hasn't really done anything of use." She flicked a glance at her mother to see if this would upset her, but Frida continued to stare out the door.

The bear nodded. "Askel will find bear. Another bear. Fame and wealth for your family." He made a noise like a reindeer lowing. "Will you come?"

The lass hesitated, but only a moment. There was a singing in her blood, and her heart pounded as though it would leap out of her chest. "Askel will find another bear," she reported. "He will be famous, and you all will be wealthy."

"It's not worth it," Hans Peter said.

"No, it is not," Jarl agreed.

"You come?" The bear's eyes were anxious. "All well. You safe. Family wealthy. You come?"

"Let me get my things," she said.

Hans Peter made a strangled noise, and put out one hand to her.

The lass turned and looked him straight in the eyes. "I'm going. I think I have to go. But I'll be back, and you needn't worry about me." She stood on tiptoe and kissed his cheek.

He closed his eyes and hugged her tight. The firelight made a halo out of his silvered hair, and tears ran down his cheeks. "I'll get my white parka and boots; you'll need them."

"This is madness," Jarl half whispered, sinking down onto a chair. "Madness."

"No, Papa," the lass said, going over and putting her arm around her father's shoulders. "No, it's the right thing to do. I feel it deep in my heart."

He reached up and squeezed the hand that lay on his shoulder. His fingers were icy cold. "Oh, you poor wisp of a girl. If anyone could come out the better for an adventure like this, it would be you."

Rollo trotted forward and leaned against the girl's legs. "I shall protect you," he said, giving the bear a defiant look.

The lass gave a little, nervous laugh. "And I shall have Rollo to protect me," she told her father.

"No," the bear said. "No wolf."

The lass narrowed her eyes at him, her free hand dropping down to rest on Rollo's head. "Yes, wolf. If Rollo doesn't come, then I'm not going."

The bear swayed back and forth, growling low in its throat. It was not threatening, more thoughtful. Then he heaved a huge sigh. "Wolf come," he agreed heavily.

And so she went to pack her meager belongings. A comb. A carving of a reindeer Hans Peter had made. The few tattered clothes she had inherited from her sisters. And that was all. She tied it up in her shawl and pulled on a pair of breeches that had once belonged to Torst and then Einar, before becoming so ragged around the hems that several inches had been cut off. She put on both her wool sweaters and got her mittens.

Hans Peter wrapped her in his parka, putting the

white boots once more over her own worn brown ones. Her father handed her a napkin in which he had wrapped some *lefse* and cheese. Her brother put everything into the leather knapsack he had taken on his sea voyage, and she strapped it to her back. The lass kissed her brother and father both and then her mother, who merely nodded at her in farewell.

"Get on my back," the *isbjørn* instructed.

Hans Peter lifted her onto the bear's broad back without needing to be asked.

With Rollo hard on his heels, the *isbjørn* took off into the blizzard as though he had wings. The lass held tight to his soft white fur, and prayed.

Chapter 8

Just when the lass had settled in to the strange rocking motion of a bear at full gallop, the animal stopped. They were on top of a steep crag that looked down over the ravine with the little stream where the lass had freed the white reindeer. The snow was letting up and the moon had dared to show its face, which made it easy to see the black ribbon of water. Standing beside the boulder that jutted into the stream was Askeladden.

He had pulled aside the high collar of his parka, and his breath steamed the air. Even from this height, the lass could see that he was angry, his face red with more than cold, and he was punching one mittened fist into the other. He kicked at the boulder, suddenly, viciously, and let fly with a curse.

"Get down," the *isbjørn* said.

The lass slithered off his back, and Rollo came up alongside. A thrill of fear ran through the girl. Maybe it was all lies. Maybe now the bear was going to eat her, and Rollo, and Askeladden. Or it had changed its mind and was going to just leave her here. At least, with the white fur parka, she was warm.

"Wait here," the bear said.

He loped a little farther along the edge of the ravine and raised his head, sniffing the air. He made a strange sound, a sort of hollow huffing noise that tingled the lass's ears and seemed to carry on the wind. After a few heartbeats it was answered by a similar sound that came from the south of where they were.

Then the enchanted bear stood on his hind legs. He was twice as tall as Hans Peter, the lass realized. He extended his black claws, curled his lips back to reveal long white teeth, and snarled. Down in the ravine, Askeladden was too busy cursing to notice. The bear opened his mouth and let out a roar that shook the snow from the boughs of the trees all around them.

The lass sat down with a bump in a snowdrift, her jaw agape. Riding on the bear had been exhilarating, and she had been daydreaming about the palace she was going to live in. Now it hit her, hard, that she was at the mercy of a very large and very wild animal, enchanted or not.

Sitting in the snowdrift with Rollo pressing against her, she could no longer see down into the ravine, but she could hear Askeladden's shout. There was a twang, and a crossbow bolt struck into a tree just to the left of the bear's head. The bear dropped to all fours and ran, keeping to the edge of the ravine but going in the opposite direction from the lass.

"Let's go," she said to Rollo, pushing him aside so that she could clamber to her feet.

"He said to wait here," the wolf argued.

"Do you really mean to take orders from a bear?"

And off she went, giving her pet no choice but to follow. She kept closer to the trees, not wanting her brother to catch sight of her. In the white parka and boots, he might decide she was a very small bear, and take a practice shot at her. In fact, having felt the pelt of the enchanted *isbjørn,* she was convinced that Hans Peter's parka was made of the same fur. She wondered anew where her brother had gotten it, and what the embroidery meant.

The bear's tracks curved in from the edge a little, and the lass thought that very wise. There was no way of knowing if the ground underneath the snow was stable, or was there at all. It was possible to walk on the thickly crusted drifts that extended out from cliffs, but usually only for a very small and cautious human. For something the size of the enchanted bear, it could be deadly.

The trees along the top of the ravine cleared, and she skidded to a stop only a few paces from the *isbjørn.* No, from *two isbjørner.* The second one was not as large, nor as white, but it was still magnificent. The bears stood nose to nose, growling deep in their throats.

The smaller bear began backing away, whining. The larger bear stalked toward it, a commanding note in his growl. The lass moved her hood back a little from her face, trying to hear what they said.

"No, please, brother," the smaller *isbjørn* pleaded.

"I am not your brother," the enchanted bear said, his voice angry. "Do it now."

"No, please, my lord," the other bear whined.

The larger of the *isbjørn,* the lass's *isbjørn,* softened and seemed now to pity the other. "Forgive me. I have no choice. Go now, please, and your spirit shall ascend to the stars as a reward for your sacrifice."

The other bear let out a strange, keening cry. It started to back farther away but couldn't seem to break free from the enchanted *isbjørn*'s gaze.

Then the smaller bear wheeled around and ran for the edge of the ravine. The lass cried out, knowing that the snow there was jutting out over thin air and would not hold his weight. The bear stopped just short of the most dangerous part, though, and reared up onto his hind legs. He roared, much as the enchanted bear had done earlier. And, like there had been earlier, there was a twang, and a thunk, as a crossbow bolt made contact.

Only this time, it did not hit a tree. It found its mark deep in the heart of the other *isbjørn,* and the beast fell backward into the snow.

"No!" The lass started forward, but the enchanted bear barred the way.

"Get on my back," he growled.

"We have to help him."

"He's dead. Get on now," the bear said, still blocking her. When she hesitated, he turned his head and bared his teeth. "You wanted family wealthy. So."

The lass sagged. She could hear the scrabbling sounds of her brother Askeladden climbing up the side of the ravine to his quarry. He would take it back to Christiania, and it would be made into a coat for the king. And Askeladden would be rich and famous, just as he and Frida had always dreamed.

Just as the lass had asked.

"Wish wisely," the *isbjørn* said, guessing her thoughts.

Subdued, the lass climbed on his back and the *isbjørn* began to run. He ran away from the ravine, fast and faster, and the lass kept an eye on the ground to the right, where Rollo ran alongside them. She could hardly believe that a bear, a great ungainly bear, could run so fast. Nor that her own dear wolf could keep pace with them. The cold wind tore the tears from her eyes and sent them running back beneath her hood to soak her hair at the temples. The black trees turned to a blur, and then she saw Rollo dropping behind.

"Wait, stop," she cried, thumping the bear's shoulder with her fist. "Rollo. He can't keep up."

The bear stopped, sliding a bit in the snow. He grunted. "Must go even faster," he told her. They waited for a full minute before Rollo caught up, and when he did, he fell sideways into a drift, wheezing.

"You'll have to carry him, too," the lass told the bear.

"Can't. Won't stay on," the *isbjørn* argued. "Leave behind."

"Absolutely not. I told you, Rollo comes, or I don't." She folded her arms in a mutinous pose, even though the bear couldn't see her. "Go slower."

The bear sighed. The lass almost slid off his back into the snow with the force of it. Rollo got to his feet, anxious to show that he was ready to run again, but his sides still heaved with his labored breathing.

The *isbjørn* swung his head around until he was standing nose to nose with the wolf. Every muscle in the lass's body went rigid. It reminded her of the way he had stood to stare down the other bear, the one who had been sacrificed for her sake, and her family's fortune.

But this time the *isbjørn* did not talk. Black eyes stared into gold, and the bear made a little singing sound deep in his throat. Rollo's ears pricked forward, and his hackles raised. When the bear looked away from him, the wolf shook himself, his tongue lolling and his breathing easy.

"I could run all night," he said. "I feel marvelous." He stretched, arching his back like a cat.

"Good. We go."

And the *isbjørn* ran again, covering the snowy terrain even faster than it had before. The lass had to crouch low against his back, clinging with both hands to his fur, her legs locked to his rib cage. She spared only one look for Rollo, who ran beside the bear as easily as he might have chased a rabbit across the yard. After that she dared not look again, for the wind had so dragged at her head when she lifted it that she had almost been ripped from the bear's back. Instead she buried her face in the warm fur and clung for dear life as the bear ran up and down hills, dodged between trees, and once gave a great leap across a river.

They went faster and faster, and the hills became mountains, and the bear ran up the sheer stone sides as though they were level, with Rollo at his heels. The sun set and then rose again, and they passed into a forest so thick with trees that the lass could not tell night from day, and yet the bear's pace did not flag and neither did the wolf's. The girl slept for what could have been hours, but was more likely days, until she felt the bear slowing down.

When he had slowed enough that she could lift her head to look around, she had no idea where they were. The sharp peaks and mountains of her home, dark with trees, were gone. Instead a white plain lay before them, deep with snow. To the west there was a tall crag, and on top of the crag she saw a shining thing of greenish white that looked like a crown sitting on the head of a giant.

"That is your home now," the *isbjørn* said.

"Let's go," Rollo shouted, and took off across the snow plain, yipping like a puppy.

The bear gave a bellow that might have been a laugh

and went after him. The lass put her face down once more, the wind dragging at her.

At least Rollo was excited, she thought. And her family would have wealth. That was what was important. She hardly dared to admit it, but the novelty of being taken by an enchanted bear to live in a palace had worn off.

She was simply terrified.

Part 2

Lady of the Palace of Ice

Chapter 9

It took longer than the lass would have thought to reach the crag where the palace stood. They had already traveled for unknown days, and night was falling by the time they reached the foot of the crag. The white plain had been so flat and featureless that she had misjudged its expanse. Rollo beat the white bear to it, and stood, panting eagerly, at the bottom of a steep trail that wound around the hill.

"Follow me," the bear said to Rollo. His manner was much warmer toward the wolf now. The long race across the plain seemed to have made them friends.

The lass sat up on the bear's back and looked around as he went up the path. It was barely wide enough for the bear, and so smooth that she could see their reflection in it. The crag wasn't stone at all, she realized with a start, but ice—smooth green ice covered with a rime of white snow everywhere but on the path. The peak was so regular in shape, and the path so even, that she guessed it had been created by some hands other than Nature's. But whose? Who was powerful enough to make a mountain out of ice?

She spoke this last thought aloud, and the bear answered her.

"*She* is," he said as he plodded up the path. It spiraled around the hill, and now the lass could see that the white snow plain extended in every direction as far as the horizon. "*She* is that powerful."

"Who?"

But the bear did not answer her.

It was full dark and the moon was on the rise by the time they reached the top of the crag. The palace was not much narrower than the crag: there was only a slender path going around its base. With a gasp, the lass saw that the palace itself had been made of green ice, though the massive doors were hammered gold set with diamonds and rubies the size of goose eggs.

The *isbjørn* approached the doors and let out a roar, and the doors swung open. They entered into a lofty hall, hung with banners of silk that depicted a strange crest: a pearly white *isbjørn* on a blue background, with a golden sun to one side of it and a silver moon to the other. Beneath the bear there was a disturbing symbol that looked like a saw, or a serrated knife, embroidered in black.

The lass was pleased to find that, although the palace was made of ice, it was pleasantly warm inside. She slithered off the bear's back and removed her hood, turning slowly to take it all in. The ceiling of the hall was supported by slender pillars of ice, carved all around with jagged markings.

Her gaze sharpened on these and she went forward to touch one. The ice pillar was smooth and hard, but warm and not at all wet. She studied the carvings that spiraled around it.

"I recognize these," she said in excitement. "This says something about whales, many whales, coming ashore." She looked back at the bear. "They're like the carvings my brother Hans Peter makes. He taught me what some of them mean." She ran her hand over the carvings, feeling a spike of homesickness. She would not see Hans Peter again for a long time.

"Your . . . brother?" The bear came over to her, squinting at the engraved symbols. "You can read them?"

"Yes." She held out the sleeve of her parka. "But I can't read these. I've tried, but it doesn't seem to make any sense. It looks like the same sort of thing, though, don't you think?"

Now the bear squinted at her parka, studying the red and blue embroidery that ran in bands around the sleeves and the hem. Suddenly his eyes widened and he reared back, giving a roar. The lass cowered against the pillar, and Rollo took up a protective stance between them.

"Where did you get that?" The bear's voice was thick with some emotion that the girl thought might be rage, but might just as easily have been fear. "Where?"

"It was my brother's," she said with a little quaver in her voice. "Hans Peter. The brother you met. He gave it to me. You were there."

He came down on all fours, still quivering with emotion. "Yes. I remember." Leaning forward, the bear squinted even harder at it. "Where did *he* get it?"

"I don't know," the lass said, nearly whispering. "He went to sea when I was small, and when he came back, he had it. Something had happened to him, something that made him sad."

The bear made a strange barking noise that caused the lass to start sliding sideways, hoping to put the pillar between them. Then she realized that he was laughing. It was a hollow, bitter laugh, but still a laugh.

"Made him sad?" His voice was mocking. "I wish that were my only complaint."

"What *is* your complaint?" She said it shyly, still halfway around the pillar.

The *isbjørn* stopped, and he began to sway again as he had at her house. "Can't say," he managed finally. A moment ago his words had come easily, easier than at any time before. But now his speech was labored again. "Can't say!" The words rose to an angry roar. The bear wheeled around and ran off, disappearing through a door at the far side of the hall.

"Well," the lass said to Rollo, blinking in shock at the bear's strange behavior. "I suppose it's just the two of us now. Let's explore."

It was so warm in the ice palace that she shrugged off the parka and the extra boots and carried them. They walked around the large hall, admiring the carvings and the enormous fireplace at the far end. The mantel and hearth, the entire structure was of ice, and yet the fire that burned brightly in it did not melt anything. There was a gorgeous rug laid in front of the hearth, and a chair uphol-stered in a cloth that the lass thought might be velvet, though she had never seen or felt it in real life. The chair was just the right size for her, she found when she sat in it, and there was even a small tapestry footstool placed at ex-actly the right angle. Other than the fabric and cushion-stuffing, both chair and footstool were also carved of ice.

"This certainly isn't for our *isbjørn*," she told Rollo, stretching her feet toward the fire.

"No, it's for you, my lady," said a voice from behind the chair.

The lass was so startled that she lunged forward and ended up on the hearthrug on her knees. Rollo dropped to a crouch, hackles raised and teeth bared.

"Oh, dear me," said the voice. And then a little person who stood no taller than the lass's shoulder came around the chair and into view.

He wasn't human. Nor was he an animal, or at least any animal that the lass had ever seen. The upper part of his body looked like a man's: he had a bare, muscular chest; two human arms; and a human-looking face. He had a beard and curly hair, both of the same reddish brown color. But there were two slender horns coming out of his hair, and his eyes were golden, with slotted pupils, like a goat's. From the waist down, he was very much a goat, with reddish brown fur that matched his hair and beard, and little cloven hooves. The only clothing he wore was a ribbon tied around his throat, woven of blue and red silk in a pattern that looked rather like the embroidery on Hans Peter's parka.

"What are you?" the lass gasped.

"I'm Erasmus," he said. "Oh." His brow wrinkled. "You asked *what* I am? I'm a faun." He said this as if it were the most natural thing in the world.

To the lass, however, it was even less natural than an enchanted *isbjørn*. Magical creatures such as white reindeer or bears that lived in palaces were the stuff of every fireside story she had ever heard.

Men that were half-goat were not.

"Can I help you to your feet, my lady?" The faun bent over her solicitously.

Feeling rather foolish to still be crouched on the hearthrug with her jaw agape, the lass waved away Erasmus's offer and got to her feet herself. She tapped Rollo on the head, their signal for him to "stand down," and he stopped snarling. However, he did continue to stand between his mistress and the stranger.

"I'm to serve you for as long as you stay with us, my lady," the faun continued when the lass was standing and facing him. He did come only to her shoulder, but she could tell from the fine lines around his eyes that he was much older than she was, although there was no gray in his hair or beard. "Would you like me to show you to your apartments? Or would you like something to eat?"

"Er." The lass looked down at herself. She was damp and grubby from traveling, and very tired. But she was also ravenously hungry. She had not had time to eat the *lefse* and cheese that her father had packed for her.

"Why don't I show you to your apartments," Erasmus said kindly. "You can wash and change your clothes, and then I can bring you a tray with something to eat in your sitting room."

"That would be lovely," the lass said, all the while thinking, *I have a sitting room?*

She followed the faun down a long passageway that led off the great hall, Rollo at her heels. They went up a curving flight of stairs, and along another passageway, and then stopped in front of a door of beautifully carved bronze.

"Here are your apartments, my lady," Erasmus said, and he pushed open the door. "I must say, it is a relief that you can understand me."

Jaw agape, the lass gazed about in wonder. The room beyond was larger than her family's entire cottage. Thick carpets of green and blue covered the frozen floor, a massive fireplace with a roaring fire took up one whole wall, and there were satin-upholstered chairs and couches scattered around the room. Most of the walls were covered in tapestries, but across from the door there were panels where the ice was so thin that she could see the night sky outside, only faintly distorted with a greenish cast.

"Oh, this room is too fine for me," she told the faun. "Please, isn't there something simpler?"

"No, my lady." He shook his head. "Only the servants' quarters, and you are not a servant."

He crossed the room to the right and threw open another carved wooden door to reveal the bedchamber. It was just as large as the sitting room, with a fireplace that the lass could have stood up inside, had a fire not been burning there, too, and a bed that could have comfortably slept ten people. The bed was also carved of ice, with slim posts at each corner that rose up to support a canopy of white silk. The pelt of a massive *isbjørn* lay across the foot of the bed, and another, smaller brown bear pelt served as a hearthrug.

Erasmus walked through that room as well, and into another, smaller room lined with wardrobes. There was no fireplace here; instead there was an enormous mirror and a small table covered with glass jars and bottles.

"Your dressing room, my lady," the faun told her. He opened one of the carved-ice wardrobes and pulled out a gown of stiff peach satin. "There are some gowns here, but I'm afraid that they will have to be altered."

"I can wear my own clothes, can't I?" the lass said,

defending her ragged sweater and hand-me-down trousers and boots.

"Of course, my lady, but you will be here some time, and if you wish to wear something else, you are welcome to anything here." He gestured around at the wardrobes.

"Thank you," the lass said, mollified. Then she, too, eyed the gown he was holding. "I don't think I've ever seen a woman that tall before."

The faun was holding the gown so that the hem just brushed the carpet, which meant that his arms were extended straight over his head. From the look of the gown, it had been made for someone fully a foot taller than the lass, and she was tall for a woman herself. Also, whomever the gown had been made for had had an impressive bosom indeed.

"This is not the gown of a woman," the faun said as he put the gown back.

"Is it another faun's gown? Are . . . lady . . . fauns very tall?"

"No, it is not the gown of a female of my kind, either," he said sadly. "Most females were smaller than I, but it has been many years since I have seen one."

"Are you not permitted to leave the palace?"

"Oh, my, no!" The faun shook his curly head. "I haven't been outside these walls since I arrived."

"Are you enchanted, like the bear?"

"That door beside the mirror leads to your washroom, my lady" was all he said. "I'll leave you now. When you are ready to eat, pull the bellpull beside any of the fireplaces, and I shall bring your meal." And he trotted away, the sound of his hooves muffled by the thick carpets.

"That was odd," she remarked after he had left.

Rollo looked over at his mistress. He was standing beside the little table, sniffing its contents with interest. "We're the guests of a giant *isbjørn* who lives in a palace made of ice" was his comment.

"I suppose you're right," the lass said.

She went through the door beside the mirror to see what a "washroom" was. It was a small room with an ornate washbasin, large bathtub, and chamber pot, all made of greenish ice. The chamber pot was as tall as a chair and half full of water.

Rollo and the lass stared at it for a moment.

"Perhaps it's not a chamber pot," the wolf hazarded. "Perhaps it's water for me to drink."

"But it looks like one," the lass argued.

"What does that do?" With his nose, Rollo pointed to the golden knob shaped like a pinecone that sat on the back of the strange contraption.

The lass tried spinning it, but that did nothing. She tried pulling it, but that also did nothing. When she pressed it straight down, however, the water in the pot swirled around and went out the hole in the bottom.

"That's amazing," she said. "Look at that! The . . . waste . . . will all go out and away."

"I still say it's for me to drink."

"Well, I need a chamber pot," the lass said, "so I'm going to try it. Go and lie down by the fire."

"Which one?"

"I don't care, just go." She gave him a gentle boot to the rear, and closed the door of the washroom behind him. When she was done with the odd chamber pot, she discovered that knobs shaped like acorns caused the washbasin to fill with water, and the tub as well. Little crystal jars of soft potions that smelled of flowers had been set on a shelf above the tub, and there was a bar holding soft white towels on the wall beside it.

With a sigh, the lass took off her clothes and slid into a gloriously warm bath. For the first time in her life, she was the first person to use the water. It was so relaxing, she could have fallen asleep. Rollo kept scratching at the door, though, to remind her that he hadn't eaten all day either, and that the idea of submerging oneself entirely in hot water was unnatural. With another sigh, she got out of the tub after no more than half an hour, dried herself, and put on a long robe of fur-trimmed silk that dragged on the ground behind her and slipped off her shoulders when she moved her arms too much.

As she and Rollo sat down to the supper Erasmus served in her sitting room, she looked around and smiled.

"I could get used to living in a palace. Especially since I know that soon my family will have wealth as well." She spread a snowy napkin across her lap and tore off a hunk of the whitest bread she had ever seen.

Rollo looked up from the platter of meat he was attacking. "We shall live here for only a year," he reminded his mistress. "And there is something not right about this."

"I know, but let me enjoy it for just one night," she said.

"All right, but be careful." And then he went back to gorging himself.

"Just one night," the lass murmured. "Then I shall get to the bottom of this enchantment. Of all these enchantments."

Chapter 10

The lass went down to the entrance hall as soon as she finished breakfast the next morning. With Rollo by her side, she started at the pillar nearest the golden front doors.

"Man. Reindeer. Ship. Something. Ship. Something. Man."

"That doesn't make any sense," Rollo pointed out. "None of them do."

"I'm aware of that, Rollo." The lass put her hands on her hips and sighed. "The trouble is, Hans Peter never bothered to carve things like 'run' or 'sail' or 'hunt.' He only carved things like 'reindeer' and 'man' and 'ship.' So I know that there's a man and a reindeer, and they have a ship, but I don't know what they're doing." She rested her forehead against the smooth ice. She'd been deciphering the carvings for hours. "Stupid!"

"Are you well, my lady?"

The lass jumped and spun around. Erasmus was standing behind her with a strange look on his face.

"Oh, yes, I'm fine, thank you. I just—I was—" She gestured at the pillar.

"You were just what, my lady?" There was a wary look in the faun's eyes.

It occurred to the lass that she barely knew this strange creature. He had seemed sad, and pitiable, last night when he spoke of his years inside the ice palace. But that might be an act. Could she trust him?

She decided to be wary. "I got lost," she lied. "I was . . . looking for the *isbjørn*."

Erasmus blinked as though not certain he could believe her, and the lass gave him a wide, innocent smile. The wary look left the faun's eyes. "My lord sent me to fetch you for luncheon," he said. "If you will follow me?"

The lass followed him out of the entrance hall and down a wide corridor. All along the corridor were niches with pedestals in them. On one pedestal sat a straw basket. The next held a pair of knitting needles with a half-finished mitten on one needle, the ball of yarn neatly placed beside it.

"Erasmus?"

"My lady?"

"Why are there balls of yarn and baskets and old rag dolls on display?"

The wary look came back to the faun's face. "I couldn't say, my lady."

The *isbjørn* was waiting for them in a long, narrow room that was dominated by a long, narrow table. The lass counted two dozen chairs, though a golden plate and gleaming silver were set at only one place. The *isbjørn* was hunkered down near that chair, waiting for her.

Feeling a cold thrill down her spine, the lass sat in the place that had been set for her. It unnerved her to see the huge bear sitting there so calmly. As kind as he seemed, she could not forget that he was still an animal, a predator large enough to eat her and Rollo both.

"Did you sleep well?" The rumbling voice sounded genuinely interested.

"Er, yes, thank you."

"That's good."

"Yes."

Erasmus took several platters covered with silver domes from a sideboard and laid them in an arc around the lass's plate. One by one he lifted the covers to reveal delicately seasoned fish, roasted chicken, soft white bread rolls, honeyed fruit, and pickled vegetables. She had never seen most of the things before her, and the things she could identify (fish, chicken, potatoes) she had never seen cooked that way. Her mouth watered and her stomach gave a lurch and a growl.

With a rumbling laugh, the *isbjørn* told her to eat.

"But I had breakfast only a few hours ago. And that was so much . . . fruit and sweet rolls and porridge . . ." She trailed off. "I've never seen so much food in my life."

The bear blinked at her. "But . . . is it so bad? Where you live?"

"The winter has lasted a long time," the lass said, not wanting to give the impression that Jarl was a bad provider. "No one has very much. But my family doesn't starve."

Blinking again, the bear said, "Of course not."

"Aren't you going to eat?" The lass took a piece of succulent fish, then a large portion of the chicken.

"No."

Something in his tone warned her not to ask any more questions about his eating habits. She deboned the fish and started to give it to Rollo, but then she saw Erasmus uncover a platter of raw steak and lay it on the hearthrug next to the wolf.

"Thank you, Erasmus," she said.

He bowed and left.

After eating until she thought she might be sick, the lass staggered out of the dining room. She realized when she was halfway to her rooms that she had forgotten to ask the *isbjørn* about the displays of strange artifacts. But the bear had gone off somewhere, possibly to eat his own luncheon in private.

He had talked a great deal while she ate. He told her that she had the run of the palace, but not to go down into the servants' quarters because it might bother them. He asked her about her family, where her other siblings lived now and what they were like. She answered as best she could while trying not to disgrace herself eating strange food with the almost as strange silver utensils.

Now she started to go back to the entrance hall and look at the pillars again, but the thought of going back down the stairs made her groan aloud. Instead she and Rollo went to her apartments and lay down on the bed.

When they woke, it was time for dinner, and Erasmus was there to lead them to the dining room once more. He took them by a route that had fewer niches with balls of yarn and knitting needles on display. It was also farther from the entrance hall, so not a glimpse of a carved pillar was to be seen. The lass wondered at this: clearly her curiosity made the faun nervous. But had he told the *isbjørn*? And was he upset about it?

So, since she was still full from luncheon, she picked at the magnificent dinner that was spread before her and put some questions to the bear instead. Had he been born here in the ice palace? Did he know what the carvings on the ice pillars meant? Why were there worn-out household tools on display in the hallways?

And the *isbjørn* replied, "Have you tried the beefsteak? It smells wonderful. Do you care for carrots? What about strawberries? I believe that your dessert will be a strawberry tart this evening."

"Would you like some?" The lass gave up trying to get any information out of the bear. She guessed that the enchantment kept him from saying anything.

"Yes, I might try a bit," the bear said, and then turned the conversation to skiing, strangely enough. He took it for granted that the lass knew how, but wondered if she was keen on jumping and the like.

Her brother Einar had recently taught the lass to jump on skis, since prior to being named she had been afraid to venture too far from the cottage. Busy answering this and other questions, she ate more than she meant to, and tried to go to the entrance hall afterward, to walk off some of the dinner, but got lost.

"I told you not to snoop," Rollo said.

"Yes, you did." She rolled her eyes. "Now could you please help me? Can't you smell the dining room, or the entrance hall, or our rooms?"

"No." Rollo shook his head and then sneezed. "Ice doesn't have a very strong smell. And the meat smell makes it even harder to find anything."

"What meat smell?" The lass thought he meant from his dinner but wasn't sure.

"You know, that meat smell everywhere."

"I have no idea what you're talking about," she said as she pushed open a door she thought might lead to the stairs that led down to the entrance hall.

Instead she found herself in a long, high-ceilinged chamber that was only dimly lit by the moonlight filtering through the window panels. She took a step forward, wondering what all the tall shapes in the room were, and stubbed her toe on something. Curious, but not wanting to stub any more toes, she went back into the hallway and got a lamp. She held it high over her head, letting the golden light shine down on—

Rollo plopped back on his haunches in surprise. "Looms?"

"Looms," she agreed.

The room was easily four times the size of her family's cottage, and entirely filled with looms. They were all shapes and sizes and made from all kinds of materials. There was one of elegantly carved whale ivory right next to a battered pine loom that still had a plain gray piece of cloth strung on it. One, of very rough-hewn wood and weighted with rocks, held a shimmering tapestry of breathtaking beauty. Beside it, neatly arrayed on a piece of black velvet, were several small handlooms for making belts.

"This is very odd," the lass said after a minute.

"Yes. It is. Can we go now?"

She looked down at Rollo and was surprised to see that his hackles were raised and he was backing toward the door. "What's wrong with you?"

"These smell like death. And more of that meat."

"All right." She sniffed the air, but all she smelled was furniture polish and wool. But knowing that Rollo's nose was far keener, and his instinct for danger better than hers, she let him lead her out. Farther down the hall, they found the door that led to the right set of stairs and made their way to the entrance hall.

"Rats," the lass said. She was still carrying the lamp

she had taken from the upstairs hallway, but it was the only illumination in the entrance hall. All the torches had been doused for the night, and in the cavernous space, her lamp shed little light. By holding it right against a pillar and leaning in, she could read a few of the symbols at a time, but it soon gave her a headache, and she let Rollo take hold of the hem of her sweater and drag her up the stairs to their rooms.

Vanity overcame her at last, and she pulled one of the silk shifts out of a wardrobe to sleep in. It was far too long and kept slipping off her shoulders, but since no one would see her, she didn't think it mattered.

She had just begun to dream about Hans Peter sitting atop a mountain of *isbjørn* pelts and weeping when a noise startled her awake. It was the sound of the bedchamber door opening.

"Hello? Erasmus?"

No one answered her. She reached for the candle by her bedside but couldn't find it. She fumbled in the drawer of the bedside table, which she could have sworn held both matches and candles, but it was empty.

Soft footsteps approached the bed.

The lass pulled the covers up to her chin. "Rollo?" The wolf didn't reply, and she remembered that he had gone out to sleep by the sitting room fire. Whoever this person was, they had passed by Rollo. She hoped that the wolf was all right.

The stranger pulled aside the bedclothes on the opposite side of the bed and got in. There was a sigh, the mattress shifted as the person settled in, and then nothing.

The lass was rigid with shock. It was too dark to even make out the outline of the person now lying beside her. "Hello? Who are you?"

No answer.

"Who are you?" She managed to say this in a louder voice.

The intruder made a grunting noise and then pulled the bedclothes up over its head. A minute later she heard a faint snore coming from under the bedclothes.

The lass wondered if the *isbjørn* had brought another human back to the palace. As company for her? Whatever the reason, she didn't want to put up with it, she decided. She got out of bed and went to the door that led to the sitting room.

It was locked. Or stuck. The latch wouldn't turn at all. She knocked on the door and called to Rollo, but he didn't respond. She felt her way to the fireplace and pulled the bellpull, but there was no response. She went to the door of the washroom, thinking that she could pad the bathtub with towels and sleep there, but it wouldn't open either. And in a room normally filled with candles and lamps, she could not seem to find one of them.

In the end, she dragged the topmost blanket off the bed and curled up on the divan by the fireplace. The fire had gone out, and the room was dark and chill. Despite the thoughts that whirled in her head, she fell asleep a little while later.

When she woke in the morning, it was to Erasmus setting her breakfast tray on the table beside the divan.

"There was someone in my room last night!" The lass looked indignantly at Erasmus. She noticed that there was a box of matches on the bedside table, right next to the candle that she was certain had not been there the night before.

Erasmus just smiled, a tight, strained smile, and told her that luncheon would be at noon.

Rollo came in, stretched, and begged for a sweet roll. He was unaware that anything unusual had happened in the night, and just looked puzzled when the lass asked him where the devil he had been.

The intruder was gone.

Chapter 11

The lass was more determined than ever to find out why an enchanted bear and something called a faun were inhabiting a palace of ice, and why they needed her. Unfortunately, those same two creatures seemed determined to divert her.

Even though there was a comfortable, human-sized chair in the entrance hall, if she ever spent more than a minute there, Erasmus would pop up and distract her, or the bear would. They didn't mind if she looked at the rest of the palace, though, so for the time being, she turned her attention to that.

Rooms led to rooms that led to still more rooms. All the chambers along the passageway where the lass's apartments were located were similar to hers. Each one was decorated in different colors, but each one had a sitting room, sleeping room, dressing room, and washroom. Hers was the only one occupied, however, so no fires were lit in the other fireplaces, and no strangely oversized gowns crowded the wardrobes.

Other passageways took her to rooms filled with

musical instruments, or strange scientific contraptions, and even more chambers devoted to homely items. She found the loom chamber again, right next to one filled with butter churns. There were washboards and clothes irons and anvils. Hammers, knitting needles, and spinning wheels. There was an entire floor that held only books, with each room devoted to a different language. The lass could only read Norsk, though, so that rather reduced the books available to her.

At least twice a day she saw the *isbjørn*. He would eat luncheon and dinner with her in the long dining room. Well, she would eat, and he would sit on the floor near the table and talk to her. He was never very articulate, but he would ask her what she had done that day and request that she tell him stories from her childhood.

At first she thought that meant the fireside tales that Jarl had regaled them with, which the bear was politely interested in, but then she found out he wanted *real* stories. He wanted to know what it had been like to get up every morning in the freezing cold and gather eggs. He wanted to know about the time they had almost butchered the white-faced doe because of a hidden fox bite. The *isbjørn* positively hungered for stories of everyday life in a woodcutter's cottage. The lass obliged, but she thought his interest very strange.

Any questions about the bear's habits or history were met with stony silence. Once or twice he looked like he wanted to tell her something, but in the end he shook his head and walked off, leaving her to eat the rest of her meal in silence. She didn't press him for information, since it was clear to her that he couldn't just tell her what the nature of his enchantment was. She would have to find out for herself.

She would also have to find out for herself about the stranger who came to her rooms every night. After her second night in the palace, the stranger was her constant bedfellow. The first two times the stranger climbed into bed with her, she climbed right out and slept on the divan, but the third time the lass tried this she was awakened by someone lifting her. Without a word the stranger carried her to the bed and tucked her in. Then the visitor walked around to the other side, got in, and went to sleep, back turned to her.

The lass gave up. She was tired and stiff from sleeping on the divan. Her suggestion to Erasmus that either she or her midnight visitor be moved to other rooms had been met with a question about whether or not she liked custard.

So the lass slept with a strange man in her bed.

She knew it was a man, because on that third night, after he had carried her back to bed, she dared to reach over and touch him. She ran her fingers over his face: he had high cheekbones and a shapely nose. His hair was straight and very thick, worn long so that it brushed the collar of his nightshirt (and she was relieved to feel that he had one).

His chin was slightly stubbly. His breathing continued to be even while she ran her hands over his face and shoulders like a blind person, but she wondered if he was really asleep or just pretending.

Rollo seemed to doubt the stranger's existence, and Erasmus and the *isbjørn* were deaf to any mention of him. She was on her own. She would have thought it was just a dream, but every morning when she woke there was a dent in the pillow beside her, and once she found a single dark hair caught in the lace at the edge of the pillowcase.

The wolf was never in the room when the man appeared, and just looked puzzled when she asked him why he didn't try to stop the intruder. Rollo never saw or heard anyone coming in. He did admit that the bed smelled like a man the next day, but had no idea how this person could have gotten past him.

Another concern that took up the lass's time was clothing. She was not fond of sewing, and the thought of altering those ridiculously ornate gowns had made her shudder. But after two weeks of sitting on silk cushions and dining off fine china while wearing a frayed sweater and patched skirt, she began to feel self-conscious.

Other than her nightshirted bedfellow, she was the only person in the palace who even wore clothes, so she knew that no one else cared. But vanity pricked her for the first time in her life. She was an attractive young woman, and all her life she had worn the much-mended castoffs of eight older siblings. True, these gowns were not new, but they looked like they had been worn only once, and they were of such fine cloth that she was almost embarrassed to touch them with her work-worn hands.

The lass spent a week taking in seams and cutting off excess cloth with a long, sharp pair of shears. It almost made her sick, the first time she did it. Selling one of these gowns would keep her family for a year. And here she was with dozens of them, cutting them up at will and altering their hems with her uneven stitches.

Often the gowns had pearls or precious lace that had to be removed before the seams could be taken in. The lass took some care with this, removing the lace and clusters of pearls and putting them in a scented wooden box in her bedroom. She didn't reattach them to the gowns, preferring her clothing to be plainer, but she had a plan for them.

When the year was over she would return home. The bear had promised wealth for her family—she had seen the sacrifice that would bring it to them—but she wanted to be sure. She knew Askeladden: he was far too lazy and fond of merrymaking. It would hardly surprise her to find that his fame was tarnished and whatever fortune he had found squandered in a few years. But if she could smuggle the pearls and other jewels from these gowns out with her, she could sell them to help her family.

Worrying that she would not be permitted to carry

anything with her when she left, she cut up a hideous gown of puce silk and made herself a belt with ten pockets hanging from it. In each one she placed pearls, coils of gold bullion thread, and even some rubies she removed from the décolletage of a magnificent ball gown. Then she sewed the pockets shut. She wore the belt day and night, taking it off only to bathe, to ensure that no matter what happened she would have some wealth.

That done, and the upper levels of the palace explored, she went lower. She had never seen the kitchen where her sumptuous meals were prepared, or the servants' quarters that Erasmus had spoken of. She had wondered at first if the food was prepared by magic, and Erasmus the only servant, but as the faun grew easier around her, he came to refer to other servants.

"Who are they? Are they fauns, too?"

But Erasmus wouldn't say. The lass remembered the faun's sad look on her first day in the palace, when he had said that it had been years since he'd seen a lady faun. Clearly the other servants were not fauns, and she was certain that they were not human. Why else would they be kept hidden?

Curiosity filled her. What could they be? *Isbjørner*? Dragons? More creatures, like the faun, that she had never known existed?

But Erasmus was adamant that the servants' quarters

were no place for a lady. The lass had argued that, as the daughter of a poor woodcutter, she was certainly not a lady, but he shook his horned head.

"You *are* a lady. You may not have been born in a fine palace, but you live in one now. The kitchens are no place for you."

"I know how to make *lefse*," she cajoled him. "And fruit tarts. I've been in lots of kitchens." Which wasn't quite true: other than her own, the only kitchen she had ever set foot in was her sister Jorunn's.

"I'm sorry, my lady," the faun had said, firmly but gently. "The kitchen is no place for you."

So the lass had no choice but to follow him. Rollo refused to come, saying that it was rude to sneak up on a creature you did not intend to eat. He stayed in his favorite spot by the sitting room fire instead.

Meanwhile, the lass waited until Erasmus removed her breakfast tray, counted to ten, and then slipped down the passageway after him. It was very easy to follow someone through the halls of the palace, since there were niches containing hammers or crochet hooks every few paces. If Erasmus stopped or started to turn around, the lass ducked into a niche, counted to five, and then slipped out again.

In this fashion she followed the faun down six flights of stairs into the bowels of the ice mountain. It was colder here, but only the cold of any cellar. The halls were lit by torches held in ice formations shaped like human fists. Erasmus had to travel quite a ways to reach her when she rang, she realized.

Resolving to call the faun less often and spare him the journey, the lass came around a corner and stopped dead. Before her was a great arch that led into a kitchen the size of the entrance hall three floors above them, but that was not what froze her in her tracks.

It seemed that there *were* other servants to help Erasmus in his work. But the reason why she had never seen them before was clear as soon as her eyes adjusted to what she was seeing: the little goat-legged man was by far the most human looking. The lass couldn't help it; she screamed.

The kitchen exploded into chaos as the servants squawked and roared and hissed and shouted. A half-dozen bizarre creatures rushed to the door of the kitchen and then stopped there, not certain what to do next. It was Erasmus who came forward and calmed them all.

Shaking his head at the lass, he turned to the other servants. "This is our new lady," he told them solemnly. Then he turned to the lass. "My lady, please allow me to present the staff." He clapped his hands and they arranged themselves into a row.

Erasmus went to the end where three orange lizards stood on their tails, tongues flickering and all four feet gently paddling the air. "The cooks: Zah, Szsz, and Sssth," he said, pointing to each in turn. Seeing the question on the lass's face, he added, "They are fire-dwelling salamanders."

"Oh, of course," she said. She smiled at them, trying to look as though she had not just been screaming at the sight of them cavorting in the hearth minutes before. "Your meals are wonderful," she said with perfect sincerity. The three salamanders blushed deep red. All over.

"The scullions: Garth, Kapp, and Nillip. Garth is a minotaurus, Kapp is a brownie, and Nillip is a pixie."

Garth and Kapp both bowed, and Nillip, who seemed to be female, made a curtsy in the air where she hovered. It was Garth who had really made the lass scream. He was easily seven feet tall, with a body like a brick wall and covered in fur that may have been clothing and may have been his own . . . pelt. He had the head of a massive bull, with great black horns and a brass ring in his nose. Kapp and Nillip were not as frightening. The former was about three feet high and looked like a little man made of bark, and the latter was less than a foot high, with butterfly wings.

"How do you do?" the lass said.

"My lady," all three murmured together.

"The chambermaid, Fiona," Erasmus continued, coming to a tall woman the lass had not noticed before. She was beautiful, with white skin and long dark brown hair that hung in curls to her waist. Her big dark eyes flashed as she curtsied to the lass, and she kept one hand clutched at the throat of the fur cloak she wore.

"How nice to meet you," the lass said, wondering how she could have failed to see that there was another human in the room.

"Fiona is a selkie and cannot speak." Erasmus went on, turning next to an ugly, gray-faced woman with enormous bat wings folded against her back, who wore a long black dress and an immaculate white apron. She—or it, rather—looked as if she were carved from stone. "And this is Mrs. Grey, the housekeeper, a gargoyle."

"How do you do?" The lass had no idea what a selkie or a gargoyle might be, but they looked pleasant enough. Well, Fiona the selkie looked rather sullen, but at least she didn't look dangerous, as the minotaurus did.

"A pleasure to serve you, my lady," the gargoyle said. Her voice sounded like two stones being rubbed together. "If there is anything you need, just tell us."

"Yes, thank you, you're doing a . . . wonderful job," the lass said lamely. She had never had servants before, and now that the initial shock of seeing what they were had worn off, she didn't know what else to do. She did recover from her embarrassment enough to notice that they, like Erasmus, all wore an embroidered ribbon around their necks.

"Perhaps you should return to the upper levels, my lady," Erasmus suggested.

Relieved by the suggestion, the lass smiled and nodded and did as he said. Back in the entrance hall, with its huge fireplace and comfortable chair, she sat for a while and thought. This was an enchantment beyond the ordinary fairy-tale kind she was used to.

First of all, there was the *isbjørn* that lived in a palace made of ice. But for the first time she asked herself why. *Why* did an *isbjørn* live in a palace of *ice*? Why did he live in a palace at all? And what did he need her for, for just a year? She had suspected that he came to her because she could understand him, but he didn't seem to want—or to be able—to tell her what was wrong.

Now there were the servants. A faun, salamanders, a gargoyle, and . . . those other creatures. Where were they from, and why were they here? Erasmus would not answer such questions either. She would try to ask the others, but she had a hunch that they would be just as evasive.

It all came back to the white bear. The servants were here because of him. She was here because of him. Perhaps even this palace was here because of him. But why? Why was he so special? And what, for a bear, would be so terrible about living in a palace and being waited on by servants? What would be so terrible about it for anyone?

"The heart of the matter is who or what enchanted them," she said aloud. "If I can find that out, I can find out why, and how."

"Who are you talking to?" The *isbjørn* lumbered over to the fireplace.

"Myself." She blushed.

"Oh. Am I interrupting?"

"Er. No. I can talk to myself anytime, I suppose." She blushed even harder.

He sat on his haunches beside her chair and looked uncomfortable. "Erasmus told me that you met the other servants," he said after a while.

"Oh, yes, they're all quite nice." Then, for lack of anything else to say, she added, "Why can't the selkie talk? What *is* a selkie?"

The bear gave a little grunt of laughter. "A seal who can turn into a woman. Fiona *can* talk, and frequently does, but she is under orders not to talk to *you*."

"Why is that?" The lass was offended. The seal-woman was the closest thing there was to a human in the palace, and she had been wondering if there was some way they could communicate so that they might be friends.

"Because if a selkie talks to a human, the human is bewitched by their voice. Before you knew it, *you'd* be waiting on *her* hand and foot," the bear explained.

The lass shrugged. "It makes about as much sense as her waiting on me. I'm only the daughter of a woodcutter."

"Yes, but you make a much kinder mistress than the selkie would ever be. Believe me."

"Oh?" The lass arched an eyebrow at him.

The *isbjørn* gave his rumbling, growling laugh. "Her kind delights in singing to sailors so that their ships run aground on the rocks."

The lass shuddered. "Oh, I see." She reconsidered her idea of courting Fiona's friendship. "Is the person who enchanted you the same person who brought the servants here?" She blurted out the question quickly, hoping to take him off guard.

The bear reeled back, one massive paw waving in the air. "What?"

"Is the person who enchanted you the same one who brought the servants here?" she asked all in one breath.

"Yes!" The word sounded like it had been wrenched out of him.

They sat in silence for a while.

"Are you happy here?" The *isbjørn* almost shouted it.

"What?" The blurted question aimed back at her took the lass by surprise.

Rather than running all the words together, as she had, the bear repeated his question more distinctly. "Are you happy here? Do you like it?"

"Well, yes. It's beautiful, and I've never had such wonderful food." She gestured at her awkwardly tailored gown, which was of peach silk embroidered with gold. "And I've never had such fine clothing."

"Do you miss your family?"

The lass froze, one hand still smoothing her silk skirt.

The first few days at the palace, she thought that she would be sick with longing for Hans Peter and her father. She told herself over and over again that they were well, they were safe, they were rich, the *isbjørn* had promised. And then the excitement of exploring the ice palace and refitting the beautiful gowns had captured her attention. While she still missed her family and their little cottage, the pain of it had faded to a dull ache that she mostly ignored.

"Do you?" the bear pressed.

"Yes," she said in a halting voice. Guilt that she had not thought about Hans Peter all day made tears rush to her eyes. "My brother Hans Peter most of all."

"I'm sorry," the bear sighed. "I will see if arrangements can be made."

"What kind of arrangements?" For a moment, a flutter of hope rose in her breast. Would he bring Hans Peter here to stay with her for the rest of the year?

"I will try to have letters sent to them, and from them to you," the bear clarified.

"Oh." The lass felt her elation ebb, but consoled herself that letters would be better than no contact at all. And she had been in the ice palace for a month now. There were only eleven months left of her stay here.

The bear lumbered away. "I will see you at dinner," he said over his shoulder.

Moody, she got to her feet and wandered over to

poke at the fire with the silver-handled poker that hung from the mantel. While she jabbed at the half-burned logs, she rested her free hand on the carvings of the mantel. It felt like her dress: slick and slightly cold. Something about the pose stirred her memory, and for a moment she had a strange doubling sensation, as though she were simultaneously in the bear's palace and back at home in the cottage.

The fingers holding the poker felt numb, and the lass dropped the heavy instrument with a clatter. She stumbled back from the fireplace, not wanting to catch her skirt on fire in her dizziness. She half sat, half fell into the chair, and when her head cleared she rubbed her face and looked up at the mantel.

The ice mantel felt exactly like the mantel back in the cottage. She got to her feet and moved closer, squinting at the greenish white patterns on the mantel. It showed more of the same angular symbols that graced the support pillars of the great hall and ran in bands around the white parka.

"It doesn't just look like the carving on our mantel at home," she mused aloud, her breath misting the air a little because her nose was only inches from the mantel. "It's an exact copy of the mantel at home. Or rather, the cottage mantel is the copy."

Two years ago Hans Peter had said that he "wanted a change" and made over the cottage mantelpiece. He had worked for days, fitting some new wood across the top, reshaping the old, and then finally carving those strange symbols that had captivated his youngest sister since his return from the sea.

"Do they mean anything?" the young lass had asked, tracing the raw new markings with a finger.

"It's a story," Hans Peter had told her as he mixed some oil to rub into the wood.

"What story?"

"A wonderful story," he had said, his voice grim. "A wonderful story about a princess in a palace who is more beautiful than the dawn and longs for a handsome young man to love her."

"It sounds silly," the lass had said. She had been at the age when she scorned anything remotely girlish.

"It's actually a horrible story," Hans Peter had told her, his voice darker than ever. "Because it is all a lie." And then he would speak no more of the carvings or the strange story.

"I bet I can piece it together," the lass said now, frowning at the marks and moving to the far left of the mantel. "Love." She traced a familiar mark with her finger. "Liar, man, sorrow, alone, tower." She frowned harder, and then on a hunch, she walked to the right side of the fireplace. "The symbols run backward," she said with satisfaction, upon seeing the marks for "long ago," "princess," and "beautiful." "It's a language, a backward language. And I can read it!" She slapped her hands on the ice in triumph. Then another thought came to her, and her hands fell to her sides like weights.

I can read this because Hans Peter taught me how. He can read this language. He knows this story. He has been here.

Chapter 12

Once she interpreted the story on the mantel, the strange language began to open up for the lass. Some of the nuances were lost on her, and she didn't know all the words, but she could get the gist of the stories. She read two of the pillars and the elaborate bands of carving over the golden door. There were a great many mentions of the beautiful princess, and her endless search for love, but the tales seemed to be more menacing than romantic. To the lass, it looked as though the princess was ordering every man she came upon to love her. It was time for supper when she turned around to see Erasmus and Rollo standing behind her, looking quizzical.

"Hello," she said, dropping her hands self-consciously. She had been running her fingers over one of the doorposts.

"What are you doing?" Rollo cocked his head to one side. "You missed luncheon *and* tea." There was no greater sin than missing a meal, in the wolf's mind.

"Well, then, you should have come to find me," she told him.

"The fireplace was too warm," he said, and then stretched languidly. "And when Erasmus came to take away the uneaten tea tray, I thought I'd better follow him to the kitchen, and see if you were still down there. But you weren't, so we came to look for you here."

"I was worried that you were still, er, shocked from this afternoon," Erasmus said, blushing. "But then Rollo assured me that you would be fine, since he was fine, and convinced the salamanders to give him cake." His blush faded and he smiled at this.

"Yes, I'm sorry for the inconvenience," the lass apologized. "For *all* the inconvenience I've caused." Now that Rollo had mentioned the missed meals and the uneaten trays, her stomach growled loudly. "Pardon me!"

"You must be starving," the faun said with a laugh. "Dinner is ready, if you are."

"Yes, please!" She gestured for Erasmus to lead the way to the dining room. "I'm so thirsty I could lick the walls!"

"The walls taste terrible," Rollo told her. "I tried it on our first day here. The ice tastes like rancid meat." He shuddered and then shook out his pelt with a look of distaste.

"What?" The lass stopped in her tracks, putting out a hand to touch the nearest pillar. "It does?" She almost licked the pillar, then and there, to see if Rollo was right. Ice that didn't melt and wasn't cold obviously wasn't regular ice, but why would it taste like rancid meat?

"Please, my lady, dinner is getting cold," Erasmus said,

his face pale. "And you should not be licking the walls," he told the wolf in a severe voice. "They are . . . you must realize this isn't . . . the sort of ice you're accustomed to."

"Oh, of course." Smiling innocently, the lass resolved to lick the wall of her bedchamber as soon as she was alone.

In the dining room the white bear was already waiting, sitting by the side of the lass's chair. She greeted him politely, and took her seat. Erasmus served her a meal of the usual magnificence: clear soup seasoned with strange herbs, vegetables roasted with honey, fish coated in hazelnuts and drenched in cherry preserves. Afterward there was cake that had been soaked in cream and drizzled with caramel.

"Please thank the salamanders," she sighed when she was finished. She leaned back in her chair and laid her napkin aside. "They are fantastic cooks."

"I shall tell them, my lady. They will be thrilled."

By the fire, Rollo rolled over and let his tongue hang out of his mouth. He'd had a fine cut of meat and a bit of the cake, which the lass had dropped into his bowl. The bear had also had a piece of cake, but otherwise had made only idle conversation while the lass and Rollo ate. He'd asked her if she'd seen the paintings in the long gallery, and did she like them (not really, they were all quite gruesome battle scenes) and had she read any of the books in the library (yes, and they were delightful).

"So you do like it here?" The bear's voice was wistful.

"Yes, of course!" She leaned sideways out of her chair and patted one of his huge paws. "And don't worry, I'm going to figure out this enchantment."

"No!" He reeled back and his claws and teeth flashed at her. The lass shrank back in her chair, and the *isbjørn* relaxed. Slightly. "Be careful," he said, his voice rough. "It would be better if you just waited."

"Waited for what?"

"For the year to end."

"And then will you tell me where this palace came from?"

"Yes." He nodded gravely.

"Who carved the mantel in the great hall?"

The bear blinked at her change in subject. "I don't know."

"So you didn't build this palace? Who did?"

Silence. The bear slowly shook his head at her, as though her endless questions disappointed him.

Nevertheless she forged on. "Can *you* read the carving on the pillars?"

"Sometimes."

"What do you mean?"

"Bear eyes are not good for reading," he said, his reluctance clear in his voice. "It's late. Good night." He lumbered to his feet and out of the dining room.

"Wait, please! Would you like me to read them to you?" She followed him out of the dining room. Perhaps between the two of them they would be able to decipher every symbol. "*Isbjørn,* would you like that?"

But he just lumbered away, through a large door that locked behind him.

"Humans are too nosy," Rollo said as he followed his mistress to their own rooms.

"Oh, hush," the lass said, thinking hard. "If you knew what was carved on those pillars, you would be curious too."

"I don't want to know. I don't want to know why the walls smell rotten. It's only going to lead to something bad."

"Rollo!" The lass was exasperated by his lack of curiosity. "Don't you want to know why we're here?"

"Yes, but I'm willing to wait until it's time to know."

They continued on to their rooms in silence. In silence, Rollo watched the lass take off her gown and put on a nightrobe. In silence, she brushed out her reddish gold hair and washed her face. The wolf sat beside her chair as she read a chapter of a book, a history of the first kings of the North.

Finally, when she was getting into bed, Rollo whined.

"What is it?" One foot on the floor, one foot in the soft bed, she looked at him. "Do you need to go out? The door isn't locked."

"No, I do not need to go out." He sounded testy.

"What is it, then?"

"My curiosity is getting to me," he said in a disgusted growl.

"About what?"

"About what it says on the pillars," he snapped, as though it should have been obvious. "You don't tempt a wolf by saying you've read something curious, and then not tell him!"

"Well, and who's nosy now?" The lass put her other foot in bed and gave the wolf an arch look.

"Just tell me," Rollo pleaded, embarrassed.

"Well, from what I can tell it's the story of a princess who lived in a palace and dreamed of finding a handsome man who would love her. But the man, or it might be men, she found insulted her, and she was very sad. Or maybe it was bitter." The lass drew up her knees under the comforter and wrapped her arms around them.

"Humph" was Rollo's comment. "That's not *that* interesting. Humans are always doing things like that."

"Who said they were humans?" The lass raised one eyebrow at him.

"What are they then?"

"I don't know what the princess was; it just says that she's a princess. But all the other symbols for people have a mark underneath that Hans Peter told me meant, well, people. It says that she's looking for a handsome *man*. Very clearly. But on the pillars there are stories about warriors and princes and ladies, and there are different marks underneath, which I think mean they are different creatures. Like Erasmus and the rest of the servants."

"What are the other stories about?"

"Well, there's one about the beautiful princess seeing some maidens in a forest. I'm not sure, but I don't think they're human. The princess speaks to them and they run away, screaming. Except for one, who taunts the princess. The cruel maiden is stricken dead, and her betrothed attacks the princess. She has mercy on him, however, and takes him to live in her palace so that he can learn what goodness and beauty really are."

"That sounds terrible."

"It does?" The lass gave Rollo a surprised look.

Rollo nodded. "First of all, why did the maidens run when the princess appeared? What did she do that scared them?"

"I didn't think of that."

"Sounds to me like this princess isn't all that beautiful, if all her lovers betray her and other females run screaming when she appears."

"Well, maybe it's just like when I saw the servants today. They're all very strange, you know, but once you get over the shock, they are quite striking in their different ways."

"Maybe," Rollo said, but he sounded doubtful. "But then I don't think what the princess did next was very nice, either."

"Taking the betrothed to live with her?"

"To teach him a lesson, you said. His lover just died,

and this strange princess whatever-she-is takes him away from his home to her palace to be her slave."

"I never said he was her slave, just that—"

There was a crash from the doorway of her bedchamber. Rollo leaped to his feet and the lass shrieked before she saw that it was Erasmus. He was staring at her in shock, and at his cloven hooves was a dented tray and a broken mug. Hot chocolate was seeping into the rug.

"Erasmus, are you all right?" The lass hopped out of bed and hurried over to the faun.

"Who—where—how—do you know that story?" he gasped.

The lass was temporarily offended by the thought that Erasmus had been eavesdropping on her. "Why?"

"I—n-no reason," he stuttered. "It sounded . . . familiar."

"I read it off one of the pillars in the great hall," she said, her mood softening. Erasmus looked gray with shock.

"You can read the—the language of the tr—of the pillars?" He stared at her in a mixture of awe and fear.

"Yes, my brother taught me," she said, taken aback by his reaction.

"Your brother?" The faun looked openly astonished now.

"My eldest brother, Hans Peter," she clarified, though it seemed silly, as the faun didn't know her brothers' names, or indeed that she had any.

"Hans Peter *Jarlson?*" The faun's voice was barely a whisper.

The lass grabbed Erasmus's slender shoulders. "How do you know him?"

Erasmus slipped from her grasp. "A terrible mistake has been made. *She* will be so angry." His face was white and tight with fear.

"Who will?"

The faun shuddered. "I hope you never know." His voice was bleak. "I will send Fiona to clean up." He scurried away.

Fiona entered a few minutes later. The lass had stacked the pieces of the broken mug on the tray and set it on a side table.

The selkie used wet towels to blot the stain and carried away the tray of broken china without saying a word. The lass had started to make several comments, but Fiona's grim expression caused the words to die in her throat.

When her bedfellow came in at midnight, the lass was still awake. Annoyed, she hopped out of bed as soon as he got in. She tripped over her slippers, struck her arm on the divan, and shouted in anger.

"I am not in the mood for you," she said between gritted teeth. "One of us is going to sleep on the divan." She waited, but there was no answer. Of course. "Fine then, I will," she snapped. She yanked the white bearskin off the bed, dragged it over her shoulders, and lay down.

Her visitor didn't even wait until she had gotten comfortable before he got out of bed, picked her up, and tucked her in on her side of the bed. She tried to jump back out, but he pinned her down. When she finally relaxed, he let go and went to his side of the bed.

"If this is part of the enchantment, it's a very stupid part," she griped. But, tired and wanting to think over all that she had seen that day, she stayed in the bed. Her bedfellow heaved a sigh that reminded her of Rollo and went to sleep.

The lass was awake until nearly dawn, thinking about princesses who made people run screaming from them, and the expression on Erasmus's face when he had heard the story.

And the fact that Hans Peter had most certainly been a guest in the palace of ice.

Chapter 13

The next morning, feeling irritable and out of sorts, the lass leaned over to pummel her bedfellow's pillow. Her irritation vanished as she spied a dark hair on the pillowcase. She fingered it, but it felt exactly like one of her own. Finally she coiled it around one finger and put it in the wooden box with her stash of lace and pearls.

She did not see Erasmus all that day. Instead, Fiona served luncheon and dinner and brought the lass her nighttime cup of cocoa. The next day it was the same: no Erasmus, but the sullen selkie instead. The *isbjørn* was now ignoring her questions about both the carvings in the ice pillars and Erasmus's whereabouts. She felt like she was being punished for something, but she didn't know what. What did it matter how many questions she asked? Especially if no one answered them.

It was almost a week before she saw the faun again. Walking through the great hall, she came upon him standing with his nose just inches from one of the pillars, hands behind his back. He rocked back and forth on his black hooves, and the lass deliberately scuffed her kid slippers on a rug to announce herself.

"Oh!" The faun whirled around. "My lady!"

"Where were you?"

"N-nowhere."

"Well, I'm glad that *you're* talking to me, now that you're back," the lass said. "I'm sorry if I upset you before."

"It is not your fault, my lady," the faun said, edging away from the pillar.

Realizing that he couldn't read the language inscribed upon it, the lass pointed to another pillar. "That's the one," she said quietly.

"Oh." Erasmus glanced at it, licking his lips. He looked over his shoulder, and then past the lass, but there was no one else to be seen. Rollo had gone for his morning "constitutional."

The lass walked over to the pillar in question, and after a moment's hesitation Erasmus joined her, his hooves clicking loudly on the ice floor. She read the story out loud, pointing to each symbol with her finger.

"I don't know what this means, but I know that the sign above it means that they were young females," she said.

"Faun," he breathed. "That must be the sign for faun in . . . this language."

"Then do you know what this is?" She pointed to the symbol that was under the sign for princess. "I know that this"—she traced the "princess" symbol—"means 'princess.'"

"I can guess."

"What is it?"

The faun paused, his face white. "Troll." He breathed the word into the still air, not looking at the lass, but staring at the symbol her finger touched as though it were poisonous.

The lass didn't know what to say. "I thought that trolls were all ugly," she said finally. "But I suppose that even troll princesses are beautiful."

The faun only shuddered.

A thought struck the lass and she felt her stomach drop into her slippers. "Troll magic built this palace, didn't it? It's a troll's enchantment that holds the *isbjørn* here."

Another shudder. "I've said too much," Erasmus said, real fear in his voice. "I must go." He clattered away.

"No, wait! Please? Tell me more!" But as fast as the lass ran, he was faster, and he only shook his head without looking around.

When he reached the door that led down to the kitchens, he started down the steps but then stopped and half turned. The lass stopped as well, a few paces away, one hand outstretched in apology or pleading, she wasn't sure which.

"The name of the faun maiden," Erasmus said suddenly,

his voice strangled. "The one who defied the troll princess and died because of her wicked tongue."

The lass had to lick her lips to make any word come out. "Yes?"

"It was 'Narella.' In our language, it means 'bright one.'" And then he hurried down the dark stairway to the servants' domain.

"Narella," the girl said. It was a beautiful name. She had a natural envy of beautiful women's names, having gone so long without one of her own. She stilled the envy by thinking of the name bequeathed by the white reindeer, which to her was the most beautiful name of all. She stilled it, too, by thinking that the faun maiden, Narella, was dead.

"The white reindeer," she breathed. "The white reindeer," she repeated, louder this time. She smacked the side of her head, feeling like a fool. So many years had passed, and so much had happened since then, that she had forgotten what she had first asked the reindeer for: a cure for Hans Peter. And the reindeer, upon seeing the embroidery on the white parka, had drawn back and said that Hans Peter was troll-cursed. "I should have put these things together long ago," she muttered to herself, feeling both foolish and frightened now.

Subdued, she went back to her apartments, where Rollo lay in his usual position before the fire. His middle was noticeably thicker from the rich steaks and sweets he had been eating and he barely stirred when she entered. She sat in a chair by the fire and put her slippered feet on his rib cage.

"Narella," she said.

"God bless you," he replied.

She rubbed her feet in his fur in irritation. "I've just been talking with Erasmus. You remember the story of the maidens who were frolicking, and then the princess discovered them and they fled? The one who didn't run, the defiant one, was named Narella. She was a faun." The lass took a deep breath. "And her betrothed was named Erasmus. Our Erasmus is the person being taught goodness and beauty."

Rollo rolled out from under her feet and sat up. "Did he tell you this?"

"No. And yes. I found him looking at the pillars, and I showed him the right one, and he said that the symbol I couldn't figure out, beneath the symbol for maiden, means faun. Then I asked him what the symbol under the one for princess meant."

"What does it mean?" Rollo's ears were pricked forward, and he was leaning in close to her, his chest pressed against her knees.

"Troll." Saying it again made her shiver.

It was nothing compared to the shudder that racked Rollo, raising his hackles and curling his lips over his white teeth. "Then that rotten smell is the smell of troll," he said.

He went into the bedchamber. The lass, following, saw

him go through the chamber and into her dressing room. He stood in the middle of the rug there, looking at her.

"What are you doing?" She stopped in the doorway, putting one hand on the frame. She felt tired, drained, and sick. Troll magic.

"Put on your old things." The wolf's voice was tense. "We're leaving."

"We can't."

"Nobody said anything about having to live in a troll's lair." Every muscle in Rollo's body was tense.

"Rollo, I gave my word that I would stay here for one year. It's only been two months."

"And the bear promised that you would not be harmed."

"But I haven't been. We're perfectly safe."

"It's not safe. How could it be safe? Trolls! *Trolls!*" He paced nervously. "Erasmus is trapped here, the *isbjørn* is trapped here, Erasmus's female was killed—we need to get out!"

"I can't. I've given my word!" She clung to the slick doorway. Rollo's fear fueled her own and her knees turned to water. She thought she might be sick. This was a troll's house.

"We were tricked! A promise given to a liar is no promise," Rollo argued.

"But he didn't lie. He didn't say anything. He couldn't; he's trapped too! We have to help him!"

"Why? What is he to you?"

"Nothing . . . no! He's my friend, and yours," she said. "I won't leave the *isbjørn* here to suffer under this enchantment. And if I can help him, I can help Hans Peter." She felt a strange stirring in her breast, though, and suddenly knew that even if it weren't for Hans Peter, she would not leave the *isbjørn*.

Rollo whined and pawed at the door of the wardrobe where his mistress kept her old clothes. "I don't like this. I think we should go."

The lass's attention went to the wardrobe. Everything else faded away. The wardrobe. Her old clothes. The white reindeer's words. Hans Peter's coat.

"The troll language," she blurted out.

Rollo stopped midwhine. "What?"

"The embroidery on Hans Peter's coat is in the troll language," she said, racing over to the wardrobe and ripping open the doors.

Pulling out the white parka, she sank to the floor with it. The bands of embroidery glared at her, the whorls and spikes at last taking on meaning before her eyes. The symbols here were more jagged, and more menacing, than those she had seen carved, and embroidery was harder to decipher than carving. She looked over her shoulder, certain that she was being watched, but there was only Rollo, whining and pacing.

The blue ribbons, embroidered with white, told a

story about love, and loss, and a strange place "beyond the moon." The red ribbons, also embroidered with white, told a similar story of love and loss, but this one was full of betrayal and anger. For the first time she noticed that the blue ribbons overlapped the red, obscuring some of the symbols, and that they seemed to have been embroidered by two very different hands. The blue bands were marked with small and skillful stitches; the red were larger, coarser, and yet more forceful in their execution.

"What does it say?" Rollo crowded in close, nudging the parka with his nose.

"It says that the wearer lived here, in the palace of ice," the lass choked out. "No, he . . . must . . . live here. One year, and one day, with a maiden as a . . . bride . . . who never sees his face."

"Like the *isbjørn*," Rollo butted in, "except you are the wrong species to be his bride."

"Also I've seen his face," she pointed out absently, still reading. "That's what the red parts say. They say that he will be betrayed, and then he must go to the princess and . . . love her always," she finished in a rush.

"The troll princess?"

"Yes," the lass said. "That awful troll princess again. I agree with you: she is *not* a good person."

"She's not a person at all, she's a troll," the wolf said, as if that settled the matter.

For the lass it did. This poor, misunderstood princess

who was only looking for love, according to the stories, was really a hideous creature trapping innocents with her magic. She had enslaved Hans Peter, but he had somehow escaped. Or had he?

"There is still some trollish curse on Hans Peter," the lass said. "That is why he is still so unhappy. And why his hair is turning white when he is still so young."

"You won't let us leave until you break this enchantment, will you?" He groaned. "We'll never get home!"

"What makes you think that I can't?"

"Because it's a *troll*. *You* can't fight a troll. *I* can't fight a troll. No one can, and live." He shuddered and shook himself. "Look at the carvings all around this palace. It's nothing but stories of creatures who have been killed or enslaved by this troll."

"Well, perhaps they didn't know what they were facing. But we do," the lass said, feeling rather insulted. If Rollo didn't believe in her, who did?

"Gaaah," Rollo said. Then he changed the subject. "What does the blue part say?" He nosed the parka.

"Oh, yes." The lass frowned down on it. "It's not as articulate as the red. It says 'love you always, miss you always' and then something about running, night and day, leaving the place of sun and moon, of ice and snow. 'Never look back, never forget.'"

Chapter 14

The lass was so caught up in trying to read the story from the parka that she didn't notice the time passing. Just like when she had deciphered the pillars in the great hall, she worked through luncheon and tea, poring over the markings. When she grew frustrated with the way the blue bands crossed over the red, she took out her little sewing scissors and delicately snipped the threads that held the blue ribbons in place. Carefully lifting up the loosened blue ribbons, the dire message of the red grew all the more clear.

"There's something strange here," she told Rollo. "I don't quite understand it. Something about trapping him without chains, making him beautiful and terrible where before he was only beautiful. I can't figure it out."

There was a growl from the doorway. Startled, the lass dropped the parka and scrambled to her feet. Rollo snarled and raised his hackles, then relaxed when he saw who it was.

"Are you all right?" The *isbjørn* stood on all fours in the doorway.

"Yes. You just, er, startled me," the lass squeaked.

"I knocked," he said, sounding apologetic. "But you did not answer, and I got worried."

"Oh, yes, I'm sorry, I was . . . busy." She got to her feet and hastily stuffed the parka back in the wardrobe. The white bear was always uncomfortable around any talk of the enchantment, so she didn't see the point in telling him about her recent discoveries.

"I have something for you," the *isbjørn* said, his great, rumbling voice shy.

"What is it?"

"I had to leave it back in the sitting room," he told her, turning around. "Please come and see."

She followed him back through the bedroom and into the sitting room, with Rollo at her heels. The *isbjørn* went over to a small table by the fire and sat on his haunches. With a long black claw he pointed to a slim book that lay on the table.

The lass went over and picked up the book. She could see faint dents in the leather cover where the *isbjørn*'s teeth had marked it as he carried it in his mouth. Otherwise it was very plain, bound in brown leather with nothing printed on the cover. She opened it, and it was blank inside as well. There were only ten pages or so.

"A diary?" She thought it sweet of him, but rather odd.

He laughed. "Not quite. You should not write . . . secrets . . . in it. Your family has its mate. What you write, they will see. What they write, you will see."

The lass stared at the book, and then at the *isbjørn*. "How wonderful!" She put the book down and threw her arms around his thick neck. "Thank you! But will they know how to use it? How did you get it to them? Did you see them? Are they well?"

The *isbjørn* laughed again at her flurry of questions. "No, I did not see them myself. I had a messenger deliver it, with instructions. They would have received it just this morning." He stopped, his brow furrowed. "I warned them in the note not to tell anyone about it, and you must not tell any of the servants here. This is not a thing that you should have, but I . . . I didn't want you to be too homesick."

"I understand." Then she hugged him again. "Thank you, thank you a thousand times!" She took the little book over to the writing desk and got out a pen and ink. "I'm going to write to Hans Peter right away!"

"I thought you would," the *isbjørn* said. His voice was wistful. "Will I see you at dinner?"

"Of course," she said, her mind already on the book. "Just as usual." She didn't hear him leave.

Dear family, she wrote in the little book, *It's me, the pika. I hope that you are all well.*

Then she didn't know what else to write. I live in a palace of ice? Every night a strange young man sleeps in my bed? I'm waited on by servants who aren't human? The palace was made by a troll? These phrases all seemed both alarming and inadequate.

Not knowing what else to do, she closed the book and set her right hand flat upon it. She counted to ten, and then opened it. The words she had written were gone. She riffled through the rest of the pages, but nothing else appeared.

"Well," she said to Rollo. "Now what?"

"I don't like this" was his remark. "It's likely more troll magic."

"Of course it's troll magic," she snapped, "but if it lets me talk to Hans Peter, then I don't—Oh!"

The open page of the book in front of her now contained a word.

Lass?

Hans Peter? she hurried to write.

Are you well? he asked.

Yes! And you? And Father? The others?

The words appeared on the page as quickly as he could write them. *Very well! Askel brought down an isbjørn, and sold it to the royal furrier in Christiania. The king will have no other hunter now. Askel brings him meat for the royal table and furs for his clothing. Askel and Mother live in a fine house in Christiania. Einar is with them.*

The lass gave a grim laugh. It was what her mother had always wanted. *But you?* she wrote, *and Father?*

Father and I remain at the cottage. You would not recognize it, though. The roof is new, a gift from Askel. But we've added another room and new furnishings courtesy of Father's own good luck.

The lass stopped and read what had been written to the impatient Rollo. This last part made her catch her breath. *Father's good luck?*

Day after you left, the first tree he cut down had a treasure inside it. A steel chest of gold coins that had been buried next to the tree when it was a sapling. The tree had grown up around it, hiding it until Father came along.

The lass was very pleased about this. She knew that it would grate on her father's pride to prosper solely because of Askeladden. Now he could boast (not that he ever would) of his own wealth.

Oh, I am so glad, she wrote.

Hans Peter replied, *What of you?*

I hazard that you know what my life is. I live in a palace of ice.

It is as I feared.

You were here, weren't you?

My cowardice has cursed us all. I am sorry, sister.

What do you mean? What happened to you?

There was nothing for a long while, and the lass feared that Hans Peter had gone away and left the book, too sick inside to even respond. She paced the floor in anguish, turning every five paces to look at the book again, willing more writing to appear. When it finally did, she ran to the desk so fast that she stubbed her toe on the chair. She had to hop around and curse for a minute before the tears cleared and she could read.

I cannot say. Even after all these years and all this distance,

I cannot say. Her power is too strong. I am sorry, sister, but you must stumble in the dark as my Tova did.

"Tova?" The lass blinked and looked down at Rollo. "Who is Tova?"

"I don't know," he responded, scratching at her foot impatiently. "Ask him."

She was beautiful, Hans Peter wrote in a shaking hand, *and kind. You would have loved her. She is gone now. I can hear Rolf Simonson hailing me. I shall have Father write to you this evening when he returns.*

And her father did, joyfully begging for news of her well-being and relating the happenings of home. The gold that Jarl had found had allowed him to send proper dowries to his married daughters.

That's wonderful, Father, the lass wrote. *I am glad that you are all doing so well.*

It was late now, and she was already in her nightshift. During supper she had told the *isbjørn* about her conversation with Hans Peter, omitting the mysterious Tova and the talk of his curse. The bear had been pleased that his gift had delighted her, but again warned her not to speak of it in front of anyone else. Whenever Fiona had come in to serve one of the courses, the bear had changed the subject.

Once more, Erasmus was not to be seen.

The lass and Jarl wrote back and forth for some time that night, each desperately trying to sound cheerful and pretend that they were chatting over the table. Jarl promised that he would bring Jorunn in on the secret when she visited next, and have her write to the lass as well.

Elated but tired, the lass closed the little book and climbed into the big bed. Her mind was so busy turning over the events of the day that she hardly noticed when the strange man came and got into bed beside her. When a snore alerted her to his presence, she merely reached over and gave him a poke, much as she would have done to one of her sisters. He rolled over, and they both went to sleep.

Chapter 15

Now that the lass had unlocked the troll language—and had learned that it *was* the troll language—she could not stop searching for answers. She scoured the palace for more carvings and embroidery, and then turned to the library. Finding a blank book, she began to record what she had learned about the troll princess, the fauns, herself, and Hans Peter.

She located a Norsk dictionary and marked the troll counterparts to the words in the margins. Doing this made her realize how limited her troll vocabulary was, but she decided that such words as "ambidextrous" and "penultimate" were useless to her anyway.

"Unless I ever meet the second-to-last troll, and he can use both hands equally well," she mused aloud, with a snicker.

"Pardon me, my lady?"

The lass jumped, slamming the dictionary shut. She turned, guilty at being caught defacing a book, and saw the housekeeper, Mrs. Grey. The gargoyle was standing in the doorway of the library with a long feather duster in one hand. She didn't appear at all concerned that the lass had been writing in one of the books, and the girl relaxed.

"Hello, Mrs. Grey," the lass said. She put the book behind her back anyway. "How are you today?" She really wished that people would stop sneaking up on her.

"Very well, thank you, my lady," Mrs. Grey said. She hovered in the doorway, looking uncertain. "Shall I go to another room, my lady?"

"Not at all." The lass made an expansive gesture. "I don't want to stand in the way of your duties." It had just occurred to her that she had not spoken to the rest of the staff since she had met them.

The lass went over to a chair by the window and sat down. The ice windows were much clearer than the yellowy, bubbly glass that the lass was used to. Unfortunately, the only thing there was to see out of any of them was an endless plain of white snow.

The housekeeper hunched her shoulders self-consciously as she went about the room. At first her dusting efforts were only perfunctory, but as the lass sat humming and writing in the dictionary, Mrs. Grey seemed to relax. Her cleaning became more thorough, and her shoulders unknotted.

The lass struck: "Mrs. Grey, where are you from?"

"Pardon?" The duster clattered onto a side table.

"Where do you come from? You weren't born here in the palace, I'll wager." The lass smiled at her.

"No, I wasn't." The housekeeper picked up her duster with a firm grip, like it was a sword.

"Where, then? I'm sure I've never seen any . . . person . . . like yourself in the North."

"I'm from south of there," Mrs. Grey said primly.

"Where? Danemark?"

"No."

"Prussia?"

"No."

"Italia?"

The housekeeper sighed and looked at her. "My lady, if it will end this questioning: I am from France."

"Really?" The lass put aside her dictionary and sat forward. "What is it like there? Are your . . . kind . . . common in France?"

Mrs. Grey's eyes misted over. "It's as different from the North as turnips and oranges," she said softly. "My people are fairly populous: the French build a great many churches, and we live in the belfries."

The lass cast aside the rather disconcerting image of being watched at prayer by a family of gray, winged things. "Don't you want to go back there?" she asked.

Her spine straightening, Mrs. Grey turned back to her work. "That doesn't matter," she said. She finished dusting quickly and left without another word.

The lass wondered what it would be like to be from Frankrike, as she had grown up calling it. "Frahnce," she said aloud, savoring the word the way that Mrs. Grey had. Would it be strange, she thought, to be from France? No stranger than having gray skin and bat wings, she supposed.

"It would be stranger to be under a troll spell, I suppose," she told Rollo later. She was sitting on the floor in the middle of her dressing room again, carefully sewing the blue ribbons back onto the parka. She felt guilty about defacing her beloved older brother's property.

"At least we aren't yet," Rollo said darkly.

"How do you know?" The lass was curious. She didn't feel cursed, but who knew what that felt like? Rollo had sounded completely certain, though.

"Because I tried to leave the palace," Rollo explained. "I got quite a ways before I thought I'd better come back." He yawned, showing his long white teeth. "But I didn't feel anything forcing me back. So I think that we're free to go."

"*You* are," she said primly. "But I gave my word that I wouldn't leave."

"And I gave my word to your brother that I would stay with you," the wolf countered. "So I shan't leave you, even if you are enchanted. But I don't think that you are. You don't smell like the others."

"That's because I'm the only human," she said with a shrug. She went back to her sewing.

"No, it's because you're not enchanted," Rollo argued. "Everyone here smells different, that's true enough. But there's also another smell, over their regular smell.

That rotting meat smell." His long nose wrinkled. "You don't smell that way, though."

"But the servants do?"

"And the *isbjørn*."

"Maybe they just don't bathe," the lass said, but it was only a halfhearted joke. She believed Rollo; his nose was too keen. "So I *don't* have to stay."

"Only to honor your word," Rollo agreed. "Which, as you know, is a completely arbitrary custom," he added.

"A 'completely arbitrary custom'?" The lass looked at Rollo in amusement. "Who taught you that?"

"Hans Peter told me that before we left," Rollo said. "He said to use it if things got bad; to help convince you it was all right to leave. And if you still wouldn't come, I'm supposed to bite you." He sounded uncomfortable.

They were both silent while they digested this information. For Hans Peter to tell Rollo to bite their beloved lass meant that he expected dire things indeed.

"Well, he *has* been here before," the lass pointed out. She grimaced. "It makes me wonder how bad things were for him, that he would even suggest it. Something tells me he wasn't draped in satin and fed such wonderful food."

At the mention of food, Rollo's stomach growled. "I have been out running on the snow plain all day," he said with great dignity. "And it is time for supper."

"Very true."

So they joined the *isbjørn* for supper. The lass had read a play that the *isbjørn* had recommended, and they discussed it at length. The lass thought that the main female character was too histrionic, but the *isbjørn* argued that when the part was performed right, it was very moving. The lass wanted to know where a bear would have seen a play, and the *isbjørn* changed the subject to poetry, of which he was also fond. The lass knew only a few of the old eddas, so the bear suggested some modern poets for her to try. She promised to read one of them aloud to him at luncheon the next day, and they said their goodnights.

When the lass undressed and went to bed, she checked her little magic book one last time, but there were no new messages from her family. She tucked it under her pillow, along with the diary and the dictionary she was making, and went to sleep.

Tonight her midnight visitor did not snore. During a dream, however, the lass kicked him, then found herself half-awake and patting him on the shoulder in apology. He just grunted, and she rolled over and went back to sleep.

Chapter 16

The days passed in much the same way after that. The lass would read and discuss poetry and novels with the *isbjørn;* she would make notes in her diary and dictionary and meticulously search the palace for clues. She started visiting the kitchens and talking with the other servants, and continued to be waited on in her rooms by Fiona the sullen selkie.

She learned that the minotaurus was from a small island near Greece, and that Erasmus was from another Greek island. She discovered that Mrs. Grey looked as if she had been carved of stone because she really *was* made of stone, and that she would sometimes sit on the top of the palace for days, not moving or even breathing, completely unaffected by the weather.

None of this told the lass how the servants had come to be here, although one of the salamanders did let something slip about Fiona's vanity being her downfall. Unlike the story of Erasmus's beloved Narella, the trolls had not felt it necessary to carve the others' stories into the walls of the palace. The trolls, or Hans Peter.

"I remember your brother," one of the salamanders announced one day. "He was very tall."

The salamander came only to the lass's knee, so she supposed that everyone was tall to him, but in this case he was correct. "Yes, he is tall."

"Is? Is he still living?" The salamander was plainly astonished.

"Yes, of course." The lass was startled by the assumption that he wouldn't be.

"Well, how interesting!" It scampered back to the big kitchen fire and held a hissed conference with the three others. "How interesting," it repeated, climbing back out of the fire.

"What else do you remember about my brother?" Then something occurred to her. She had thought that only Erasmus knew that Hans Peter was her brother. "How did you know that my brother had been here?"

The salamanders exchanged sly looks. "The faun told us," another said, also coming out of the fire. The lass had trouble telling them apart, but that didn't seem to bother them. "But we haven't told anyone else."

"No, not safe," the first agreed. It looked around, but they were the only ones in the kitchen. "Erasmus knew we wouldn't tell."

"That's very kind of you. Now, what was it that you remember? Anything . . . interesting?"

"He liked to read, when he could, and to carve. He

studied the books in the libraries, then carved things into the mantel. Not the pillars, though."

"Who carved those?"

"Some of it has always been here, longer even than we," said the third salamander. It had a higher, softer voice than the others, and the lass suspected that it was a female. "And some was carved by one of the other poor humans."

The other two salamanders shushed her and they all ran back to their fire. They wouldn't say anything more, so the lass went back upstairs.

Every morning after breakfast she would write to her father and Hans Peter, and they would write back. That morning when she opened the book, there was already a message waiting for her, this time from Jorunn.

Dear sister, it said, *I am sorry to tell you this, but Father has been badly hurt.*

The lass gasped, and held the book closer to her eyes, as though that would help her read faster:

Yesterday the tree he was cutting fell on him. His right leg and arm were badly crushed. He was close to Haraldson's farm; their eldest boy found him. The doctor here could do little, so Hans Peter took Father to Christiania. Father was already feverish. I wanted to go, but am too close to delivering this babe. Tordis and her husband came in their sleigh and she went on with them.

I know you cannot come, but I wanted you to know so that you might pray for Father.

All my love,

Jorunn

Numb, the young lass just sat at her elegant little writing desk for a while. Eventually, Rollo woke up from his morning nap and came over to ask what news had come. It wasn't until he put his wet nose into her empty palm that she started and looked at him.

"I think Father is dying," she said, her voice barely a whisper. She swallowed, then choked and coughed and began to sob. "Father is dying!"

She grabbed the little book and ran through the palace. She raced through the library, through the room filled with spinning wheels, the butter churn room, the great gallery full of tools and paintings and printing presses. As she ran she shouted.

"*Isbjørn! Isbjørn!*" She felt stupid, yelling this way. It had never seemed strange to her that the white bear did not have a name—after all, she hadn't told him hers—but now she felt a pang at never having inquired. "*Isbjørn! Isbjørn!*"

"What is it?" He was running toward her down a long corridor, lined with unused bedchambers.

Eyes and nose streaming, out of breath, she held up the little book, not caring how foolish she looked. "My father is dying," she sobbed.

The *isbjørn* squinted at Jorunn's cramped handwriting and then sat back on his haunches. He looked up at the painting hanging on the wall above them—some creatures with horse legs and human torsos cavorting— and then down at her creased and bunched skirts of blue velvet.

"I have to go home," she sobbed.

"You cannot."

"Please," she begged. She reached up and clutched at the fur of his neck, forcing him to look at her. "Please. I will come back. I need only to see him."

He gave one of those sad, growling moans of his, that almost sounded like a cow lowing. "You will come back?"

"Yes, if you still want me."

"I need you," he said. "I will take you to your family today, but you must promise to come back. You must live here one year."

"Yes, of course." She pulled out a lace-edged handker-chief and mopped up her face. "Thank you so much, thank you!"

"You must promise me something else," the bear said, his voice heavy.

"Anything!"

"Promise me that you will not tell anyone the secrets of the palace."

"What?" The lass stopped blowing her nose to stare. She hadn't thought that he knew about her discoveries. "You mean about the tr—"

"Hush! Do not speak of *any* of our secrets. To any-one."

"All right." She scrambled to her feet, feeling much better now that she knew she would be seeing her family soon. "I'll go pack." And she all but ran to her rooms.

Rollo came in a few minutes later. "Where have you been?" he panted.

"Talking to the *isbjørn*. Where have you been?"

With a loud rip, she tore the skirt of an ugly yellow dress free of its bodice. Then she laid the skirt on the bed and began placing gowns and shifts on it. Her old knapsack was not large enough to hold her new clothes, and she refused to go to Christiania looking shabby.

"I was looking for the *isbjørn* as well," Rollo huffed. "I found Mrs. Grey instead. Then the bear roared down to the kitchens that we were going to Christiania, so I came here to tell you."

"I know; I'm trying to pack." She added some shoes to her pile.

"Here, my lady." Mrs. Grey came in, holding a large leather knapsack.

"Oh." She looked down at the dress she had just ruined. "Thank you, Mrs. Grey." The lass changed into her old trousers and the white parka while the gargoyle repacked the lass's things and put them into the knapsack.

In less than an hour she and the *isbjørn* were on their way across the snow plain, Rollo hard on their heels. The sun was so bright on the gleaming snow that the lass pulled the hood of the parka down over her eyes and buried her face in the bear's fur. She dozed as they ran across the snow plain and into the forest. Less frightened and confused by this journey, she was able to see more of the landscape through which they traveled. They ran over hills and across frozen fjords. Night fell as they were running up the side of a mountain, and when the lass woke, the mountain was far behind them. She didn't remember this from their first journey, and sat up as much as she could on the bear's back.

"Where are we?" She had to shout for the sound to carry up to his ear.

"In the North," he called back.

"This is not how we came before," she shouted.

"We are going southwest, to Christiania," he said.

Then he lowered his head and ran even faster through the foothills, dodging trees and boulders. Rollo scampered beside them, hardly even panting. The lass had to duck to avoid being struck by a tree branch.

In this fashion they continued on for another day, stopping only once to eat the food the salamanders had packed. By nightfall of the second day, they had reached the outskirts of the great city of Christiania, where the *isbjørn* had to leave the lass and Rollo.

"Christiania is no place for a snow bear, I suppose," the lass said, trying to sound cheerful. She was anxious about her father, but she also felt a pang at leaving the *isbjørn*.

"No," he said. His speech had become slower and more labored the farther they got from the ice palace. "Remember promises."

"Yes: I shall be with my family for only five days, and

then I will meet you here to return to the castle," she said. It was an awfully short visit, but the *isbjørn* was insistent that she not stay one day longer.

"And?"

"And I shall not speak of any of our secrets," she added. Then she reached out and laid a hand on his head, a lump rising in her throat. "Be safe. Don't let anyone see you."

"Won't."

She blinked back sudden moisture in her eyes and turned away. "Come, Rollo." They hurried out of the little copse of trees that concealed them and onto the road that led to the city. "We'll be back in five days," she called back to the bear.

The bear gave a roar in answer, and the lass saw a flash of gleaming white as he turned and loped off into the deeper forest. "Just five days, and then we'll be back home—I mean, at the ice palace," she said to herself.

"Do you know how to get to Askeladden's house?" Rollo's nails clicked on the hard paving of the road.

"No, but once we get into the city, we'll just have to ask," the lass said, hiking her huge pack up higher on her back. "Surely someone will know where the king's hunter lives."

Rollo just grunted in a skeptical way. With the *isbjørn's* influence fading, he was panting more and his head hung low. "Just as long as it's close," he said.

"Stop complaining," she told him. "In an hour or so,

we'll be sitting in front of a warm fire with Father and Hans Peter, just like old times."

"Or so we hope," Rollo muttered.

The lass didn't ask about his dire statement. She felt strange too. It wouldn't be just like old times. Her father was injured, perhaps dying. She knew some of Hans Peter's secrets, and the family's fortunes had drastically changed.

All because of a bear.

Chapter 17

It was nearly dawn before they found Askeladden's house. The streets of Christiania were confusing to someone who had never seen a village of more than fifty inhabitants. And since it was the dead of night, there was no one from whom they could get directions.

Finally they made their way to the gates of the palace itself. The human palace was square and made of warm yellow stones that looked friendly even in the dim light of the torches placed around the outside. A fatherly *vaktmann* inquired as to her business, and she said she was looking for the home of Askeladden Jarlson.

"Oh, the king's hunter? Are you one of his many sisters?" The man laughed kindly. "Just down the road there, that big gray stone house," he said.

The lass's head reeled a little. Askel lived in a big gray stone house? Just "down the road" from the palace of the king? She glanced down at Rollo, who looked startled as well.

"Thank you," she told the man when she had recovered. When she got to the house she was sure there was some mistake. It was such a grand house, with a slate roof and rich curtains covering all the windows. A fine carriage with a pair of matched bays stood in front of the house, and the servant holding the reins looked at her curiously.

Feigning confidence for the sake of the man watching her, the lass raised her hand and knocked loudly on the door. Almost before she unclenched her fist, the door was flung wide.

A young man stood there in a wash of bright light. He was wearing a nightshirt half tucked into green trousers. "Are you the nurse?"

She goggled at him. "Einar?"

"Pika?" Her next-oldest brother rushed to embrace her. "I can't believe you're here! I thought that *isbjørn* had eaten you!" He squeezed her hard and then turned to thump Rollo's ribs, which the wolf bore with dignity.

"No, no," she wheezed, breathless. "I'm fine! But how is Father?"

Einar pulled back, his face tightening. He looked less the young man now and more the boy she had seen last. "He's bad. The doctor is still with him. Askel called in the king's own physician." His voice was awed. "And now he's sent for a private nurse, too. I thought that's who you were."

"I heard." She forced herself to laugh. "Can I—can I see him?"

"Of course! Tordis is here. And Hans Peter. We've sent word to the others, but I don't know when it will reach them." Einar led her across the high-ceilinged entrance hall to a broad, curving staircase of polished wood. Then he stopped. "Oh," he said, dismayed. "I'm supposed to wait at the door for the nurse."

"It's all right. I found my way this far."

"The first room at the top of the stairs, on your right," Einar said. Then he gave her shoulders another quick squeeze and went back to his post.

With Rollo padding along beside her, the lass went up the stairs, her heart in her throat. There was a gorgeous rose-patterned carpet to muffle their steps, and at the top of the staircase stood a small table holding a vase of Oriental design. The lass wasn't sure which was more alarming: that her brother Askeladden lived here, or that the door just beside the small table concealed her injured father.

Mustering even more courage than she had needed before, she knocked softly on the bedroom door. Her knock pushed the door open, for it had not been properly latched. The scene within the room was much as she had expected: her mother, her sister Tordis, her three eldest brothers, all gathered around a bed where her father, pale and swathed in paler bandages, lay. A storklike man dressed in black leaned over him: the doctor.

"Hello?" The lass clutched at Rollo's ruff for support.

All eyes turned to her, even the bleary eyes of her father. For a moment, no one reacted. Then it was as if the room exploded.

"Lass!"

"Sister!"

"Daughter!"

"How did you get here?"

"Silence, all of you!" This last came from the physician. "Master Oskarson needs quiet!"

Hans Peter reached the lass first, hugging her tightly. Then Tordis, followed by Torst. Askel did not embrace her, but stood with his hands in the pockets of his fine breeches.

"It's all right, Dr. Olafson. This is my youngest sister," he said in a pompous voice.

Their mother did not embrace the lass, either. She stood behind Askeladden, playing with the long silk fringe of the shawl she wore.

"Daughter." Jarl reached out his good hand.

The lass moved slowly toward him. As she went, the warmth of the room made sweat break out on her forehead, and she cast aside the white parka.

Jarl's right arm was splinted and swathed in bandages. The blankets had been folded away from his right leg, which was splinted and wrapped in even more white linen. Both his eyes looked swollen, and there was a massive bruise on his left cheek. The girl knelt beside the bed and reached out to clasp his good hand.

"Father, I'm so sorry," she said with a sob in her throat.

"It wasn't your fault, my daughter," he said, his voice weak, and gave her hand a little squeeze.

She shook her head. She had a horrible feeling that this had something to do with her situation. Not for nothing was bad fortune called "troll-luck" in the North.

"Yes, well . . ." The physician cleared his throat, uncomfortable. "When the nurse arrives, I shall give her the medicines for the pain and fever. She will know what to do."

"Thank you, Dr. Olafson," Askeladden said. He stepped forward and shook the physician's hand. "I will show you out."

The lass couldn't help but stare after her brother. He was so polished, so polite, it was eerie. Seeing her expression, Hans Peter gave a barking laugh.

"As you see, Askel has found his place in the world," he said in his dry way.

"And a good thing he has," their mother said severely. "Where would your poor father be, if Askeladden was not able to call upon the king's own physician?"

Bowing his head, Hans Peter said nothing. Their mother turned on the lass.

"Have you broken your word?" Frida's face was stiff, but the lass thought she saw a hint of fear in her mother's eyes.

Momentarily confused, she blinked, then shook her head. "No, the *isbjørn* brought me to the city so that I could be with Father. I have to go back in a few days."

Frida nodded curtly. "See that you do."

The light dawned on her youngest daughter. Frida was

afraid if the lass broke her word to the bear, their newly acquired wealth would be taken away.

"Such a short visit," Jarl muttered. Then he slipped into sleep.

His youngest daughter watched, fearful, until she saw his chest rise and fall in the rhythm of natural sleep. Then she loosened the hand she still clasped and pulled the blankets over it.

"The physician gave him medicine to ease his pain," Tordis told her, coming to stand by her side. She put an arm around the lass's shoulders. "He said it would make him sleep."

"Will he be all right?"

"Of course he'll be all right," Torst said, his voice gruff. His face was as white and strained as everyone else's, but now he mustered a grin. "He just has to rest. That's what the doctor said."

But Hans Peter was frowning. "We should let him sleep," he said abruptly, picking up his parka and heading out the door.

Frida and Torst followed him, but Tordis and the lass stayed by their father. A few minutes later, an efficient-looking woman with gray braids wrapped around her head and a long apron came in. She smiled at the two girls as she felt their father's wrist for a pulse.

"Are you the nurse?" Tordis whispered.

The woman nodded and put her finger to her lips.

Exchanging looks, the lass and Tordis slipped out of the room.

Still hushed from the sickroom, the two sisters made their way down the wide staircase in silence. Tordis led the way into a sitting room where the rest of the family was gathered.

The lass sat on a sofa beside Tordis and accepted a cup of tea and a slice of bread and cheese. She surveyed the room, which was luxuriously furnished, and then her family. Tordis looked much the same, in clothes that she had made herself, brightly colored and fancifully cut. Hans Peter was dressed in heavy, simple wool clothing, as usual, but there were no patches or frayed cuffs. Askel, Torst, Frida, and Einar were all in fine city clothes, though somewhat disheveled.

"Will Father be all right?" This time it was Einar who asked the dreaded question.

"Of course he will," Askeladden said with false heartiness. He took too large a gulp of coffee and choked. Torst pounded him on the back.

"It will be a miracle if your father ever walks again," Frida said. "He won't lose his arm, but his hand may be of no use. Praise the skies that Askeladden is able to provide for us. At least one of my children was not a waste," she sniffed.

"Father has sufficient means to care for himself," Hans Peter said. He was still clutching the white parka in his hands. With one thumb he rubbed the blue ribbon that ran down the sleeve, and the lass wondered if he had noticed that it had been taken off and then reattached. "Of course, we had to sacrifice our youngest to an enchantment to get where we are. But I'm sure it was all worth it." His voice dripped with sarcasm.

"Yes, it was." The lass put her chin up and spoke the words firmly. "Father will survive this accident. He will be treated by the best doctors and cared for by a professional nurse. Askel and Mother have a comfortable home—"

"You shall have one, too," Askel interrupted her. "When you come back for good, you can come here."

She knew how much it cost Askel to be generous, so the lass smiled at her brother, and thanked him.

"If I hadn't gone with the *isbjørn*," she continued, "we would all still be huddled in a little cottage with a leaky roof. And when Father had his accident, we would have been caring for him ourselves in front of the kitchen fire." She finished this with a curt nod, and took a sip of her now-cool tea.

"You're assuming that Father would have had this accident if the *isbjørn* had never come to us," Hans Peter said, voicing the lass's fears. "I'm going to get some sleep." He stalked out of the room.

The lass hurried after him, catching her brother's sleeve as he reached the bottom of the staircase. "Hans Peter," she said in a low voice, "if you know something about this enchantment that would help me, I would very much like to hear it."

"Be careful. Wait out your year. Come home," he said. He shrugged out of her grip and took the stairs two at a time.

She followed more slowly, allowing Tordis to catch up to her. Upstairs, the lass found a bedchamber had been prepared by one of Askel's numerous servants. She couldn't help but notice that it was much smaller than her bedroom at home—the ice palace, rather. There was no private washroom, only a chamber pot and a washbasin with a ewer of hot water beside it. She did a quick wash, pulled out a clean shift, and climbed into bed.

She told herself that she had trouble getting to sleep because this bed was narrower than she was used to. The sheets were coarser, and the furniture made different shadows.

She refused to admit to herself that she was waiting for a familiar weight to settle itself in the bed next to her. For familiar breath to blow softly against her cheek. In the end she made Rollo get in the bed, where he proceeded to snore and kick and keep her awake until dawn, when she finally gave up and got dressed.

Chapter 18

Three days passed in a blur. The lass spent most of each day in her father's room, holding his good hand and talking to him. She "invented" stories about creatures called fauns and salamanders and selkies that inhabited a fantastical palace of ice. She described books she had read in the palace library. She said she was trying to teach herself a new language, but when he asked what it was, she hastily said, "Fransk." She didn't want him to know that she was learning troll.

She sent Einar to the nearest bookstore to buy a stack of popular novels, and she and Tordis took turns reading to Jarl. They left his side only when the nurse changed his bandages or bathed him, and even then it was a wrench for the lass to be parted from her father.

The day after her arrival, Hans Peter hitched up the reindeer and returned to their old cottage. Everyone had begged him to stay, but he refused. He said that he had things to do ("Ha!" was Frida's response to this), and that Jorunn would be frantic with worry.

"I wish I had brought my little book, so we could have

written to her," the lass said, stroking the nose of the white-faced doe while Hans Peter put his small bundle of clothes and a large hamper of food into the wagon. "Then you could have stayed."

"I wouldn't have stayed anyway," he said tersely.

"I need to talk to you," she insisted. She had been insisting for the past day and a half. She wanted to talk to Hans Peter, alone, and ask him about the ice palace and the enchantment.

"No, you don't," Hans Peter said. Then he sighed and sat down on the driver's seat. "All right, dear little lassie, listen well. You are right: I *was* there. I have seen the great snow plain and the palace of ice. I know Erasmus the faun, and the salamanders that make such fine meals. But I also know the mistress of that house, and the extent of her designs on those who dwell within. Which is why I say to you: be careful, wait out your year, and come home."

"But I think that I can—"

"Be careful. Wait out your year. Come home," he repeated. He gathered up the reins and released the brake on the front left wheel. "You can keep the parka for now, but I would like it back when you return."

He shook the reins and whistled, and the lass hurried out of the way as the reindeer set off. Hans Peter looked back briefly when he reached the end of the street, and waved. His hair shone almost completely white in the sun, making him look like an old, old man.

"Well!" Frida came down the steps and glared after the wagon. "Is he gone, then? And not even a good-bye to his mother, or the brother whose hospitality he took advantage of?"

Her mother's shrewish voice set the lass's teeth on edge. "You know that Hans Peter isn't much for good-byes. And neither is Askel. It would have only embarrassed them both."

Her mother merely sniffed. "I'm going back inside. It's chill out."

All too soon the end of her visit came, and the lass found herself packing her knapsack one morning. Askel said that he would drive her outside of the city to meet the *isbjørn* at dusk, but Jarl was taking a nap and no one else was around, so she began to stow her things. She wore a pretty blue dress for now, but had left out her trousers, a sweater, and the parka to change into later.

There was a knock at the door. "Pika? It's me," Tordis said, sticking her head into the room. "Anxious to go?"

The lass picked up her hairbrush and smiled at her sister. "No," she said. "I just didn't want to waste my last hour with Father by having to pack."

"Can't you stay longer?"

The lass made a face. "I promised that I would go back today. The longer I stay, the longer my year will be."

Tordis stared at her. "What do you mean?"

"I have to stay with the bear for a year and a day. Since

I've been here for five days, that means I have to stay five days longer at the *isbjørn*'s palace."

"Is everything really . . . all right . . . there?"

Now the lass laughed. "I live in a palace with a giant *isbjørn*," she reminded her sister. "It's as 'all right' as it could be." She shook her head, laughing, as she continued to pack. "And it will be a relief to get away from Mother," she muttered, half to herself.

"Mother is much happier now, you know," Tordis said.

"Oh, I'm sure. But her happiness seems to have made her rather nosy," the lass replied. "She's been poking and prying all week. 'What do you eat? How many servants are there? Does the bear have courtiers?' " She pitched her voice higher in imitation of Frida.

It was Tordis's turn to laugh. "That's her exactly," she said. "But it's not like you have anything to hide," she continued. Then her gaze sharpened on the lass, who had lowered her eyes. "Do you?"

"N-no."

Tordis came around the bed and put her arm around the lass. "What's bothering you, little sister?"

"Nothing," the lass said, folding and refolding a shift. The lie sounded obvious even to her ears.

"Nothing?"

"It's just that—" The lass brought herself up short.

"It's just that what?"

Two voices warred in the lass's head. One was the voice

of the white bear, warning her not to tell any "secrets." The other voice was her own, almost crying with loneliness as her sister embraced her. She enjoyed the bear's company, but there was a vast difference between being with him and being with another human, especially one of her sisters.

"It's that . . ." She still hesitated, not sure how to begin. "Well, don't tell Mother or Father, but every night someone gets into bed with me," she said in one breath.

"Someone gets into bed with you? Who?" Tordis's brows drew together.

"I don't know." The lass shrugged. "I can never find a candle at night. It's a huge bed, and . . . they just get in on the other side and go to sleep. They're gone in the morning."

"They?"

"Um, it? I can't see. . . ."

Tordis put her free hand to her throat in dismay. "Is this thing that's sleeping with you human?"

"I think so."

"How can you be sure?"

The lass blushed. "I felt his head," she muttered.

"It's a man?" Tordis's eyes narrowed.

The lass didn't have to speak. Her flaming cheeks said it all.

"A strange man is lying beside you every night? You poor child!" Tordis clucked her tongue. "Just because you think it's a man doesn't mean that it really is, you know."

The lass pulled away to get a better look at Tordis's face. "I don't understand."

"This is an enchanted palace," her sister pointed out. "This . . . man . . . who shares your bed may be under an enchantment as well. It could be a horrible troll, who *feels* human only to lure you into a sense of security."

"I really don't think so." And the lass didn't. There was something so . . . solid and ordinary about her nightly visitor. Compared to the minotaurus in the kitchen, he was almost boring.

"What if this whatever-it-is is playing some game with you? Trying to convince you that it's innocent, so you'll forget it's even there?"

"But what good would that do?"

"Living as deep in the forest as I do, I've heard some horrible stories," Tordis said with solemn certainty. "You don't know what this creature could do to you."

"I don't *feel* threatened," the lass argued.

Tordis just shook her head. "That doesn't matter. You must look at this creature in good light, to make sure that it is not some hideous monster."

"But I told you: I can't ever find any candles at night, and the fire goes out."

Tordis tapped her lips, then went over to a candelabrum on the dresser. The lass had not burned any of those particular candles because they were the herb-scented kind that made her sneeze. Her sister took a small pair of scissors from the pocket of her apron and cut off the top of one. She handed the stub to the lass along with a box of matches she took from another pocket.

"Take these and look at this monster that shares your bed," Tordis advised her. "Our priest says that a candle made in a Christian home can banish any illusion. It's the only way you may be sure that you are safe."

"And if I'm not?" The lass felt an icy trickle down her spine.

"Do what you think best: lock yourself away at night, or escape the palace and come home." Tordis pressed the little box and the short bit of candle into the lass's hands. "Have it with you always. Promise me."

"All right, I will," the lass said, more to reassure Tordis than anything else. She took the proffered items and put them into the bodice of her gown while Tordis watched. The herbs in the candle tickled her nose, and she itched where it rested against her skin. She wiped her fingers surreptitiously on one of her shifts as she packed the last away.

"I'll just go and see if Father is awake yet," she said, edging around the bed. She regretted saying anything now.

Troubled, the lass went to spend the last few precious hours with her father. She could not concentrate on the novel they were hurrying to finish, and she found that the candle itched even worse as her skin warmed the wax. By the time she took leave of her family she was cross, tired, and breaking out in a rash.

"Let's just get back to the palace so that I can have a bath," she grumped to Rollo as they waited in the little copse of trees outside the city. Askel and Torst had driven her there, but she had made them leave at once, knowing that the *isbjørn* would be shy of her brothers.

"You came," the *isbjørn* said, coming out of the trees as though summoned by her thoughts.

Despite her rash and her bad mood, her stomach fluttered when she saw the bear, and she couldn't stop a smile from spreading across her face. "Of course," she said. "I gave my word!" And she scrambled onto his back without being invited, kicking his ribs with her heels as if he were a horse. "Let's go." She rubbed at her chest, willing it to stop itching.

The bear rumbled something that might have been a laugh or a complaint, and began to run. Rollo came after, tongue lolling in anticipation. They were going home.

Chapter 19

Back at the palace, things soon settled into their old routine. The lass would read and try to teach herself the troll language. She and the *isbjørn* would have their meals together and talk, and sometimes she would ride on his back as he raced Rollo across the snow plain. Whenever she thought the bear or one of the servants was off his or her guard, she would blurt out a question and try to surprise them into answering.

She didn't make much progress, though. The servants and the *isbjørn* were all accustomed to her startling questions, and they remained silent on the topic of trolls or enchantment.

But not everything was back the way it used to be. She knew that she had upset Erasmus with her questions, but she had hoped that in time he would shake off his fears and wait on her again. Fiona was hardly a cheery companion, and the lass knew that Rollo missed Erasmus as well.

"Mrs. Grey?" The housekeeper was folding linens at one end of the long kitchen table. "Where is Erasmus? I've been back from my visit for over a month, and yet I haven't seen him. Is he angry with me?"

The housekeeper's sturdy, gray-skinned hands closed on the napkin she was folding, crumpling it into a tiny ball. Her stone eyes closed, and she breathed heavily through her nostrils. This made them flare, taking the gargoyle's face from merely homely to downright hideous.

The lass drew back. "Mrs. Grey?" The salamanders stopped cavorting in the kitchen fire. Garth dropped the knife he had been sharpening and lurched out of the kitchen with a muttered oath.

Mrs. Grey's hands unclenched. Her nails had gone right through the fine linen of the napkin. She smoothed it out, surveyed the holes, and then tossed it into the fire, where one of the salamanders turned it to ash with a burst of breath. The housekeeper flexed the gray wings that were always folded against her back, something the lass had never seen her do. When they had settled again, Mrs. Grey looked at the lass and said, "Erasmus is no longer here."

"Where is he?"

"He is no longer here," Mrs. Grey said again. She cleared her throat, a sound like rocks tumbling in a barrel. "Perhaps you should not spend so much time in the kitchen with the staff, my lady. It isn't seemly."

Knowing that she was being dismissed, the lass got to her feet and left the kitchen. She went upstairs and found Rollo lying in front of the fire in the great hall. She looked at the carving on the mantel, but she'd read it so many times it was a blur. Poking Rollo in the ribs with her toe, she went up to her apartment and checked the blank diary to see if there was any news, but no one had written that day. Hans Peter had not written at all since she returned.

"Well, I'll just *make* him write," she grumbled.

Sitting at the elegant little ice desk, the lass took up her pen. She wrote a note at the top of the page, apologizing to Jorunn because what followed was for Hans Peter's eyes only. Then she described Mrs. Grey's words, her sudden agitation, the salamanders' silence, and the minotaurus's abrupt departure.

I know that Erasmus was here when you were here, and so were the others, she wrote. *Do you know where Erasmus might have gone? I don't think he returned to his home. But did he run away? I'm concerned about him.*

She signed the page with a flourish and closed the diary. Feeling much better, she went into the dressing room and took down a green gown she wanted to refit. She had never cared much about clothing before, having never really had any to call her own. But now that she had endless supplies of beautiful gowns, she was becoming vain.

She held up the gown for Rollo to see. "Whoever these used to belong to was frighteningly tall, don't you think?" When she held the dress high enough so that the skirt didn't puddle on the ground, the bodice was over her head.

"Frighteningly tall," she said again, freezing. "Wealthy.

Vain." She dropped the gown as though it had burned her. The bodice, heavy with gold bullion embroidery, landed on Rollo's head, and he yelped.

"Why did you do that?" Backing out from under the gown, the wolf shook himself.

"It's a troll's gown." She looked at herself in the tall mirrors, seeing the pale blue morning gown she wore in a whole new light. "They're all troll's gowns." She gave Rollo an accusing look. "Does this have the smell?"

"Er. Well. They also have a flower smell, from those little bags of dried petals hanging in the wardrobe," he told her soothingly. Then he added, "With a little hint of rotten meat."

"Bleah!"

The lass ripped the lace of her blue gown in her haste to get it off. She shed her shift and ran into the washroom to fill the bath with water as hot as she could stand. She scrubbed herself raw and then stood in the middle of the dressing room, wrapped in a towel, staring at the doors of all the wardrobes. In the end, with a sigh, she put on one of her old ragged sweaters and much-mended skirt.

"You smell better," Rollo said, nudging her hand in a consoling way. "Like your old self."

"That's good, at least. Still, I wish there were some clothes here that hadn't been worn by a troll. There must be something that used to belong to a selkie or a faun or what have you!"

She began pulling gowns out of the wardrobes, piling them onto the floor in the middle of the room. She made a careful stack of her own things: Hans Peter's parka and boots, her other sweater and skirt, her trousers.

One of the troll gowns caught on something as she yanked it out of the wardrobe, and ripped. Cursing, the lass reached in and felt around, and felt a sharp chunk of loose ice at the back. She lifted it aside and found a bundle shoved into a hiding space between the wardrobe and the wall.

It was a knapsack not unlike the one Mrs. Grey had given the lass. Inside she found a linen shift with long, full sleeves embroidered with flowers, a dark wool skirt and red vest, and a pair of scuffed leather shoes. All the things were worn soft, of good quality but not expensive. What horrified the lass was that they had obviously belonged to a girl of about the same size as she. Where had the owner of the clothing gone?

Underneath these everyday clothes was the worst thing of all. Wrapped in muslin was a wedding *bunad* that had never been worn. It was gorgeous, but in a far different way than the heavy velvet skirts and pearl-encrusted bodices of the troll gowns. The skirt of the *bunad* was black wool, with a deep hem of embroidery in bands of red and blue and green and yellow. The red vest had silver buttons up the front, and the white blouse was of fabric as fine as gauze. There was even a set of silver earrings, and a circular brooch with dangling medallions. There were white stockings and a pair of black buckled shoes that were too stiff to have ever been worn.

The lass sat on the floor in the middle of the dressing room and cried over those shoes. Some other young girl had come here, to this cold palace of ice, expecting to be made a bride. But what had happened to her? Had she died? Had she tried to escape across the snow plain? Or pined so for her family that she had wasted away? Or maybe she had just disappeared one day, like Erasmus.

Picking up the everyday vest, the lass saw that there was a single long hair clinging to the back of the wool. It was so pale as to be almost white, but when she held it up to the light, it caught glints of gold.

She coiled the hair carefully around one of the buttons of the wedding *bunad,* so that it would not be lost. Her sobs faded to hiccups, and Rollo licked the tears from her face.

"It's just some clothes," he said, confused.

"Don't you understand? Some other girl was brought here, and she left without her things. That means that she's . . . dead . . . or something." A fresh flow of tears ran down her cheeks. "I think . . . it must have been Hans Peter's Tova."

Rollo sniffed the clothes. He shook his head over the *bunad;* it was too new to smell like anything other than wool and maybe the lingering scent of the hands that had made it. He snuffled the everyday clothes more thoroughly.

"She was human," he reported. "And clean, very

clean. She liked strawberries and books. And Hans Peter. And she didn't die in these clothes."

"Are you sure?"

Rollo sniffed the shift again and then nodded his head. "They smell like *isbjørn,* but not *our isbjørn.* And they also smell like Hans Peter. Or at least this does"—he nosed the shift—"faintly."

The lass caught up the shift and gave it a good sniff herself, but couldn't smell anything. Well, she smelled dried flowers from the wardrobe, and leather from the knapsack. But no strawberries, or books, or Hans Peter.

"Your nose isn't that good," Rollo reminded her, with just a trace of smugness.

"It *was* Tova's," the lass said with certainty. "When Hans Peter was here there was a beautiful girl named Tova with him, and they loved each other very much."

"Even I couldn't smell all that," Rollo said.

"But I can feel it," the lass insisted. "I think she's the one who embroidered the blue parts on Hans Peter's coat. The red bits are some sort of enchantment, and Tova changed it.

"I wonder what happened to her, and to their *isbjørn,*" she finished, a final tear slipping down her cheek.

"Their *isbjørn?*"

"You said that it smelled like one, but not ours."

"Ye-es." But now Rollo didn't sound as sure as he had been. "Really, these smells are quite confusing. One sniff and it's *isbjørn,* the next it's Hans Peter. There's a whiff of troll, too."

"There is?" Again she lifted the shift to her nose, but again the smell eluded her. "What does it mean?" Her hands shook a little. "What did the trolls do to her? What do they want with—" She started to say "me," but changed it at the last minute, unable to even voice her fear. "With my *isbjørn?*"

"I don't know," Rollo declared, "but I think we should stick to Hans Peter's advice. Wait, be careful, and go home."

"But don't you want to help?"

"I don't think we *can* help," Rollo countered. "I think we can just make things worse. And when this year is over, maybe Hans Peter will tell us what happened to him. And this girl." He nosed the *bunad.* "I think her mother helped her sew it," he added. He turned his head aside, and sneezed. "Somebody who liked rosewater, and freshly dug potatoes, did the seams on that skirt."

The lass sat for a long time in the mess of her dressing room and pondered all that she and Rollo had discovered. When it was time for dinner, she packed Tova's things neatly into the knapsack and put it in the first wardrobe with her own clothes. She left the troll dresses where she had thrown them.

The *isbjørn* looked taken aback when he saw her old clothes. They appeared even shabbier in the light from the chandelier over the dining table, but he said nothing. He made conversation as best he could, and the lass answered in monosyllables. Rollo's words about them only making things worse were haunting her, and she didn't try to winkle any information about the enchantment out of the bear that night. Subdued, she went to bed early.

When the young man came to lay with her at midnight, she rolled close to him as though she were having a dream. When she thought he was asleep, she sniffed him. He smelled like soap. She wished again for Rollo's sensitive nose, or at least that he would wake just once when her visitor came. But she didn't have a wolf's keen nose, and Rollo wasn't even in the room, so she gave up. He didn't smell like troll, or even potatoes.

Chapter 20

The next day, the lass was sitting in the library making notes when Mrs. Grey came in to dust. Remembering how she had gotten the housekeeper to volunteer the information that she was from Frankrike the last time, the girl prepared herself to ask another question. The only problem was deciding which one. Her plea for information from Hans Peter the day before had been rewarded with only the brief message: "Be careful. Don't ask." She had mentioned the clothes she had found to the *isbjørn,* but he had no idea whom they belonged to.

So she opened her mouth to say something about her nighttime visitor. The strange visitor who smelled of soap and linen, who snored but never spoke, and surely must be known to the servants.

"My lady?"

The lass's mouth snapped shut and then opened again in surprise when Mrs. Grey spoke first. "Yes?"

"Erasmus is dead."

"What?" The lass leaped to her feet, dumping her books onto the floor. Her elbow joggled the inkpot sitting on the table next to her chair and it fell to the carpet, spilling ink like black blood across the floral pattern.

"He said too much and now he is dead," Mrs. Grey said. She was wringing her duster in both hands, shedding feathers all over the ruined carpet. Her hideous face twisted with grief. "I shouldn't say anything, either, but Erasmus was a good friend to me. You're not to blame yourself: he knew better. But we've never had one of you who could understand us before."

"How did she find out?"

The gargoyle snuffled and fingered the ribbon at her throat. "I'm sorry to distress you, my lady. But I wanted you to know." Her bat wings flapped miserably. "I wish that I had tears to cry for him, but my kind don't." Then she fled, dropping her mangled feather duster into the widening pool of ink.

The lass sank back down into her chair. She watched the pool of ink seep into the carpet. Her troll dictionary was on the edge of the puddle—actually, it was *in* the puddle now—but she didn't care. Erasmus was dead. Because she had asked him questions. And he had answered. He was six hundred years old. Had been. But now he was dead. *She* had taken him away.

"The troll princess," the lass said. Then she started to cry. Once she started she couldn't stop, and when Rollo found her a few minutes later, she was down on the floor in the puddle of ink, eyes swollen and nose streaming, sobbing and pounding her fists into the cushion of the chair.

"Are you all right?" Rollo hopped around the black mess, pushing his nose into the lass's shoulders and arms, whatever he could reach without getting his clean paws in the black mess. "What's wrong?"

"Erasmus is dead! He's dead, he's dead, he's dead! Because he talked to me, *she* killed him!" The lass howled and beat the cushion with even greater ferocity.

"Who killed him?" The wolf's hackles rose.

"She did, she did, that troll, that troll . . . hag!" The lass picked up the fallen inkpot, now mostly empty, and hurled it at the window. It smashed into the ice, leaving a spiderweb of cracks before falling to the floor with a *thunk*.

Rollo breathed heavily on his mistress's hair and then turned and ran out of the room. The lass thought that she had finally chased away her last friend, and began to cry even harder. Hans Peter wasn't talking to her; Erasmus was dead; Rollo had abandoned her. Who was left?

The great white *isbjørn*'s paws were so large and soft that he made no noise entering the room. He stepped right into the inkstain and laid his huge head on top of the lass's. The low rumbling of his voice vibrated her skull.

"I'm sorry."

"I'll kill her," the lass hiccupped.

"Who?"

"You know who. The troll princess, the one who killed Erasmus's Narella. And now Erasmus. I'll kill her." She raked her nails down the cushion of the chair, snagging the fine silken embroidery.

Another rumble from deep in the bear's throat. He sat back and the lass leaned against his warm, furry torso. Even though she'd thought her tears had dried, a new wave swept over her, and she wept into the bear's soft fur for a long time.

"Better?" He waited until the last sob faded away and she had pulled a handkerchief out of her pocket to mop up her face.

"I suppose. I still want to kill her."

The bear growled. It rattled the lass's bones and made Rollo whine.

"You shouldn't even know she exists," the bear warned the girl. "Don't speak of her again. Don't ask questions; don't threaten her. Soon the year will be over."

"That's what Hans Peter says," the lass snapped, pushing away from the bear's embrace. "Wait and be careful, don't do anything, just wait and then go home. Well, I can't! Erasmus was kind to me, and now he's dead."

"Asking more questions won't bring him back. It can only make things worse," the *isbjørn* warned.

"How could things be any worse?" the lass raged. She

stomped around the library, ripping books off the shelves and throwing them to the floor. "My brother's life is ruined. Erasmus is dead. All the servants, their lives were ruined by her. Your life, my life. The girl whose *bunader* I found, she's probably dead, too! There has to be some way to fight *her*."

"No, there is no way. We can only wait, and see, and hope." The bear was watching her rant with an uneasy expression.

"What does that mean?"

"I can't tell you," he said.

She rounded on him. "You!" She pointed a shaking finger at his broad white face. "You're afraid of her!"

"Of course I am," he shouted, getting to his feet. "Do you know what she's—" His words cut off abruptly. He stood there, silent, for a moment, and then snarled in frustration. "I can't—if you had any sense, you would fear her, too!" He came over to stand nose to nose with the lass. On all fours, he was as tall as the lass standing upright. "Believe me: things can be much, much worse. She can make you regret you were ever born." And then he left.

The lass plucked a globe of the world inlaid with precious stones from a table and hurled it through the already cracked window. The ice pane made a creaking sound as it broke, and the globe hurtled through the air like a falling star, to smash on the jagged ice at the foot of the palace walls.

The next day, the salamanders tearfully told the lass that Mrs. Grey was gone. *She* had come in the night and taken her away.

The lass didn't leave her rooms for two weeks.

Chapter 21

After Mrs. Grey was taken, the lass did as her brother and the *isbjørn* had pleaded. She stopped asking questions. She stopped begging Hans Peter for information. Having been rejected by her mother at birth, the lass wasn't all that frightened by the threat that she would regret she had been born. But she was sickened by the thought that Erasmus and Mrs. Grey had suffered because of her.

And yet the lass couldn't just sit there, day after day, idle. She asked Fiona if she couldn't have some new cloth to sew clothes for herself. She refused to wear the troll gowns, and she had ruined her best skirt by kneeling in the puddle of ink. Tova's clothes (for she had decided that they were Tova's) would fit her with a little alteration, but somehow it seemed sacrilegious. Fiona nodded, and the next day the sitting room was filled with bolts of silk and velvet, fine linen, and spools of silk thread.

With a self-deprecating laugh, the lass made herself the kind of clothing she was used to, rather than the kind she had been wearing. Fiona removed the troll gowns, and the wardrobe slowly filled with long bell-shaped skirts, tight vests, and shifts with gathered sleeves such as any farmgirl of the North would wear. Not that the farmgirls of the North had ever worn skirts of rich blue velvet and vests of peacock green satin.

Sewing kept the lass's hands busy, and even her mouth. When she sewed, she pursed her lips, or chewed them, or stuck her tongue out. Her siblings had always made fun of her for this, but no matter how she tried she couldn't break the habit. She decided that it was a good thing, now, for it prevented her from asking questions. But her rage over the troll princess caused her fingers to fumble or move too fast. She sliced through the fabric with reckless abandon and angrily threw great lengths of cloth into the fire when she couldn't get the seams straight.

Once she was done with the new wardrobe, she found her resolution not to ask questions waning. The trouble was that servants avoided her now, and so did the *isbjørn,* except for dinnertime. Even the salamanders, those chatty little cooks who had enlivened her early days in the palace, were monosyllabic when she visited the kitchens.

The lass had searched the palace top to bottom already. But now she did it again, determined to gather information without endangering anyone else. She turned the strange rooms upside down, rummaging in piles of carding combs, overturning butter churns, and sorting through spindles, spinning wheels, and looms. She even managed to push over every anvil in a room full of metal-working tools, to see if there was anything written or carved underneath, but there was nothing.

She did ask the *isbjørn* about the rooms full of household tools. She didn't think it could hurt, just to ask why there was a room in a palace full of old butter churns.

He shook his head, equally puzzled, and told her that there was just something about the tools that attracted *them*. He didn't need to say which "them" he meant. The lass knew: trolls. The silent, never-seen rulers of this strange kingdom of barren ice.

"It's like Rolf Simonson's spoon," Rollo said, looking up from his dinner.

The lass and the *isbjørn* exchanged confused looks.

"Rolf Simonson's Fransk silver spoon," Rollo explained. "You remember: it sat on the mantelpiece, and everyone admired it, but no one actually ate with it, because it was foreign."

"Oh, of course!" The lass nodded. "One of his sons traded two reindeer for it, in Christiania. It was very elegant." She wrinkled her nose and looked at the spoon she was eating with. "Although not as fine as this."

"Hmm," the *isbjørn* rumbled. "Perhaps Rollo is correct. Perhaps such things attract *them* because they are foreign."

Fiona the selkie was serving dinner during this discussion. She looked sharply from the bear to the girl as they talked, and cringed when the bear spoke of "them." The lass had never seen the tall, proud seal-woman cringe before. As she carried out the dinner tray, she did it awkwardly one-handed; her other hand was curled into a strange sign that she pressed to her side as though to ward off evil spirits. The bear and the lass both observed this, but neither said anything about it. It was almost embarrassing to see Fiona behave in such a way.

The next morning, the lass woke at dawn to find Fiona hovering over her. The selkie grimaced and frowned in the pale morning light. The lass gave a shriek and slid to the other side of the bed. Her nighttime companion was gone, but the bed was still warm where he had lain.

"What is it?"

More grimacing and frowning from the selkie.

"Oh, just speak," the lass said with impatience, recovering from her surprise. "I don't yearn for your beauty or want to marry you. What on earth are you doing?"

As though summoning all her strength, the selkie drew herself up to her full height, opened her mouth, and then blew out all her breath in a gust. Sucking in another breath, she finally spoke.

"You foolish little girl," she snarled. "What do you think you're playing at? Do you want to kill us all?"

"I'm only trying to help!"

"But you're *not* helping! None of you has ever helped! You poke your little button noses into things that don't concern you, or you cry and whine and mope about, but you *never* help! Then it all explodes in your rosy little faces and you run away home and the masters are forced to go away with *her*."

"You mean the troll princess? And what masters? The *isbjørner*?"

The selkie gave a scream of rage. "Stop asking questions! How many of us must die to satisfy your stupid curiosity? All you have to do is wait out the year. . . . Is that too much to ask?"

"Yes!" the lass shouted. "It is too much!" Her outburst startled Fiona into silence once more. "Aren't you a prisoner here? Don't you want someone to free you?"

"You can't help me; you're just a silly human girl!"

"But I want to try!"

Clapping her hands to her ears, Fiona shook her head and left the room, slamming the door behind her.

When Rollo came cautiously into the room after the selkie's dramatic exit, he found his mistress pounding a pillow ferociously. He went and got the *isbjørn* again, who growled over Fiona's harsh words and patted the lass heavily on the back.

The next day the minotaurus, Garth, brought the lass's breakfast tray. The lass looked at him curiously, said good morning, and received a grunt in reply. She went down to the kitchen after she got dressed and asked the salamanders if there was anything new with the staff. They didn't answer her. Nor did the brownie and pixie she found in the scullery. None of them would meet her eyes. None of them would talk to her.

She went and found the *isbjørn*. He was in a room full of knitting needles and small belt looms. He was holding a belt loom up to a window and squinting at it. When he saw the lass, he dropped it with a clatter.

"Fiona is gone," he said, confirming the lass's fears.

"But why?" She clenched her fists and shook them at him. "She yelled at me, but that was all! Was that so terrible? Why did you . . . ?"

She hadn't thought of it until the words were out of her mouth, but when they burst into the air she realized what was really bothering her. No one beside the *isbjørn* could have known that Fiona had shouted at her, unless Fiona had told the other servants. The bear had been angry at Fiona for hurting the lass's feelings, but Fiona hadn't told her anything that would have gotten her into trouble with the troll princess, as far as the lass could tell. So had it been the *isbjørn* who told the troll what the selkie had done?

"She was under orders not to talk to you," the bear rumbled. "Not my orders, either. I said no word about her shouting."

"Then who? Garth?"

"Nothing happens within these walls that *she* does not know about. I'm sorry. Truly sorry. I liked Fiona and her pouts."

"I liked Erasmus and Mrs. Grey, too," the lass sniffed.

To her annoyance, she was crying. It felt like all she did lately was cry or sew. Sometimes both.

"So did I."

They sat together for a while in silence. Then they both went down to the kitchen. The salamanders didn't speak, but they did give them cake and cider. Garth and the others came in, and they all raised a glass in a wordless toast to Fiona and Mrs. Grey and Erasmus.

That night Rollo went out and mourned them in his own way, howling at the moon for hours. The lass lay in her bed and listened to the muffled sounds of his howls coming through the ice-paned window.

Chapter 22

The lass did not tell Hans Peter what had happened. His responses to her letters in the blank book were always terse, and she sensed that he was angry with her for being so curious and endangering the servants. She learned that her father was doing well, and could now walk with the aid of a crutch. The king's physician had recommended lightly exercising the injured leg and arm, to strengthen them.

And then there was a puzzling letter from Tordis. Well, it was puzzling to Jorunn, at least. She reported to the lass via the magic book that Tordis wanted to know, urgently, if the lass had done what she had asked and used you-know-what to look at you-know-who.

I am completely at a loss, Jorunn wrote. *But Tordis said that you would understand. She wants to know at once. As soon as you write to me, I am to write to her.*

But the lass didn't write "at once." She had *not* done what Tordis asked. She still had the little stub of candle and the matches. The candle had given her a rash and made her nose itch, and she had stuck the candle and matches in one of the pockets she wore under her clothes. She supposed that she could use it at any time, but why? Tordis was convinced that she was in bed with a monster, but the lass was not so sure.

True, when she had asked Rollo to smell the hair she had found, it had carried a hint of troll. But he had also smelled bear and human, so it was hard to say which smell was more accurate. She herself smelled rather like bear, lately. And her nighttime visitor felt like a human. She had touched him, kicked him, and rolled against him by accident in her sleep. She thought that she would know if he were some hideous beast.

After lunch, she made up her mind to lie. She got out the little book and wrote to Jorunn: *Tell Tordis yes, and all is well.* There, the lass thought, that should soothe her sister for a time.

But then the guilt began to gnaw at her. She was lying to Tordis. And maybe her sister was right. Just because the back she had felt in the darkness seemed to be the back of a human man, that didn't mean that it really was. And along with the magic that kept her from finding any candles or getting out of the room in the night, maybe there was an enchantment that made him feel human when really he was . . .

"A troll," she breathed aloud.

As soon as the idea entered her head, it wouldn't leave. This was a troll palace. Everyone raised in the North knew that the trolls had magic, terrible magic, and they played with the lives of other creatures like dolls. After what had happened to Erasmus and the others, she knew that as well as anyone. How could she have been so foolish? For all she knew, she was lying beside the troll princess herself! Perhaps the feeling that she was lying with a young human man was there to reassure her while the princess did . . . what? Sucked out her soul slowly over the course of a year? Made herself young by aging the lass? The lass had a name, but she had never been baptized—how much protection did her name really provide?

She ran into her dressing room and studied her face in the mirror there, but couldn't see any difference. Well, that wasn't quite true. She did look a bit older, but that was probably just from having traveled so far and seen so much. Her face had rounded out, but that was thanks to good meals.

"Well, it's not that," she said aloud.

"What are you doing?" Rollo came into the dressing room.

"I just thought that . . ." She let the sentence trail. Rollo would only be upset by her suspicions that a troll shared her bed. He would want to protect her, but there was no way that he could. At midnight every night, a deep sleep came over him that lasted until dawn. Even when he fell asleep on her bed, her visitor lifted him off and put him by the sitting room fire. She suspected that her visitor also hid the candles before climbing into bed, but he was so quiet that it was hard to tell.

"I thought I had a gray hair," the lass said. "But it was just a trick of the light."

"Hmmph. Vain" was Rollo's comment.

By the time they went to meet the bear for dinner that night, the lass had made up her mind. She couldn't continue to sleep beside someone—or something—that she had never seen. She knew it would be risky, so she made preparations.

After dinner, she filled her secret pockets to bursting with pearls and rubies and coils of gold wire thread. She packed her troll dictionary and clothing into the knapsack Mrs. Grey had given her. She begged food from the salamanders and they gave her bread, dried meat, cheese, and apples. As an afterthought, she attached Tova's pack to her own knapsack with silk scarves. She laid the awkward bundle by the hearthrug where Rollo slept and told him to keep an eye on it.

"Why?"

"Never you mind, dog." She put the candle and the matches under her pillow, and then she cleaned her teeth and slipped into bed.

She had worried that she would fall asleep and not wake up until after her visitor had gone, but that wasn't a problem. She lay, rigid as a board, while her thoughts screamed at her: run, hide, run, hide!

She told herself over and over that she had done it for months, she could do it one more night. The memory of all those past nights curdled her stomach. She could not go on like this. She would look, and then in the morning, as soon as he? . . . she? . . . it? . . . left, she would grab her pack and Rollo and run home. It was possible that she would die somewhere in the forest or on the snow plain, but it would be better than having her life sapped away by a troll.

By the time the creature climbed into bed with her, she was vibrating like a fiddle string. When the weight of her nighttime guest hit the mattress, she almost bolted. Instead she gripped the edge of the blanket and concentrated on breathing deeply. This calmed her somewhat, and she was able to keep up the pretense of sleep until she heard a soft snore from her companion. She counted to fifty, just to make sure that it hadn't also been feigning sleep, and then she fished the candle and matches out from under her pillow and slithered out of bed.

There were thick silk curtains all around the bed, and she stood outside these, counting to twenty to make sure that she hadn't woken whatever it was. Her fingers shook so badly that it took three tries before she could get the wick lit. Then, cupping her free hand carefully around the flame, she crept around the bed.

Biting her lip, the lass parted the curtains and leaned into the bed to see what had been lying beside her all these months.

A man.

A handsome, young man. Dark hair, a fine straight nose, long eyelashes fanned on a smooth cheek. He looked older than the lass by a few years—perhaps he was twenty, twenty-one years old. He wore a linen nightshirt, and the collar was open to reveal a glimpse of smooth, muscular chest. The lass leaned over him, studying the planes of his face, but could see no flaw, no sign of a monstrous nature.

And then.

And then the burning wick reached one of the scented herbs Frida put in her candles. The herb sizzled, making the flame sputter. A little streamer of smoke curled up the lass's nose.

She sneezed.

Hot wax dripped off the candle as the sneeze jolted through her body. It fell on the shoulder of the young man's white nightshirt, and he woke. His wide eyes fastened on the lass's. They were violet.

"Oh, no," he breathed, an expression of horror creeping across his handsome face. "What have you done?"

"I only wanted to s-see what you were," she stammered, backing away from the look on his face. "I thought that maybe—"

"One year and one day. You had only to endure one year and one day of my company. Bear by day, man by night, just like your brother. Tova failed too. They always fail. And then we have to go." He shuddered and his eyes closed.

"Go where?" She could barely speak; a terrible coldness was coming over her.

"To *her*. I must marry her and live in her palace east of the sun and west of the moon."

"But isn't there any other way? Can't I . . . do . . . something?" The cold was making her face numb, and her hands. She dropped the candle; the flame went out as it fell, plunging the room into darkness once more.

"If you had waited three more months—just three—I would have been free," the young man said. "We both would have been free." Then: "She comes!"

"Isbjørn!" The lass called to him as the cold rose up and swallowed her. The wind rushed in her ears. She fainted.

Part 3

The Lassie Who Should Have Had the Prince

Chapter 23

The lass awoke to Rollo nosing her face and whining. Her head was pillowed on her bulging knapsack, and she was cramped and cold. Blinking the sleep from her eyes, she sat up and looked around.

"Rollo? Where are we?"

"I don't know, and I couldn't wake you for hours, and I didn't dare leave you," he whimpered. He lowered himself down until his upper half was in her lap, something he had not done since he was a puppy. "What happened?"

What had happened was that the palace had disappeared, the lass thought, looking around. She and her wolf were deep in a forest somewhere. Judging by the thickness of the trees, they were far from the ice plain. Or perhaps they were right in the middle of the ice plain, but the trolls had taken away the palace and replaced it with this forest as part of her punishment.

"I saw him," the lass told Rollo. "I lit a candle, and I looked at him."

"Who?" He raised his head and looked at her.

She looked off through the trees, but didn't really see them. "I think he was a prince. He was so handsome. Our *isbjørn*. Every day he was an *isbjørn,* and every night he was human and lay beside me. If I could have gone one year and one day without looking at him, without being curious and asking too many questions, it would have broken the enchantment. But I looked, and now he's gone."

Rollo whimpered. "Gone where?"

"To a castle east of the sun and west of the moon," she said, remembering the words as clearly as if they had been written on the inside of her eyelids. "To marry *her*.

"Hans Peter did this as well," she continued after a long silence. "He was an *isbjørn,* and Tova was the girl who had to lay with him and not look. But she looked, too. I guess we always look."

"But Hans Peter didn't marry the troll, did he?"

"I don't know." She reached over to her parka, Hans Peter's parka, which lay to one side of the knapsack. "But I think that Tova did this, this embroidery, to change the spell. She must have found this somewhere and done it, to help him get away."

Another long silence. The lass was very cold, sitting in the snow in just her nightshift, but didn't want to move. Finally a shiver took her unawares, and she sneezed. It reminded her of the sneeze last night, the sneeze that had spilled the wax and woken the prince. She got to her feet and shucked off her wet shift.

Rollo scrambled to his feet and stared at her. "What are you doing?"

She opened up her knapsack and pulled out a clean shift, a heavy velvet skirt, and a vest of stiff brocade. "We're going to find him," she declared, dressing as quickly as she could.

"I did this," the lass went on as she fastened the ties of Hans Peter's parka. "I caused the deaths of Erasmus, Mrs. Grey, and Fiona. I caused the poor *isbjørn*"—a sob shook her—"*my isbjørn*, to be taken away, and now he'll be forced to marry a troll. I caused it, and I'm going to fix it." She wiped her nose on her sleeve. "I never even knew his name," she said in a whisper. "I should have asked his name."

"All right," Rollo said finally. "Which way do we go?"

"What's east of the sun and west of the moon?"

"Nothing."

"If it's easter than east and wester than west, it must be north," she reasoned. She was thinking of the globe from the library, the one she had recently hurled through a window. The top of the globe was a white disc of gleaming opal where her reading had told her "no man lived." No man, perhaps, but trolls might.

"Or south," Rollo interjected.

"But trolls don't like to be warm," the lass reminded

him. "So it must be north. The lands to the south are all deserts, like the one the salamanders came from." That thought brought her up short. "The salamanders!"

"What? Where?" Rollo looked around in confusion.

"Not here," she sighed. "What if everyone who was in the ice palace is dead now, because of me?"

Rollo gave an inarticulate whine.

"We have to stop this," the lass said. "There will be no more deaths." Her heart thudded. "And I don't want *her* to have *him*."

She began to march. A little while later the thought came to her that the servants wouldn't be put to death just because she looked at the prince. Tova had looked, and the servants hadn't been harmed. This cheered her, and she was able to walk in a faster rhythm.

When her legs screamed with fatigue and she was sweating beneath her parka, they stopped. Rollo went off after a rabbit whose tracks they had seen, while the lass ate some bread and cheese. She sucked handfuls of clean snow to quench her thirst. When Rollo came back, looking pleased and licking his chops, they went on.

For a day and a night and a day they walked, seeing no one. They came across a fox, and a wolf who could have been Rollo's twin. The lass called out to them, but they sniffed at her and then ran.

"We smell of troll," Rollo said, grim.

"It doesn't matter," the lass said, and walked on.

They traveled for another day, another night, and another day. The lass ate the last of the food the salamanders had given her, and was forced to stop and build a fire to cook the rabbits that Rollo caught. Every moment that she sat by her little fires, every time she lay down to sleep because her body could go no farther, her mind and heart raced, thinking of her lost companion and the horrors he might be facing. She would clamber upright as soon as she could, and march on.

After two weeks of this, as near as she could reckon, the lass expected any moment to come through a cluster of trees and find a fabulous palace. Perhaps of ice, perhaps of gold or ivory or silver, but gleaming and grand and dangerous, whatever it was built of. She felt certain that they must be nearing the top of the world, where the trolls' palace simply had to be.

She did not expect, deep in the frozen woods, to find a weird little hut made of turf bricks with an old woman sitting in front of it, paring apples.

"*Morn'a*," the old woman said cheerfully.

"*Morn'a, moster*," the lass said politely.

" '*Moster?*' " The crone cackled with glee. "I like that! '*Moster!*' No one's called me '*moster*' in years!" She dropped her paring knife in her lap and slapped her thigh. "And I'm old enough to be your *moster's moster's moster's* moster's *moster,* besides!" She wiped tears from her eyes, still laughing.

"She's insane," Rollo said, hunching against the lass's legs. "Let's go."

"I'm not insane, you young pup," the crone said, picking up her knife and shaking it at him. "I'm just starved for fresh company!" She cackled some more. "Set down your pack and have some apples," she invited in a calmer voice, though still cracked and thin with age.

The lass was footsore, and it had been hours since breakfast. Thinking that anyone who could speak Wolf could not be all bad, she set down the knapsacks on the cleared space in front of the hut and sat on a stump opposite the old woman. Rollo, more cautious, came and stood beside her, not taking his eyes off the crone.

"Can I help?" The lass took off her mittens and loosened the ties of her parka.

"Surely, child." The crone took another knife out of the pocket of her apron and handed it to the lass.

Taking up an apple and beginning to peel it, the lass stole glances at the woman across from her. She was the oldest person the lass had ever laid eyes on. Her wrinkles had wrinkles. Her hair was as white as the snow, but very thin, and scraped back into a small bun that was mostly covered by a little red bonnet. She wore a *bunad,* or rather, several *bunader.* The lass could see at least four skirts in various states of raggedness peeping out from the hem of the uppermost one. She had on three vests, too, which explained how she could sit outside in the snow without a parka.

Of course, it didn't explain why her breath didn't cloud the air the way the lass's and Rollo's did. But the lass didn't think it polite to remark on that.

After she'd peeled and cored three apples, she helped the old woman carry the basket of peeled fruit over to a big black pot that hung over a fire behind the hut. The pot was half-full of boiling water, and they spilled in the apples. The old woman produced bags of spices from her apron and poured them into the pot, replacing the lid with a sigh.

"By tomorrow morning that will be the sweetest apple jelly you ever did taste," the old woman said, smacking her lips. She did have all her teeth, which seemed odd in one so decrepit.

"That's kind of you, *moster*," the lass said. "But we must be going. We have a long road ahead of us."

"And where is it you're going?" Bright blue eyes peered at the lass from the web of wrinkles. "There's naught but snow and trees and trolls from here till doomsday, the direction you're headed."

"That's rather the point," said the lass, twisting her fingers in the fur edging the white parka. "I'm looking for the castle that lies east of the sun and west of the moon, you see. Do you know where it is?"

Sucking in a breath, the crone stared at the lass. "At it

again, is she? So you're the lassie that should have had the prince she's stolen?"

"*Is* he a prince?"

"Oh, yes. Always has to have the royals, she does. I heard one time that she made an exception, for a boy of especial beauty, but he got away from her."

"I think that was my brother, Hans Peter," the lass said, feeling her skin tighten with gooseflesh.

"Aye, that was the name the last little girl said to me," the crone said, nodding.

"Tova? Did Tova come this way?"

"That was the other name she said, yes," the old woman agreed.

"Then where did she go? Am I going in the right direction? *Do* you know where the palace is? Did Tova make it there?"

The old woman shook her head to stop the lass's questions. "You'll reach the castle, late or never, I suppose. If you are determined to see it. For myself, I never dared to face her. Not even when she took my Lars." Tears fogged the old eyes. "Trolls live a long time, but human husbands do not."

"Oh, I'm so sorry, *moster*." The lass put her arms around the old woman and hugged her. The crone felt as light and fleshless as a straw doll.

"No sense crying, no sense now," said the crone, wiping her face with a ragged sleeve.

"Who's out here blubbering, when there's wool needs carding?" Out of the hut popped another old woman with a face like a walnut and bright blue eyes.

If the lass had thought the first *moster* to be the oldest woman alive, she was mistaken. The crone standing on the doorstep of the hut, smiling with remarkably white and even teeth, was even more withered of form and thin of hair than her friend. Her white hair was so fine that her pink scalp showed through, and she was bundled up in even more layers of worn clothing. In her gnarled hands she held a basket of snarled wool and a pair of carding combs.

"*God dag, moster,*" the lass said.

"This is the lassie that should have had the newest prince," the first *moster* said in the loud, clear voice you used around the hard of hearing.

The second old woman had a laugh like a creaking gate. "No wonder her was in such a taking when she flew by t'other day," she said. "It's another lassie, and another husband, and another fine mess, it is."

"Yes," the lass agreed loudly. "Do *you* know the way?"

"Oh, saints be praised no, child! I only ever made it this far after my sweet Finnish prince was whisked away. Lovely dark eyes he had," she sighed.

"He's dead now," the first *moster* announced. "Hand me the wool."

"Yes, yes," the second said, irritated. She handed the

wool to her friend, and gave the lass the carding combs. "It's too late now to be going on. The sun will set soon. But we'll see what we can do for you in the morning."

"All right," the lass agreed.

She settled back on her stump, with Rollo sprawled at her feet, and began to card the wool. The *mosters* produced two more sets of combs, and together they made short work of the basket of wool, though the sky had grown quite dark by then.

"Very nice," the first *moster* said when they had finished. "Supper time!" She poked Rollo with a bony finger. "We've enough for four but not for five. Go get your own fat rabbit."

"Four?" The lass and Rollo exchanged puzzled looks.

"You haven't met the Eldest yet," the second *moster* told her. "Bring the basket of wool into the hut, dearie, and I'll introduce you."

The lass felt a surge of fear. The hut was small and dark, with no windows. What if this was some trick? How could anyone be older than these two crones, unless she was a troll or some other monster?

"I'll get my rabbits in a moment," Rollo said casually, eyeing the first *moster*. "Let me pay my respects to the Eldest first."

"Yes, Rollo. That would be the polite thing to do," the lass said, feeling slightly relieved.

The *mosters,* as though sensing her fear, cackled and

went into the hut, leaving the rough wooden door open. The lass and Rollo followed slowly, and the girl held the basket of wool in front of her like a shield.

Inside it was dim and smoky, with a single fire in the center of the one round room. The only furnishings were a large wooden bed covered with reindeer hides, and a table with three chairs. Seated in one of the chairs was the third *moster*.

She was only identifiable as a woman because she was wearing the faded remnants of what once might have been a gown. It wasn't like the skirts and vests that the lass was used to, though. Instead, the patched fabric formed a long, straight robe that had no definite waist or bodice. This crone had more hair than the other two, more hair than the lass herself, even. Her two long braids, yellowed white like old ivory, were as fat as the lass's wrists and hung down to the ground. The ends were clasped with bands of tarnished gold.

With a face so withered and wrinkled that it was impossible to see her expression, she raised her head to the lass. In her clawlike hands she held a worn wooden drop spindle. She dropped it with a practiced gesture. It spun in a little dent in the hard-packed earth floor, smoothed by the years, and she pulled a fine white thread from it without any effort.

"Who's this then?" Her voice was like twigs rubbing together in the wind.

Feeling only comfort and kindness emanating from the three *mosters,* the lass set her basket of wool on the table. "I'm the one who should have had the prince who lived in the palace of ice," she explained. "I'm looking for the castle that lies east of the sun and west of the moon. Do you know how to get there?"

"My Eirik was her prince," the old woman said as she continued to spin. "More years ago than I can count. I nearly died of the curiosity, lying there night after night, and had to look."

"Yes, *moster,* as did I," the lass said.

"As did we all," the first *moster* remarked loudly to the second.

"Moster?" The Eldest tilted her head and sniffed the air, and for the first time the lass realized that she was blind. "Yes, I suppose that is what I am now. Once I was a princess, and my father's ships sailed the world over. My brothers fought the *skrælings* in the lands to the west, the dragons to the east, the trolls to the north, and the dark men to the south. But never did they reach the castle that lies east of the sun and west of the moon. Nor did I, for I was not strong enough to stir beyond this place."

"I—I'm sorry . . . Your Highness," the lass stammered.

" '*Moster,*' child, for that is all I am now. An old blind woman, spinning away the years." She shook her head and the gold band on her left braid struck the leg of her chair with a gentle chiming sound. "The last young girl to pass through here called me *'moster'* as well." The old woman sighed. "Now if you'll help me spin the new-carded wool while the others prepare supper, we'll see if we can't help you on your way tomorrow."

The lass sent Rollo to catch his own meal, and took up the spindle offered her.

Chapter 24

"None of us have ever ventured farther than this little clearing," the first *moster* told the lass the next morning.

They all three stood before their hut, the Eldest leaning on a tall walking stick carved with flowers. In the gray dawn light they looked even older and less human, but the lass knew them to be kind and good.

"But our horses were gifts from our neighbor, and know well the way to his house," the second *moster* said. She walked to the edge of the clearing and whistled a long, sharp note.

"*His* house?" The lass was surprised. "I thought I would go on and on through a long trail of women who got lost searching for the troll palace."

The Eldest shook her head. "Many have passed through, over the years, but where they ended up we've no notion. We help those who are polite, and bar our door to those who are not."

"Oh." The lass felt very grateful that her parents had taught her good manners. The two hot meals she had eaten at their hearth and the warm soft bed had done wonders for her.

"Here is your pack," the first *moster* said, holding it out. "We've stuffed it full of apples and bread, and a little cheese."

"Oh, thank you!" The lass felt guilty: they were so old, and she had Rollo to hunt for her. "Are you sure you can spare it?"

"Of course, child," the Eldest said. "And more besides." She pointed imperiously at the pack. "Show her," she ordered the first *moster*.

"A jar of my apple jelly," the first *moster* said, flipping open the knapsack and showing the lass where it nestled inside. The jar was shaped like an apple, and the jelly inside made it shine like pure gold. "The jar is carved from crystal," the crone said with pride. Then she held up a set of carding combs, and these really did appear to be made of gold, finely worked and set with small jewels. "Carding combs, and a ball of new wool, from that one." She nodded at the second *moster,* still standing a few feet away and just now emitting a second whistle.

"And this from me," the Eldest said. She felt inside the pack and pulled out a spindle of gold, as elegant as the carding combs. "A blind woman has no need for such trinkets. But if you wish to enchant the troll princess . . ."

The lass thought of the ice palace, with its rooms full of anvils and knitting needles, and smiled. "Wonderful," she said. "Tova was polite, wasn't she? Did you help her?" She wanted very much to know about Hans Peter's beloved. Not just if she had survived, but what sort of person she was.

"Tova was a good girl," the first *moster* said brightly, repacking the lass's bundle. "We gave her useful gifts as well."

The Eldest smiled at the lass, her ancient face transformed by the expression. "We send you as well armed as we sent the last lost maiden, if you can find a way to use these weapons," she said.

Doubt fluttered in the lass's breast, however. "Do you really think that I will get to the palace?" she asked.

The old woman paused. Her gnarled, ancient fingers reached out and touched the lass's cheek. As softly as snowflakes, she stroked the girl's face. "Yes," she said, her hands still resting lightly on the lass's cheeks. "You will find the palace east of the sun and west of the moon." She shook her head, the motion rippling down her long braids. "Poor thing."

"But will I be able to free my prince?"

"That I cannot say."

The lass sighed deeply.

"Come now," the Eldest said, taking her stiff old hands from the girl's face. "You are too young for such despairing sighs. We will loan you our horses, and they shall carry you to the home of the east wind."

"The east wind?" The lass gaped at the Eldest *moster*.

"Indeed," she said. "Who else would live so far from human habitation?"

A third whistle from the *moster* at the edge of the clearing, and three horses came trotting out of the forest. One was black as ebony, the second gray as a stormcloud, and the third white as snow with a bloodred mane and tail.

"This is Hjartán," the first *moster* said, stroking the black horse's nose.

The horse's name took the lass aback. At first it sounded like an endearment, but then the crone crooned to the horse in the older tongue of the North for a moment, and the lass realized what the name meant. In the old tongue, it meant "heartless."

The *moster* saw the lass's expression and cackled. "I was a wee bit bitter over my fate when he was given to me," she said. "Ride him as far as he can go, then flick his left ear and send him home."

"Then ride my Falskur," the second *moster* said, slapping the gray horse on the shoulder.

"Falskur?" Another strange name.

"Aye." The old woman grinned. "The horse is not faithless, but it was faithlessness that brought me here.

"Ride him until he tires, for he is stronger and faster than his brother Hjartán. When he begins to slow, flick his right ear and send him home."

"And then you will mount my dear Vongóður," the Eldest said.

"Hopeful?" The name was startling, considering what the other crones had named their horses.

"We must always have hope, child," the ancient princess said. "Even when it seems that there is none in sight."

Fighting back another despairing sigh for which she was too young, the lass stepped up on a stump and then mounted Hjartán. She had never ridden a horse before, but Hjartán stood very still despite her scrambling. He was not as broad as her *isbjørn,* and his coat was smooth, but his mane was thick and she thought she would be able to hold to that well enough. She settled her pack on her back as best she could, made sure that Rollo was on his feet and ready to follow, and then smiled at the three old women.

"Thank you, dear *mosters,*" she said.

They smiled back, and for a moment, a ghost of beauties lost passed over their faces.

"May the old gods protect you, child," the Eldest said. "When you have reached our neighbor, tickle Vongóður under the chin and he'll find his way back."

The first *moster* patted the lass's knee and then brought her hand down with a crack on the horse's rump. "Go!"

Squealing, Hjartán shot out of the clearing, heading north and east. Rollo and the other two horses followed hard behind. The lass clung to Hjartán's mane and prayed that a branch wouldn't whip her in the face. She might be blinded—with a thrill of terror, she wondered if that was how the ancient princess had lost her sight. She crouched low on the horse's neck, hiding her face in her white hood again. Her muscles soon cramped and locked into place. After some hours, she tried to stop Hjartán so that they might all rest, but he would not be halted. She thought of leaping off, but the snow looked hard and icy, so she resigned herself to hanging on.

To pass the time, she thought of her bear, who was also a prince, and their time together discussing plays and poetry and stories about the lass's childhood. She remembered telling him about finding the white reindeer, which only Hans Peter knew about, and how the *isbjørn* had not been all that surprised at the tale.

Thinking of the white reindeer made her think of her name.

The lass, who possessed in her heart the most beautiful name ever heard, firmed her resolve. She would find the castle east of the sun and west of the moon. She would atone for her faithlessness and make things right with the prince. She would find Tova, and bring her to Hans Peter so that they could be happy. Surely someone gifted by the white reindeer, who had befriended fauns and *isbjørner* and who had traveled so far, would succeed.

Surely she would.

She whispered her name into the wind. Hjartán surged through the trees, his brothers just behind. With a yip, Rollo sped up to match the stallion's pace. The lass hung on, and the miles flew by.

Chapter 25

Wind does not need translation. It speaks the language of men, of animals and birds, of rocks and trees and earth and sky and water. It does not eat or sleep, or take shelter from the weather. It *is* the weather.

And it lives.

The east wind lives in a forest dark with trees. The trees do not grow straight or tall, for the wind is too forceful to allow that. But they grow strong, with deep roots and trunks like stone. The branches have been twisted and twined about each other, thrust out at impossible angles from trunks that curl like smoke.

The aged princess's horse slowed as they reached this strange forest. The lass was able to sit up straight and look around at the bizarre living sculptures that surrounded them. Rollo, panting hard, dragged along behind them, twigs and leaves caught in his fur and little balls of snow tangled in the long feathery hairs on the backs of his legs and tail.

There was no snow on the ground here, though some was pushed up against the trees in hard drifts. The ground looked polished: there were no twigs or fir needles littering it. They came to a great rock that had been smoothed into a shape like a throne twice the height of a man. Vongóður stopped, and the lass slithered off his broad, pale back.

They stood there for a while, all three of them. The horse plainly thought that its duty was fulfilled, and refused to go farther. The lass was hesitant to send the stallion on his way, however, and Rollo was just glad that they had stopped. He flopped down on the hard ground and fell instantly asleep.

"Hello?" the lass dared to call out at last. "East wind? The three old . . . *mosters* . . . who are your neighbors sent me."

In truth the lass was not expecting to see anything more extraordinary than a man. A strong man, perhaps, a strange man, most likely. But just a man all the same. The *mosters* had said that their neighbor was the east wind, but the lass had not taken that literally. Jarl used to regale his children with tales of great heroes and ancient gods riding into battle on the backs of the winds, but the lass had always suspected that the heroes, if they did exist, had simply ridden horses like everyone else.

And now as she stood in this alien landscape and called out to the east wind, exhausted in body and mind, she just hoped that whoever answered had a sleigh she could ride in as they continued their journey. That is, if he would help her continue her journey.

The air swirled around her. It rose to a frenzy that tore her hair out of its braid and whipped it around her face. Vongóður dropped his head and flattened his ears but didn't shy. Rollo looked up, sighed, and staggered to his feet to stand protectively by his mistress's side. The lass clung to the horse's mane, closing her eyes against little icy particles of dirt or snow that blew into her face.

When the wind calmed, she opened her eyes, and the east wind was sitting on his throne.

The east wind didn't look human, because it wasn't human. It was a great swirling concoction of leaves and twigs and mist and smoke and rain and dust that at last collected into the shape of a wolf, sitting upright on the stone seat of the throne.

"Why are you here"—its voice howled and whispered and whistled in her ears, and a tendril of wind snaked out to tap up and down her body from head to toe and back again—"human maid?"

"You're *real*," she breathed, and could say nothing else for a heartbeat. When she found her voice again, she said, "I'm looking for the castle east of the sun and west of the moon."

A great shudder racked the east wind. It flew to bits, and then gathered itself into wolf-shape once more. "Why would you want to go there?"

"I lived in the palace of ice with the prince who was an *isbjørn*. Because of me, he is being forced to marry a troll, and I wish to help him."

"Mortal creatures are so strange," the wind mused. "Here is another one looking for a human male she barely knows."

"Did you help Tova?"

"I suppose that was her name. I carried her to the plain where dwells the west wind."

This news made the lass's shoulders sag. "So you do not know the way to the troll's palace?"

"I have never blown so far, nor have I ever wanted to. The magic of trolls is an evil even the winds cannot defend against. You would do wise to emulate my neighbors: build a hut and abide where fate has taken you."

"I can't," the lass said, shaking her head with vehemence. "I must find the palace. I must free the prince. I *must*."

"Then all the help I can offer you is to carry you to the west wind."

"Thank you."

A huff of air blasted her hair straight back. "Will you still thank me later?" The form on the stone throne shivered. "No matter. We shall blow to the home of my brother."

The lass sent Vongóður home at last. Rollo melted into the twisted trees and returned with feathers around his muzzle a few minutes later.

"You have some fine birds in your forest," he complimented the east wind.

"I *did*," the east wind replied.

"Sorry," the lass said, hunching her shoulders in embarrassment. She gave Rollo a hard look.

"We can't all live on bread and love," he said.

" 'Love'? What do *you* know about love?"

"It's at the heart of every story," Rollo said with authority. "If humans could avoid falling in love, you would never get yourselves into any trouble."

The lass closed her eyes for a long minute. Was she in love with the prince? Maybe. She had loved the *isbjørn,* in a way. And in a different way she loved her brother Hans Peter and wanted to help him. So it was for love that she was doing all this. But would she be happier if she just went home?

Could she live with herself if she did?

She opened her eyes. "Can we leave now?"

Being carried on the back of the east wind was a very strange experience. The writhing mass of twigs and leaves and wind and feathers and ice swooped down from its throne and lifted her high off the ground. She had not yet shouldered her pack, but when she looked back she saw that it and Rollo had been gathered up as well. Her wolf alternately howled in fear and growled to show how brave he was as they ascended. Up in the air the east wind gathered itself, a wolf the size of a ship running over the treetops.

The lass hovered, suspended, atop the wolf wind of the East. She stretched out her arms and leaned back, feeling it cradle her. It was like riding on the back of the *isbjørn,* only better. Now she truly was flying, free of the ground. She laughed.

The east wind surged forward, and the laugh was ripped from her throat. Beneath them trees whipped the sky and crops lay down. They passed over mountains and hills, whistled down fjords and over the sea. At one point the wind rose until it was swallowed up in clouds, churning and driving them like egg whites swirled with a wooden spoon. More ocean lay beneath them when the clouds dissipated, then beaches and forests and fields of wheat.

And then nothing.

Dirt. Sand. Cracked, dry ground on which the only growing things were scrubby little bushes that looked half-dead. The earth was red and the rocks were raw and jagged.

And then they were smooth.

As fantastical as the forest of the east wind had been, the west wind's palace of living rock was stunning. Red and purple and gold stone had been twisted and shaped like clay. Great arches passed overhead, pillars, caves, hollows as smooth as a worn wooden bowl, filled with purple shadow that looked like water as the sun set. There were mounds of rocks like pillows, like mushrooms and beehives.

The east wind slowed here, and the lass was able to gape at the formations of stone as they passed over and around them. Soon they came to an open space like a great shallow bowl. Dozens of little whirls of sand and grit spun merrily about in the bottom of the hollow.

The wolf wind set the lass down and shrank until he was only slightly larger than an *isbjørn*. The stone bowl was blazingly hot, like being inside an oven. The lass shucked off her parka and boots and still sweat poured down her face, plastering her disarrayed hair to her neck. Rollo was panting, and he danced in place to avoid burning his paws.

The little funnels of grit danced together and became one giant spinning pillar of wind and sand. A dry, rasping voice issued from it.

"My brother East, what have you brought me?"

"A human who is looking for the palace east of the sun and west of the moon," the east wind replied. "Have you ever blown that far?"

"Never!" The spinning column wavered and then steadied. "I have no dealings with the trolls."

"I thought not," the east wind said. "But she is determined to go. Can you help her? You have blown farther than I ever have."

The west wind swayed back and forth in its hollow. "Why should I take this human anywhere? I do not meddle in the affairs of trolls. Perhaps the troll queen will hear of what I have done, and take her revenge upon me." The column of wind shuddered.

The lass looked from one gathering of wind to the other. "The troll *queen?*"

"Her daughter is the princess who turns humans into northern bears, to toy with them before she marries them," the west wind said. "But the queen is far more terrible: older and uglier, and wicked to her stone bones. No entity in this world dares to cross the queen of the trolls."

The lass raised her eyebrows. "I do."

"That is because you are nothing more than a foolish human child," the west wind retorted.

"And you are nothing more than a rude little breeze, blowing sand in my eyes and quivering," the lass snapped back. She had not come this far just to be turned away by a *wind*. "The princess, and the queen, must be stopped."

"Then find someone else to help you, if you want to kill yourself," the west wind said.

"Coward," the lass said, without heat. She shook her head in a pitying way. "You won't even blow me to the north wind's home. I feel certain that such a strong wind as he would know the way, even if you don't. And I have no doubt that he would take me all the way to the palace east of the sun and west of the moon."

A little gust came from the west wind, as though it had snorted at her ploy.

"Well, that's all right then," the lass went on, hands on

hips. "I've come this far without your help. I've been helped by three kind old human women, with little more than the clothes on their backs and more to lose to the troll queen than you. I've been helped by this good east wind, your brother.

"Your brother wind was convinced that you would help me. He said that you had blown far and wide, and would surely know the way. But he was wrong." She put out a hand and stroked the back of the east wind, as though comforting it. "What a shame." She shook her head. "Dear east wind," she said in a fond tone. "You have been so kind, and blown so far to help me, I couldn't ask you to help me go any farther. But could you at least direct me toward the domain of the north wind? Rollo and I shall walk there." At her feet, Rollo groaned.

With a hiss and a scrape, the west wind shot up into a towering shaft of swirling sand. Then it collapsed, raging out to encompass the east wind, the lass, and Rollo, along with the stony desert around them. The wind howled through the rocks, picking up more grit and sand and scraping the surface of the rock formations with it. The force knocked the lass off her feet, and she huddled next to Rollo, burying her face in his fur to protect her eyes. She smiled into his flank, where no one else could see it.

"If you wish to take your chances with the north wind I'll not stop you," the west wind said. "But not even I know where he resides. The North is the greatest of us all."

"Oh." The lass had felt certain that the west wind would help her. But if it didn't know the way. . . .

"But the south wind knows where our brother dwells," the west wind continued. "They are forever chasing each other over and around the world. It may even be that the south wind has blown to the trolls' palace. But if not, then South knows how to reach North."

"Thank you."

"We shall see if you still thank me in a week or a month or even a day," the west wind grumped, echoing the east wind's sentiments.

Chapter 26

Riding the east wind had been exhilarating, but riding the west wind was taxing. Trapped in a spinning column of sand, the lass felt as though she were falling, then being lifted up, only to plummet again. She wondered if the west wind were doing it out of spite, and fought the urge to be sick.

An eternity later, the west wind dropped her. She didn't fall far, landing on all fours on a stone floor. When she recovered from the shock, she sat up and looked around.

She was in the ruins of a great palace. The rich stone carvings were crumbling, and vines had wormed their way between the cracks in the paving stones and up the sides of the square pillars. Animal faces and strange, squat human figures leered at her from between leaves the size of dinner plates.

A swirl of black earth, green pollen, and warm dew skirled through the ruins and languidly took the shape of an enormous bird of prey.

"What is *that?*" Its tone was ripe with disgust. "What is it doing here, Brother West?"

"This foolish human is looking for the palace east of the sun and west of the moon," the west wind replied. His collection of grit and heat wafted across the broken floor tiles, exhausted.

The green-and-black bird shot in and around the pillars of the ruins in agitation, making a singing, whistling noise. "Never have I dared to blow there!"

Once again, the lass's patience snapped. "I know, I know! Because you are afraid of the trolls! But *I* am not, and maybe that makes me a fool, but I don't care. If you can't blow me to the palace, at least blow me to the home of the north wind, and perhaps *he* will be able to help me."

"It's a temperamental little thing, isn't it?" The south wind soared over and stroked the lass's face with a moist, feathery breeze. "Humans are so odd."

The lass flapped her hands in front of her face, trying to slap away the south wind in irritation. "Will you help me, or not?"

"I don't see why I should."

"Because somebody, somewhere, has to fight the trolls," the lass said with vehemence.

"I don't think there's any need to be so hysterical about it," the south wind said. "In fact, I think that you're overreacting. It's common among humans. The last human I carried was prone to breaking out in sobs and praying aloud for the safety of her lover."

"Tova?" The lass had forgotten to ask the west wind if he had carried Tova.

"I didn't ask," the south wind sniffed. "I picked her up on my way to visit my brother north. She was sitting on a grassy plain, sobbing and tearing her hair."

"I left the last human I carried sitting on a grassy plain, sobbing," the west wind panted. "Did she taste of strawberries and snow?"

"Indeed she did!"

"You abandoned Tova in the middle of nowhere?" The lass kicked out at the west wind but failed to do any damage to it.

"She couldn't go any farther," it snapped. "She was not as hardy as you. She feared that she would perish."

"I took her to our brother North," the south wind sighed. "Though I do not know what happened to her after that."

"If you didn't mind taking her, then you won't mind taking me," the lass reasoned.

"Our brother may not approve of me dropping so many humans in his home," the south wind said.

"I really don't care," the lass replied. "I think it's despicable that the four winds—the great and powerful four winds—are all such cowards! The trolls are causing great evil, and you will do nothing to stop it!"

"But how can the evil of mortal creatures affect the wind?" The south wind's tone was arch.

"If the trolls can't harm you, why are you afraid of them?" the lass countered. Then something about the south wind's words snagged her attention. "Mortal? I thought that the trolls were immortal?"

"The years tramp more slowly for them than for humans, and I have yet to hear of age killing a troll, but there are other things that can destroy them," the west wind said. The south wind was swirling through the broken pillars again, apparently mulling over the lass's words.

"Like what?"

"Powerful magic. Weapons of enchanted steel. Dragons."

"Oh." The lass had none of those things.

"Rest and eat," the south wind said, winding through the ruins to make the lass's skirts flap. "Tomorrow I shall carry you to my brother."

"Thank you."

Though stronger than the west, the south wind was far more pleasant. Warm, moist air scented with exotic flowers bore her up as dawn gilded the ruins of the ancient temple. Feeling as though she rode on a bed of soft moss, the lass closed her eyes as the south wind's bird shape sped over mountains and valleys, crossed oceans, and wove between treetops.

Rollo was tucked up as he had been on their other wind journeys, but this time he would occasionally raise his head and lap at the moist air with his tongue. When she did open her eyes, the lass delighted in watching the play of dewdrops on her hands, seeing them bead up and then run up her arms as the south wind sped forward. Finally even that grew tiresome, though, and she closed her eyes and slept. The south wind bore her on and on, beyond a day and a night, until it was little more than a stiff, wet breeze that could barely hold its shape. With a last puff of effort, she was set down on the crest of a snowdrift as hard as stone.

"Brother," the south wind called weakly.

The roar of the north wind blasted the snowdrift into a million sharp, cold diamonds, and the lass fell down and down, into a crevice of blue ice and white snow. Rollo landed heavily atop her, knocking the breath from both their bodies.

The north wind howled down the crevice, smashing the lass against a jagged wall of ice. She struck her head, and all went dark.

Chapter 27

When she woke, the lass found herself in a snow cave sitting propped up by a chunk of ice. A pool of water as gray as steel reflected dim light onto the roof of the cave, and a walrus was lying beside the pool only a few paces away. It was big, and brown, and had long yellow tusks.

"If you scare away my fish, I'll eat you and the wolf," the walrus said. Then it heaved its ungainly body into the pool without causing a splash. The lass assumed that it swam out of the cave, because it didn't resurface.

"Nasty temper," Rollo said from his position at her side. "Nothing but threats and insults since the wind brought us here."

"Which wind?"

"North. South was too weak."

"Will the north wind help us, do you think?"

"It won't talk to me," Rollo huffed. "But at least it brought us in here and gave us our things."

The lass realized that she was covered in the white parka, and various other items of clothing had been spread over her. She wasn't sure if Rollo or the north wind was responsible, but she was grateful all the same. It was very, very cold.

Riding the south wind had dampened her clothes, and now they had frozen stiff. She stood up and quickly undressed, then yanked on the first things she could get her hands on. In the end, she had a nightgown on over an outer shift, but she didn't care. There were layers of skirts and vests over that, and then the white parka. Besides, there was no one here to see her but Rollo and the walrus, and the walrus still had not returned.

The north wind arrived before the walrus did. A great whirl of icy particles whipped into the cave and tore at the lass's clothes and hair. Before she could protest, it lifted her off her feet and carried her out of the cave, with Rollo and her pack as well. The wind dropped her just outside, near the water, and then pulled back.

Looking around, the lass felt her jaw fall open. She was not on solid ground. She was on a large sheet of ice and hard-packed snow, floating in a sea of other sheets of ice, mountains of ice, pillars of ice. That hadn't been a little pond inside the snow cave earlier; it had been the sea coming through a hole in the floor.

The sudden realization made the lass lose her balance and she staggered to keep herself from falling. What if the sheet of ice she was on tipped? How thick was it? She had heard that the great bergs and islands of ice in the far north floated freely, ramming ships and trapping sailors. Her father thought that was what had happened to Hans Peter's ship.

"Are you ill?" The voice of the north wind was sharp and cold. It knocked the lass's hood back off her head, and burned her ears with particles of ice.

"No!" She snatched her hood back, straightening. "I just—I didn't realize—is this ice solid enough to hold me?" Then she saw Rollo, a pace away with all four legs splayed wide and his eyes rolling in panic. "Is it solid enough to hold *us*?"

The north wind's laugh sounded like icicles breaking off eaves and smashing to the ground. The lass clapped her hood tight to the sides of her head, guarding her ears from both the sound and the blast of cold air.

"I'm sorry." The wind sounded contrite. And quieter. "I had forgotten the delicacy of humans. The ice will hold you and your companion."

"Thank you." The lass cautiously took her hands from her ears. "I suppose you know why I'm here?"

"Yes."

And then the north wind took shape in front of her. From the swirling particles of ice it formed into the shape of a snow-pale man in a long robe, with blue-white hair and a beard to his waist. Clasping his hands, he looked her over. "You wish to go to the palace east of the sun and west of the moon," the north wind replied. "And you want to know if I can take you there."

"Can you?"

"Indeed I can."

Again the lass felt her jaw drop. A flutter of hope rose in her breast. "You truly can?"

"I have blown there once before, though it nearly did me in," the north wind told her. "And I will blow there again, if you are determined to go."

"I am." She bit her lip. Despite the friendly tone, and the thoughtful lowering of the wind's great voice, this was still the *north wind* she was facing. But she had to ask. "Why? Why did you blow there once before, and why are you so ready to take me?"

"Once before a girl came, and begged me to take her. I took her because she meant to cause mischief with the troll queen, and it pleased me to help in that."

"Tova?"

He raised an icy eyebrow. "Do you know her?"

"She was in love with my brother, when he was the troll princess's *isbjørn*." The lass frowned in thought. "Why do you want to cause harm to the troll queen? Your brother winds seem to be afraid of her."

"That creature has caused me no end of trouble," the north wind grumped. "She dares to order me about, to try and control *me*! She changes the weather, making the winter last too long and spread too far to the south. I know why the creator made me, and it was not to serve her purposes!"

"The troll queen is making the weather so cold?"

"Of course. I can tell from your speech that you are from the northern lands. The cold there has not broken in decades. . . . Can your people not have noticed?"

"We noticed, but what could we do about it?"

"True, true, you are very weak." Another sigh. "No doubt it was too much to hope that Tova could succeed in doing harm to her. Or that you could. Still, if you wish to go . . ."

"I must go! How soon can you take me?"

"We can go now, if you like. But I know that you humans need to eat, and it is a long journey."

The lass carefully settled on the ice beside Rollo. They had apples, and bread and cheese, and a bit of dried meat. After they had sucked some snow to rinse their mouths, the lass packed her bundles and stamped her feet to settle them in her boots. "I'm ready."

With a laugh, the north wind scooped up the girl, the wolf, and the bundle in his arms. He was growing larger by the second, his human features blurring as he expanded. "I doubt that, but there is no point in waiting longer." And with that, they hurtled into the sky, a great boiling mass of wind and ice and fury, aimed at the troll queen and her distant palace.

If she had thought the other winds had power, it was

nothing compared to their eldest brother of the North. The lass felt like some ancient goddess, one of the Valkyries, riding high over the world in a magical chariot. They soared over ocean and mountain and plain, heading steadily toward both the sun and the moon, which hung side by side this far north.

As they traveled the sun and moon dipped in the sky and then rose again, moving around them in a stately dance. In the summer months, at the top of the world, neither sank below the horizon. The sky was both dark and light, the sun a tiny pale ball and the moon a long thin crescent, lying on its back like a bowl. Then, for a time, the sun was directly below the moon, looking insignificant and weak.

And then they came closer, and closer, the north wind, the wolf, and the young woman. The sun and moon parted ways, like a curtain being pulled back. The sun moved to their left, the moon to the right. The north wind roared as it charged toward the speck that lay between them. The speck grew, reaching out taller and wider as they approached. It was a palace, made entirely of gold, sitting on an island of silver snow at the very top of the world.

East of the sun, and west of the moon.

Part 4

Beggar at the Palace of Gold

Chapter 28

The north wind's great strength failed as they drew closer to the island, and more and more of him dropped away as they went on. At last, at the edge of the island, he was nothing more than a chill breeze. The lass tumbled from the sky to land on the shore of hard-packed snow beside the green-gray water.

The little swirl of ice particles that remained wavered at her feet. "That is the limit of my strength. I must rest here a day or so, before I return." Its voice was hardly a whisper.

"Thank you, a thousand thank-yous," the lass said, holding out one mittened hand. "I will do all I can to harm the troll queen, and her daughter. For your sake."

"For the world's sake," the north wind said. Then even the small cluster of ice dissipated. "Farewell," it sighed into the air.

The lass shouldered her pack, staggering a little under the weight. Rollo shook himself and sniffed the air.

"How does it smell?" his mistress asked.

"Like trolls" was the solemn reply.

"Well, I suppose we've come to the right place, then," the lass said.

And they started walking. The island was not as large as the snow plain in front of the palace of ice had been, nor was it as flat. They trekked up a long rise, and then looked down into a hollow that had two large gray boulders lying in it. The boulders had moss growing on them, and one had a very small pine tree sprouting from one side.

"Odd," the lass said. "How could anything grow here?"

As they passed between the boulders, Rollo stiffened, and he pressed against the lass's leg. "Walk faster," he whispered.

"What?"

"Walk. Faster."

He relaxed only slightly once the boulders were behind them and they were coming to the top of another small rise. He stopped and looked back, and so did the lass. One of the boulders had changed shape. It was taller, and there was a glowing pair of—

"Eyes," the lass said faintly. Her knees started to buckle, and Rollo pushed her so that she fell down the far side of the rise. Away from the trolls.

She lay in the little hollow on the far side of the rise and shook. Rollo leaned against her, still at the alert, but the trolls did not follow.

"What am I doing here?" The lass's teeth began to chatter. "I can't face the queen of the *trolls*. I'm just a silly little girl! Father's fears have all come true: I've been taken by the trolls." She let out a hysterical laugh.

"Hush, hush now," Rollo said, more worried than the lass had ever heard him. "The trolls haven't taken you. You came here to fight. You have a name; you used to whisper it to me as a pup." And he leaned down and said the lass's name softly in her ear.

She got to her feet, squared her shoulders despite the prickling down her spine at the thought of the trolls behind her, and walked on. Her heart was still pounding, but she did not stop until they reached the doors of the palace.

There was no courtyard, and no wall around the golden palace, but then, there was no need for any. The palace doors rose to four times the height of a man and were set with precious gems in a design that showed the sun and moon eclipsed. Over the doors, dimly seen in the light from the torches that burned on each side, the lass could make out the emblem of the troll queen: an *isbjørn* on a blue background, with a crown above it and a saw-edged sword below.

Just as she raised her hand to knock, a shadow peeled itself away from a niche to one side of the doors. The lass had thought that the narrow recessed area held a statue of some kind, but it was all too alive.

Another troll, this one tall and thin, with ropes of muscles along his bare arms.

He carried a black sword with a serrated edge, like

the one on the trolls' standard, and wore livery of a sort: a blue leather vest and trousers. His boots were studded with iron, and there were iron cuffs around his wrists. He had huge ears pierced with fat rings, and a sharp, jutting nose. There was no hair on his head, but his scalp had been painted blue.

"*Ja?*"

The lass froze. Rollo's hackles raised, but he whimpered rather than growled. "I, um, the queen . . . I'm looking for work," the lass stammered.

The troll gazed down at her in consternation. "Why would you come all this way to work here? You're a human!"

"Er. Well." The lass rallied, remembering the flattering carvings of the ice palace. "But is the young princess not fairer than any human maid could ever aspire to be? I have come to serve her graciousness."

"She's a *troll*," the guard grunted. "One look at her could peel the hide off a goat."

The lass couldn't help it, she snickered. Then she covered her mouth and looked around. "Should you be saying that?"

"No, but who's going to hear me except you? They're all in there celebrating. It's all wine and dancing and feats of magic, and I'm out in the cold talking to a mad human. I'm cursed." He seemed to be saying this to himself, but it made the lass shiver all the same.

"Celebrating? Celebrating what?"

"Princess Indæll's latest marriage to some poor human fool, of course."

"Oh, no!" The lass felt tears prick her eyes. "They've already married?"

"No." The troll frowned at her. "They won't be married for four more days." He bent down and studied her face. "Are you the girl? The girl who had to live in the palace of ice?"

"Yes." Her voice was barely a whisper.

"And you made it all the way here? So quickly?"

"I had some help."

The troll looked around nervously. "If you're wise, you'll get out of here. Leave, go back to your family."

"I can't."

The troll heaved a sigh. Breath that smelled of rock and ice, not altogether unpleasant, blasted in her face. "I didn't think you would take my advice. They never do."

"Is Tova here?"

"It's better not to ask. It's better not to be here."

"Can you at least let me in? Could I talk to . . . the housekeeper, or someone, about getting work?"

The troll shook his head. "It's more than my sorry hide is worth to let you pass through these doors." He licked his lips with a blue tongue. "I did it once," he confided in a low voice, "and if I do it again . . . well, few have survived the queen's wrath *one* time." He shuddered.

"That's why I've been ordered to play sentry, as though anyone would think to attack the troll queen's lair. The humiliation of it nearly killed my family."

"But," the lass faltered, then thought of something. "I can pay you!" She let her pack fall to the hard-packed snow with a thud, and rooted around inside. A golden carding comb came to hand first. "Here! Solid gold!"

He shook his head. "Very pretty, but this entire palace is made of gold. If I wanted a lump I could just chip off a piece of windowsill."

"Oh." The lass's shoulders slumped.

"What is that, anyway?"

She fished out the other comb and held them up so that he could see them better. "They're carding combs. You know, for wool."

"Really?" This seemed to interest the troll. "You can card wool with them?"

"Well, yes. I mean, I've never used this particular set, but I'm sure they'd work just fine."

"No, I mean, *you* personally know how to card wool?"

"Of course." The lass was puzzled: idiots and children could card wool.

"Well, then, you might have something there. I'm not one for the, er, ladylike arts myself. But there's others here that are. Certain ladies of high birth, if you know what I mean." He laid a long finger to the side of his sharp nose and winked.

The lass's heart raced. "The princess? She would like them?

"She might. Especially if you were to demonstrate."

"Can you take me to see her, then?"

"Oh, no, I can't let any more humans in. But if you were to hang around the palace, and maybe do a little carding. . . . Her rooms are on the west side." The troll leaned in close as he said this.

"Thank you so much," the lass said. Without thinking, she stretched out one mittened hand and put it on the troll's. He looked startled and blushed a sort of purple color.

"I do have a weakness for human girls. I don't know what it is," he said, shaking his head. "My grandfather would skin me for a drum, if he were alive to see how soft I am."

"Skarp-Heðin! What have you there?"

The lass turned and saw a massive troll, like a chunk of mossy granite, stumping toward them. She made a choking noise, and shrank back against the gem-studded doors. Rollo took up a defensive stance but once again did not dare to growl.

"Another human, Captain Banahøgg," the sentry said uneasily. He was tiny and his features were almost human in comparison to the captain's.

"Get rid of it!" Banahøgg's gray, craggy face crumpled into a frown, a truly terrifying sight. "You weren't going to let another one in, were you?"

"No, sir, captain!" Skarp-Heðin raised his sword, bringing the point to within inches of the lass's chest. "Get away, girl! Back to the southern lands with you!" One eyelid twitched ever so slightly in what could almost have been a wink.

The lass took the hint and ran, Rollo by her side. But as soon at they had gone around a snowdrift that hid them from sight of the front doors, she turned and made her way around to the west side of the palace.

The palace of the trolls was a truly magnificent place. There were windows with panes of crystal set into the walls every few paces, and the lass stood on tiptoe to peep through them. She supposed that for a troll they would be low, but even on tiptoe she could just rest her chin on the sill. It was growing darker and darker, and inside the lights blazed. From what the lass could see, there was a great deal going on. She heard music and saw servants in blue livery rushing back and forth with silver trays. The servants were gargoyles, pixies, brownies, and other creatures like the ones who had waited on her at the palace of ice. None of the servants were trolls.

But there were plenty of trolls in attendance. Male trolls and female, dressed in elaborate suits and gowns of brightly colored satin and velvet. Jewels gleamed and sparkled in the light from the hundreds of candles. The troll ladies had their hair piled in fabulous towers of curls above their hideous gray-green faces, and the troll gentlemen had caps of leather or silver or gold covering their heads.

Then she noticed that there were a few trolls who shunned this humanlike finery. These wore layers of hides from a variety of animals. Their hair stuck out at all angles from their broad faces, and the lass saw moss and other scruffy plants growing on them. One appeared to have an actual bird's nest in his beard.

The window where the lass found the best view looked in on the ballroom itself. There was a drift of hard-frozen snow just under one of the windows, and if she stood on the very top, she could peer inside without straining. The ballroom was a sight to behold: huge be-yond belief, with pillars of carved crystal and amethyst. Chandeliers with dangling pendants that were surely di-amonds filled the room with light and were reflected on the gleaming black floor. At one end of the ballroom stood a dais with two thrones. One was of gold, set with rubies, and the other silver, set with sapphires. Beside the silver-and-sapphire throne was a stool, also of silver and inlaid with pearls. The lass's heart stopped beating for just a moment and then started back up with a painful thump when she saw who was sitting on the stool.

It was her prince.

As the trolls moved about the ballroom, drinking and eating and talking, the prince sat on his stool and stared straight ahead. The lass had a childish urge to wave at him, just to see if he would look, if he would recognize her, but she quelled it. Instead she pointed him out to Rollo, who agreed that he did not look well, and they continued to watch.

After a few minutes, when the lass's feet were starting to go numb from standing in the snow for so long, the double doors at the far end of the room flew open. A dozen servants marched into the room in perfect formation. They had the upper bodies of men and the lower bodies of horses, four legs and all. They stood at attention to each side of the large doors and raised silver trumpets to their lips. When their fanfare was over, the roomful of trolls dipped into deep curtsies or folded in half with bows.

The doors opened and an especially hideous troll woman in a scarlet gown swept into the room. She had a tall pile of unnaturally yellow hair surmounted by a crown that was more diamonds than gold. Her eyes bulged and her nose drooped down almost past her lips. There were so many gold rings in her ears that the lobes touched her shoulders. Her skin was the exact color and texture of unpolished granite.

Stories about trolls said that the females had noses more than three yards long and breasts that hung to their knees. The lass thought that this was not much of an exaggeration: the queen's nose was alarmingly long, and her wrinkled bosom threatened to burst free of her gown at any moment.

The queen surveyed the room with her glaring, scum-green eyes and sailed past her bowing subjects to take her seat on the golden throne. The centaurs—that was what the servants were, the lass remembered reading of such creatures once—blew another, shorter fanfare to herald the entrance of a second troll lady.

This, the lass thought with a gasp, was surely the troll princess. Her nose was even longer than her mother's and had a great wart on it besides. She wore a gown of sapphire-blue velvet, to match her throne, and her hair was a gleaming arrangement of flame-red tresses and diamond hairpins. She swayed across the room with the air of a woman who knows all eyes are upon her, and stopped to plant a kiss on the cheek of the human prince before sitting on the silver throne.

The troll queen clapped her hands—her ring-encrusted fingers appeared to have another set of joints—and music began to play. The lass could not see the musicians from her vantage point, and she wondered what sort of odd instruments they were playing. There was a lot of banging, a deep echoing hoot that made the bones behind her ears vibrate, and rising over it all a shrill sound that made her cringe.

"It sounds like a rabbit being killed," Rollo said, disgusted.

"Ugh, you're right," she agreed. "Oh, they're going to dance." The lass and the wolf pressed their noses closer to the window to watch.

The trolls were dividing into pairs and taking up positions on the dance floor. The lass noticed that the mossy, fur-wearing trolls did not join in the dancing, but instead stood aside with disapproving expressions on their faces and large goblets of wine in their fists. But the finely dressed trolls began to dance to the music with great delight.

Not even Rollo could think of a comment to make about the trolls' dancing. It was horrible and fascinating at the same time. In time to the beat of the thumping, wailing music, they hunched their shoulders and stamped their feet, lurched from side to side, and slapped their heavy hands on their bellies to make a counterpoint to the musicians' drumming. It was like a macabre parody of human dancing. Something about it sent a curl of terror up from the lass's stomach and into her throat, and she thought she might scream. She had three days, three days to free the prince and get far away from this awful place and these nightmarish creatures.

"Hide!" Rollo sprang down from the windowsill and began tugging at the lass's parka with his teeth.

"What? Why?" Startled, she slipped on the icy snow and one of her boots punched through into the softer snow beneath.

"A troll saw us!"

The lass yanked her foot free of the hole in the snow and flattened herself against the side of the palace to one side of the window. "Are you sure?" she whispered.

"Yes!" Rollo crouched directly below the window, trying to make himself as small as possible.

There was a scraping sound, and the window swung outward. It nearly hit the lass in the face, and she managed to put one hand up just in time to keep it from breaking her nose. The cold panes, leaded with gold, smacked against her hand and bounced back. She held her breath, squeezed her eyes shut, and prayed.

"What are you doing?" A female troll's voice rang out.

"I saw something," grunted a thick, male voice. "There's someone out here."

"There's no one out there, you old fool," the female insisted. "Close that window; it's cold!"

This was greeted by a roar of laughter from a number of trolls. Even the lass had to admit that the female was either being very stupid or very witty: here at the top of the world, how could it not be cold?

The window swung closed, and the lass heard the latch click. Still she held her breath and prayed. When she did open her eyes, she didn't dare move her head.

When she had counted to fifty, she looked down at Rollo. He was still huddled close to the side of the palace directly below the window. His golden eyes were wide and staring, the white showing all around. The lass slithered down until she was kneeling in the snow, and put out one hand to touch his head. He jumped at the contact, then relaxed.

"We've already spoken to one troll," she reminded him in a whisper, "who was not entirely unkind."

"There's a world of difference between that bored sentry out there and the fish-eyed courtiers in there," Rollo said.

He was right. The faces of the trolls within the palace were vastly different from Skarp-Heðin's. The lass nodded. Dragging her pack by one strap, she crawled along the foundation of the palace. Rollo came behind, listening with his superior hearing as they passed each window. He hissed for her to stop only once, and they spent a terrified moment crouched beneath one of the ballroom's other windows while a troll female, shrieking with laughter, leaned out the window to "catch a breath of air."

After an interminable amount of time, they came to the back corner of the palace and huddled in a blue shadow. Rollo could hear no sounds coming through the wall, and there were no windows for several paces, so they thought themselves safe. Together they dug a snow cave, and the lass made a nest out of her clothes. They snuggled in to sleep, blocking the entrance with the knapsack.

Despite their strange surroundings, and the danger that lay all about them, they were both soon snoring. It had been a long day, after a series of long days, and tomorrow promised to be even longer.

Chapter 29

The next morning the sun woke them, turning the roof of the cave pale yellow. It was far away and strange here, but it was still the sun, and it brought a little warmth. It took an effort for the lass to crawl out of her nest and stretch her limbs. She felt old and cold and worn thin. Rollo grunted but didn't wake, even when she pulled the skirts and shifts right out from under him and repacked them.

She pulled off the topmost of the skirts she wore, since it was filthy, and put a slightly cleaner one on. She had four more skirts underneath, and still she was cold. The white parka gleamed, though, without a stain or a smudge to mar its beauty. Pushing back the hood and taking off her mittens, the lass scrubbed her face and hands with snow. She combed her hair and braided it. It made her feel slightly better, and eating breakfast even more so. Of course, it was only bread, but even Rollo got up to have some, and it raised his spirits as well.

"Now what?" Rollo rolled briefly in the snow, then shook with a will. This did wonders for his fur, which was full of sand and pine needles from their journey.

"Now we have to attract the troll princess's attention," the lass replied.

They made their way along the west side of the palace. It was early, and the windows were still shielded by draperies. They couldn't be sure where the princess's rooms were, unless they ran all the way along that side.

"There's no telling which floor they're on, either," the lass fretted. She counted eight levels, and thought that she saw one or two beyond that, but standing so close to the massive building made it difficult to judge.

"It's not too late to go home," Rollo said, pacing around the hardened drifts of snow.

"Actually, it's far too late," she told him gently.

It was something that she had only realized as they were walking along the walls of the palace. The north wind had blown itself out to bring them here. And then . . . what? She supposed that when it was rested, it would go back to its own lands. She and Rollo were stranded. Perhaps, if she were able to free the prince, he would know the way back. Perhaps he could change into a bear again, and carry her.

Perhaps. Perhaps not. It was too late to worry about it. She would just have to move forward, she told herself. But at the same time she was racked with a deep longing to be riding her *isbjørn* across the snow plain, heading toward the ice palace and a rich supper.

"Well, can I at least have something more to eat?"

Rollo sat on a snowbank and looked around with a disgruntled expression.

"Yes, I suppose," the lass said. She plumped down beside him and rummaged in her pack. "An apple?"

He sneezed in distaste. "Isn't there any meat at all?"

"There might be." She rummaged some more. Her fingernails clicked against something hard, and she pulled out the bottle of apple jelly. "Oh, look!" She held it up to the weak light. The golden jelly blazed, and the refracted light from the crystal jar cast bits of rainbows on the snow around them.

"I'd still rather have meat," Rollo said.

"Well, *I* might like some apple jelly on a bit of bread," the lass said. "It's not always *your* stomach that concerns me."

She unwrapped a bit of bread and unstoppered the jelly with a flourish.

"What's that?"

The rasping troll voice scared the blood out of the lass's face. Her hands went numb, and the little jar of apple jelly fell to the ground and rolled away. A few golden globules scattered across the snow, freezing almost instantly.

"I said, what is that? Are you deaf?"

Slowly the lass turned around. The window behind the lass was opened wide, and the Princess Indæll herself leaned out of it. Today she wore peach silk, and it reminded the lass of a similar dress she had worn in the palace of ice. It made her shiver. Of course, she had not had an enormous, greenish gray bosom to pour into the bodice.

"It's apple jelly, Your Highness," the lass said when she could breathe. She bent over and picked up the little jar before any more could spill out. Taking great care, every movement seeming weighted with importance, she replaced the golden stopper and held up the jar so that the troll princess could see it.

A pointed purple tongue darted out of the princess's wide mouth, and she licked her heavily made-up lips. "Did you . . . make . . . that yourself?"

"I helped the aged woman who did," the lass replied. "I peeled apples, and she put them in the pot with the spices."

"Ah!" Another lick. "And the jar?"

"I do not know where it came from."

A shadow passed over the troll's face. "A pity. But still." She reached out one hand. Her fingers were twice as long as the lass's and her pointed nails were gilded. "Give it to me."

"Very well, Your Highness," the lass said, but she made no move to hand the jar over. She had just had a sudden insight into the trollish character: they were jealous! They were jealous of humans, who could make things, when apparently they could not. The clothing, the dancing from the night before . . . the lass now saw them for poor attempts to copy human society.

Indæll grew impatient. "Give it to me now!"

The lass feigned surprise. "But, Your Highness, I was waiting for *your* offer."

"*My* offer?"

"In the human world, no one ever gives another person something for free! We pay each other, with gold or goods or . . . other things."

"Hmm." The princess was plainly intrigued. At the same time, though, her long fingers flexed on the windowsill, making dents in the gold surface, as though she yearned to simply reach out and grab the jar. "Very well. What do you want?"

"I want to visit the human prince," the lass said promptly.

Indæll's eyes narrowed. Her wide, thick-lipped mouth drew down. "You!" She didn't bother to speak Norsk anymore: it seemed that she knew of the lass's gift. "You are *that* human wench! The one who tried to take my dear love away!"

This gave the lass pause, but she decided it was foolish to remind the princess that it was she who decreed that the lass live in the ice palace for a year. And Tova before that, and the *mosters* and countless others before that. "Er, yes, that was me."

A sudden smile stretched Princess Indæll's lips. "Of

course you may spend the night in my dear prince's chambers," she purred. "Come to the front doors at sunset." And she held out one hand for the jar of jelly.

Her heart in her throat, the lass held the jar out of reach. "How do I know you will keep your end of the bargain?"

The princess's eyes flashed red. "Trolls always keep their bargains," she said in a tight voice.

Something in the princess's greenish gray face and bulging eyes told the lass that this was the truth. The girl placed the gleaming jar in the hands of the troll princess. "I shall be at the front doors at sunset," she said.

Princess Indæll didn't say anything. The jar clutched in one hand, she used the other to pull the windows shut. Heart racing, the lass walked back to her snow cave with Rollo. There was no point in lingering under the princess's windows now; they would only risk aggravating her.

A few minutes before sunset the lass could wait no longer. For the past hours she had been poring over the symbols in her troll dictionary, in case she saw any carvings inside that would help. But now that the sun was getting lower, she couldn't concentrate. She hurried to the front doors and knocked. The guard-troll from the night before, Skarp-Heðin, came out of his niche.

"Traded your carding combs, did you?"

"A jar of apple jelly," she said. "Now the princess says I'm to be let in. Please?"

"I'm not to let you in until *she* comes," he said. "You're sure that you want this? There's still time to run."

"Why would I want to run?" The lass was almost giddy at the prospect of seeing the prince again, and the troll's question made no sense to her. "I'm so close!"

"Not as close as you think" came the reply. Skarp-Heðin leaned down, as though to confide another secret to her. He opened his mouth just as the golden doors opened as well. He straightened and turned to bow.

Dressed all in rich purple with silver lace and beadwork, the troll princess stood there smiling. "Hello, little human," she said. "I shall lead you to my betrothed's room now. Of course, he will not be there for some hours. We are having a ball to celebrate our marriage."

"But—"

"He will come back to them some time between midnight and dawn, I assure you. Of course, at dawn you must leave."

"Very well." The lass thought of the spindle and carding combs in the pack on her back, and the three nights left. She would find a way to get him free. Somehow.

The lass followed the princess through long hallways of gold, richly carpeted and hung with silk. There were vases of fine Oriental work, statues of marble, and beautiful paintings. There were also little pedestals displaying butter churns and cheese graters. A complete set of cooking pots hung from the ceiling of one anteroom they passed through.

A door opened as they went by and a faun in livery stepped out. Behind him, the lass could see a large loom with a half-finished tapestry still strung on it. The faun backed against the wall and bowed deeply until they passed. Seeing him gave the lass a surge of hope, but it was not Erasmus.

"Come along, come along," Indæll said, and clicked her long fingernails at the lass, making the girl shudder.

They stopped in front of a door made of silver and set with pearls. The princess threw it open and gestured for the lass to enter. Timid, she and Rollo stepped into the room. The door slammed shut behind them.

"You will stay in this room until dawn, and then I will fetch you," Princess Indæll called through the door.

"I don't like her," Rollo said when the princess's footsteps had faded away.

The lass just snorted, taking off her parka and outer boots. Her Highness, the Princess Indæll, was ugly, overdressed, and cruel. "She's a troll."

Together they explored the prince's chambers. They were in a large sitting room, richly furnished. Beyond, they found a bedchamber and a washroom. It was much like her apartments at the palace of ice, though here everything was made of gold and inlaid with jewels. There were books on a footstool near the fireplace, in Norsk and Tysk, and a game of chess was under way on a small table by the windows. In the bedchamber, the lass found a single dark hair on one of the pillows. She wound the hair around the top button of her vest, thinking of how she had saved Tova's hair the same way.

This sobered her even more than the situation already had. She settled in an armchair in the sitting room with Rollo at her feet. She tried to read one of the books from the footstool, and he dozed lightly. She could tell it was only lightly, because his ears moved to follow the sound of any footsteps in the corridor, no matter how faint.

The gold clock on the mantel was chiming two o'clock when the silver door opened. The lass had been nodding over her book despite her nerves, and now the sound startled her awake. She and Rollo were on their feet in an instant, the book slithering down her skirts to the floor.

A centaur entered the room. Thrown across the horse part of his body was the prince. He was facedown, his arms hanging down one side and his legs on the other.

"Is he dead?" The lass clutched at the front of her vest. Her knees were shaking and she felt her lower lip tremble.

The centaur gave her a strange look, equal parts pity and worry. "No, he's just . . . asleep." He paced through the sitting room and into the bedchamber. The lass and Rollo followed. With a small buck and a roll, the centaur flipped the prince off his back and onto the bed. "My lady," he murmured, bowing. He left.

The lass approached the bed on quiet feet. Rollo stayed

by the door to give her privacy. With a shaking hand, she reached out and took hold of the prince's shoulder.

"Wake up . . . Your Highness," she said softly.

He didn't stir.

She shook his shoulder, and said, louder this time, "Wake up, my *isbjørn!*"

No reaction.

For the next few hours until dawn, the lass and Rollo tried everything to wake the prince. The lass shouted and shook him, Rollo licked his face and even bit his shoulder gently. She pounded on the outer door, begging for help, but no one came. She poured the ewer of water from the washstand over his head, but the prince did not stir. When Princess Indæll came to collect them, the lass was huddled on the bed by his side, clutching his hand and weeping. The princess smiled smugly as the lass gathered up her parka and boots and pack.

"I have something else," the lass said in a small voice as they crossed the entrance hall. She dropped her pack and fished out the golden carding combs. Taking up the ball of uncarded wool the *moster* had given her, she demonstrated the technique with shaking hands.

The troll princess was fascinated. Other members of the court gathered around to watch as well, their rancid breath and glowing eyes making her feel faint.

"Come back at sunset," Princess Indæll ordered after a few minutes. "You shall card the wool fine for me, and then

I shall keep the combs. In return you may spend another night in the prince's chambers."

Numb, the lass nodded and put away the combs and wool. The cold outside the palace was like a slap in the face. She felt her eyebrows and lashes freeze instantly, the skin on her forehead tightening. Shrugging into her parka, the lass tramped back around the palace to her little cave. She crawled in and fell asleep with her head on Rollo's flank.

Chapter 30

The next night was much the same. After Princess In-dæll and several dozen of her court had watched the lass card the wool into a neat twist, the princess left her in the prince's chambers. The lass was still reeling from seeing the queen peering at her from the doorway to the ballroom: she was more frightening than her daughter. The lass couldn't even pretend to read while she waited for the prince to appear, and when he did, he was unconscious across the back of the same centaur.

The centaur rolled him onto the bed, bowed to the lass, and left again. She tried to stop the centaur, to ask him what was going on, and even dared to touch his arm and then his horselike flank, but he would not look at her. His eyes straight ahead, he paced out of the room, shutting the door and bolting it despite her pleas.

"Well! No help there," she said to Rollo. She remembered the compassion in the centaur's eyes from the night before, though. "Probably under threat of death if he talks to me," she reasoned.

She and Rollo spent another night trying to wake the

prince. They pulled his hair, and the lass slapped him as hard as she could, although it brought tears to her eyes to do it. He did not respond, and for their last hour together, the lass simply lay beside him and reveled in the familiar sound of his breath.

The troll princess came to fetch them at dawn, her smile even broader. The lass was too exhausted and out of sorts to remember the spindle until she had been shut out of the palace. She and Rollo went to their nest, but neither could sleep. They had only one more night.

After a restless hour the lass got up, stripped, and scrubbed herself with snow. Her hands and feet were blue and her joints ached with cold by the time she was done, but she did it all the same. She put on the cleanest of her shifts and stockings, her favorite blue skirt and scarlet vest, and then put the parka over it all. She brushed her hair until it shone, and plaited it in a four-strand braid that Tordis had taught her. Leaving her pack with Rollo, who thought she was crazy, she took the gold spindle and the hank of wool she had carded the day before and went to sit under Indæll's window.

She scraped the hard snow flat to give her a place to drop the spindle. Then she rolled a large snowball for a seat. Arranging her skirts neatly, she took the wool and began to spin.

The window behind her creaked open a few minutes later, but the lass didn't turn around. She forced herself to keep on spinning, and even hummed a little.

"What in heaven's name are you doing?"

The voice was female and speaking Norsk, but it was not Princess Indæll's. It sounded human, and young. Surprised, the lass stopped spinning and turned around.

Dressed in blue livery with an embroidered scarlet ribbon at her neck, a young woman leaned out the window of the princess's chambers. Hair so fair it was almost white was braided into a coronet around her head, and she had the milky skin and rosy cheeks of the North. Her wide blue eyes held a touch of humor, and her mouth was caught between gaping and smiling.

"Oh, no! You too?" she said when she got a good look at the lass.

"Tova?" The lass gasped. "Is it really you?"

The blue eyes widened even farther. "How did you know my name?" Then her eyes fixed on the white parka that the lass wore, and the roses disappeared from her cheeks. "Where did you get that parka?"

"It belongs to my brother, Hans Peter."

"Are you—why, you must be the youngest, the little pika!"

Tova hoisted herself up and over the windowsill and half fell into the lass's arms. They hugged and kissed each other's cheeks and cried.

"I feel as though I know you," they both said at the same time.

This set them to laughing and crying again. Tova demanded to know where Hans Peter was and how he fared; the lass wanted to know why Tova was working at the palace.

Sobered by the question, and by the news that Hans Peter was safely at home but still haunted by his enchantment, Tova sank down on the snow beside the lass. She reached out and fingered the embroidery on the white parka.

"I changed the embroidery to make it so that Hans Peter could escape from *her*," Tova said. "But I'd never done magic before and didn't think that it had worked. I came here, looking for him, and was caught." She shrugged. "I thought, too, that I might be able to break the hold on your brother completely." She pointed to some of the embroidery that ran along one sleeve. "It's a curse: not even in death will he be free. She wants them to love her, to think only of her, forever."

"You're so good!" The lass clasped Tova's hands, a fresh wave of tears running down her cheeks. "I'd like to do the same thing, but if you have been here for years and haven't made any progress. . . ." The lass sighed, feeling even more hopeless than she had earlier. "I didn't even guess that the bear and the man in my bed were the same person."

Tova giggled at this. "Hans Peter talks in his sleep. I would say things to him and he would answer, thinking it was part of his dream."

"Oh." The lass thought about this. "That explains why Torst and Askel always complained about having to share a bed with him."

Tova laughed again. She had a merry spirit, despite the shadow in her eyes. The lass estimated that she had been in service to the trolls for nearly ten years. She must have been nearing her thirtieth birthday, for all her youthful looks.

"And then we passed notes to each other as well," Tova said, lowering her voice. "When he was human, just before he would come into my bedchamber, he would leave a letter in the sitting room. And I would leave one for him there as well. The servants never knew, or the princess would have found out." She paused, smiling in reminiscence. "Did you never find your prince's parka?"

"*His* parka?"

Tova plucked at the white fur cuff. "This is Hans Peter's; your prince has one as well. If we could change his, the way I changed this one, he could get free. But there isn't much time; they're to be married tomorrow noon."

"Wait, you mean——?" The lass felt even more foolish than she had before. "This is what *causes* the transformation?"

"Didn't you know?"

The lass only blushed in reply, then a thought struck her. "How is it that *she* can make such fine parkas, if she cannot even card wool?"

"Trolls can't make anything," Tova said, shaking her head. "They aren't natural creatures: they can only destroy."

"Erasmus said something about that, that they cannot make things, which is why they are so fascinated by human tools." The lass swallowed. "And I've heard the legends about their . . . palaces. Rollo, my pet wolf, said that the ice palace smelled of rancid meat."

"It's true," Tova said, her nose wrinkled with disgust. "They take thousands of lives, filled with the creative forces they don't have, to build a palace like this. He's probably smelling the . . . evilness of it.

"*She* doesn't sew the parkas and boots, either," Tova continued. "A servant does, and from the pelt of her last husband, no less."

They both shuddered.

"Then she enchants the ribbon and has it sewn on." Tova reached out to finger one of the embroidered bands.

The lass shook her head; trolls were beyond her ken. "But Hans Peter's pelt . . . ? Hans Peter is still alive."

"She used the scraps from the one before, the same one this parka is made from," Tova explained, her expression dark. "I had to help the gargoyle who made it. It was terrible."

"Why don't you leave?" This had been bothering the lass since she recognized Tova. "Hans Peter isn't here; why don't you go?"

Tova pointed to the ribbon around her neck. "This. All their servants wear one. It's how they know where we are and what we're doing. It's too close to the skin to alter. Some of the other servants have volunteered to let me experiment with theirs, but it hasn't worked." She opened her mouth to say something else, closed it, shook her head, and then said it anyway: "A naiad, a faun, and a centaur all asked me to try with their collars. They died."

"Oh, no," the lass gasped, and put her arm around Tova. "At least you tried to free them," she consoled her. She hesitated and then plunged ahead. "Do you think that you could alter my prince's parka?"

"We'll have to hurry. You're not allowed in during the day?"

"No, but I've been bartering things for a chance to be with him at night. He won't wake, though!"

"She puts something in his wine at night so that he will sleep," Tova said. "She's taking more precautions since Hans Peter got away."

"Why does she toy with them this way? Why the year of being an *isbjørn,* and why were we there with them?"

"A good question," Tova said. "It took me two years to find someone who could answer it. It seems that the first human prince she ever married extracted a promise from her, that she would give him and anyone who came after a way out. If the prince can find someone to stay with him as a beast by day and a silent, unseen man by night, to live that way for a whole year, then he can go free."

"It seems almost crueler than just stealing them away and marrying them right off," the lass said.

"That's their nature," Tova said simply. "I'm not allowed to speak to your prince. But I prepare his meal trays. I can hide a note on one and warn him not to drink any wine tonight. And I'll see if I can't find his parka. It was more luck than cleverness that I found your brother's. He kept me awake, talking in his sleep, and as I paced one night I tripped over it."

"But how did you know what this said?" The lass fingered the embroidery. "It wouldn't have meant anything to me, except Hans Peter had taught me the troll symbols."

"My father was the captain of the *Sea Dragon*," Tova explained. "He had run afoul of trolls before, and had taught me the runes, as he calls them."

"Did he teach Hans Peter?"

"Most likely. They were stuck in the ice for many days before the troll princess found them. Most of the crew were dead." Tova's face grew sad. "I visited my parents a few months after I went to live in the palace of ice. My father thought that Hans Peter had died as well."

The lass put one hand over Tova's to comfort her. "Of course," Tova went on, "my father is now a rich merchant who owns many ships." Her voice was bitter.

Before the lass could answer, both young women were startled to hear a troll calling from inside the palace. "Hey, you! Lackwit!"

"That's me," Tova said with a tight smile.

They embraced again. Tova scrambled up the bank of snow beneath the window and the lass gave her a push to help her back in. "Sorry," she called, when Tova tumbled head over heels onto the floor of Princess Indæll's sitting room.

With a laugh, Tova leaped to her feet and shook down her skirts. "I'm all right." She looked around quickly. "I'll leave this window open. Keep spinning so that you can make your bargain for tonight. If *she* doesn't come by in the next few minutes, I'll figure out a way to lure her. And I'll get a note to the prince." She bounded off to answer the ever-more-shrill summons. The lass sat back down and began to spin.

After a little while, Rollo came wandering over. "Are you still just sitting there? Hasn't anything happened? It's been hours!"

"Rollo!" The lass dropped her spinning and reached out to take hold of his ruff. She was so excited that she kissed him on the nose, which made him sneeze. "I can't wait to tell you—"

"You can and will wait to tell him," rasped a voice behind her. "For now, you will keep on spinning."

The lass whirled, but the window behind her was still empty. She heard a cough like rock being rubbed on a steel file from above her head. Looking up, her whole body went numb. The windows of the second story were full of trolls. It seemed that the entire court, save only the princess herself, was gathered to watch the lass. The order, and the cough, had come from the queen herself.

She pointed an imperious finger at the lass. "Continue. And face us, this time."

Shaking, the lass did as she was bid. When the spindle was wound with a more or less even thread, the lass held it up for the court to admire. They applauded and began to drift away from the windows. When it looked like the queen might also leave, the lass gave a deep curtsy.

"Your Majesty, a favor?"

"What is this?" The queen scowled at her.

"Your Majesty is so wise," the lass said carefully, "she surely knows that I have bartered my wealth and skill to spend the past two nights with Princess Indæll's betrothed."

"I had heard." The queen's red-lacquered nails tapped on the windowsill.

"I thought that, since Your Majesty has gotten so much pleasure in watching me spin, I . . . might have . . . earned . . . another night? I will give Your Majesty this gold spindle, and the fine thread that I have made."

"Very well." The troll queen waved one hand. The spindle sprang from the lass's grasp and flew to the queen. "Present yourself at the front doors at sunset." Then she held up one finger in warning. "This will be the last time I allow such a thing, you understand. Tomorrow my daughter and the prince will be wed, and there will be no more dallying with human maids."

"Of course. Your Majesty is very kind." The lass curtsied again, and the window shut with a slam.

"Quick, back to our cave," the lass said to Rollo.

"What? Why?"

The lass hiked up her skirts and started off at a run without seeing if he followed. "I don't want the princess to see me standing there. She might demand that I give her something else, and I have nothing left but dirty shifts and snagged stockings. The last thing we need is for her to be angry at us tonight."

"All right, but then will you tell me what happened while I was asleep?"

"Oh, yes, I'll tell you everything. And then I need to try and sleep. It's going to be another long night."

Chapter 31

Dressed in the best that she had left, the lass followed the queen and her daughter through the halls of the golden palace. They both smirked at her when they left her in his rooms, alone save for Rollo, but she smiled back. *This is going to work,* she told herself.

Again she was too nervous to read, and Rollo paced with her. After no more than an hour, Tova stuck her head into the sitting room, grinned at the lass, and told her that she had given him the note.

"And if he didn't read it," she whispered, "I may have found the antidote to the sleeping potion."

"Thank you!"

"I have to go." Tova winked and ducked back out of the room, closing the door behind her without a sound.

The lass's heart sank when the centaur servant brought the limp prince into the room, just as he had the last two nights. But when he rolled the prince onto the bed, the centaur winked at the lass just as Tova had. He even reached down and patted Rollo's head as he went out.

"Your Highness?" The lass shook the prince's shoulder gently.

His eyes popped open, making the lass gasp. He grinned up at her. "Hello there, my lass."

Without thinking, the lass threw herself into his arms. He caught her easily and they embraced. He kissed her cheeks and then her mouth, and she clung to him, laughing and crying as she had earlier with Tova. But this was very different.

"I can't believe that you're *my isbjørn,*" she said at last.

"I can't believe that you came all this way," he said. "How did you get here?"

"I rode on horses loaned to me by three old women who had also loved and lost the princess's *isbjørner*. Then I rode the backs of the winds, east, west, south, then north, to reach this place." She gasped, out of breath when she finished her recitation.

He squeezed her tightly. "Thank you a thousand times for coming so far. It's more than I had hoped to be able to see you and speak to you as a man." Then his dark brows drew together, his expression clouding. "But tomorrow I must marry Indæll."

"There has to be a way out."

He shook his head, his mouth a thin line. He shifted her so that she was sitting more comfortably on his lap, and she put her arm around his broad shoulders. "We'll never get past the guards, even if we make it out of the palace. And there's no way off the island."

"We have to think of something. There must be a way out for us. And Tova."

"Tova, the human chambermaid?"

"Yes. When my brother Hans Peter was the *isbjørn* who lived in the palace of ice, Tova was the girl who lived with him. She followed him here, but he had escaped."

The prince's eyebrows shot up. "How?"

"Tova altered the embroidery on his parka. I'll show you." She hopped off his lap and hurried into the other room, grabbing her parka off the chair where she had left it. The prince lit more candles in the bedchamber, and studied the embroidered bands closely.

"Ah, very clever. As an *isbjørn* I couldn't see details like this very clearly."

"Why didn't you look at it in the night?"

"The enchantment. There was very little that I could do as a man, at night. Sleep would come over me quickly. It was all I could do to hide the candles before I slept." He smiled at her, and her stomach flipped.

"I wish I was strong enough to defeat the trolls and see you safely away." She remembered and snapped her fingers. "Do you have your parka? Tova can alter it."

But he was already shaking his head. "It was taken from me as soon as I arrived."

"There has to be a way," she insisted. "The winds that brought me here, the old *mosters* who gave me gifts so that I could get inside, they all hope that I can defeat her. And my brother and Tova. They deserve to be happy."

"And what of yourself? Don't you deserve to be happy? Maybe it would be better for you to leave while you still can, so that you, at least, will be free."

"I couldn't live with myself, knowing that I had given up," she said.

He nodded. "And that's why I love you."

Her breath caught. "You do?"

"After all those days talking to you about your family, and all those nights lying beside you, listening to you breathe . . . how could I not?"

They kissed again.

A knock and a cough from the open door to the sitting room separated them. Tova stood there, smiling with a wistful light in her blue eyes. "Hello?"

"Hello!" Embarrassed, the lass jumped to her feet.

"Tova?" The prince got to his feet with much more grace, but the lass was glad to see that he was blushing. "As you can see, I took your advice about the wine."

"Excellent, Your Highness. I just hope that Indæll didn't notice that you didn't drink."

"She didn't." He shook his head. "I kept emptying my goblet into a large vase at the back of the dais. Or I spilled it, pretending that it was already taking effect."

"Bravo!" Tova clapped. She took a needle and thread out of the pocket of her apron and held them high. "I'll see what I can do to help."

But the lass and the prince shook their heads in unison.

"The only thing I have from my time as an *isbjørn* is this," he said. He went to a chest and opened it. With a flourish, he drew out the soft linen nightshirt. On one shoulder was a yellow tallow stain. "Is there anything we can do with this?"

Tova's mouth turned down. "I don't know how to cast an enchantment, only alter one that already works."

The lass couldn't take her eyes off that stain. It loomed in her gaze, reminding her of that night: the smell of the herbs in the candle, the warmth of the bedchamber, the golden glow falling over the prince's face. She thought of the palace of ice and the carvings there that she had pored over, looking for an answer.

"Oh. Oh, oh, oh!" She snapped her fingers to interrupt the prince and Tova, who were talking now about the possibility of the lass escaping alone.

"What is it?" The prince turned. "What's wrong?"

"Troll weddings!" That was all the lass could think to say for a moment. In her mind she ran over everything she remembered from a certain pillar in the great hall of the ice palace. "Trolls can't create with their hands!"

"That's right," the prince said, puzzled.

"Can they make things clean?" The lass looked to Tova for the answer. "There were washboards in the ice palace. And I thought I saw a copper washtub here."

"You're right," Tova agreed. "But I don't understand what this has to do with weddings. . . ."

"I deciphered a description of a wedding on a pillar at the ice palace," the lass explained. "As part of the ceremony, the bride and groom ask each other to prove their suitability. The bride asked the groom to "provide for her," so he slaughtered a bull. And he asked her to always be beautiful, or something like that, and she did a spell that made her beautiful, or more beautiful. I think it was the troll queen, and her consort."

The prince had caught her line of thought. "What should I ask her for? Should I ask her to release me?"

"She won't do that," Tova interjected. "I'm sure every one of her husbands has asked for that."

"Ask her to do something that she can't do," the lass said. "If she can't do what you ask, the marriage is invalid." She pointed at the nightshirt, still gripped in the prince's hands. "Ask her to wash this clean."

"The princess does not like to lose," Tova warned. "Neither does the queen."

"But trolls are bound when they make a bargain," the lass countered. She turned to the prince. "You have to make her promise that she will do what you ask, or let you go. Then ask her to wash it."

Slowly the prince nodded. "It just might work."

Tova gave the lass an appreciative look. "It's a better plan than I can think of. But you had better be ready to run. There's no guarantee Her Highness won't take out her anger on you."

"That's true." The lass sighed. "I'd like to be there to watch, but I should probably be waiting outside instead." She clenched her fists. "And we'll have to find a way to free you, too."

Tova just shook her head and gave the lass a sad smile. "It will be worth it, just to see her lose another one."

"Yes, lass, you must wait on the shore," the prince said. He cast the nightshirt aside and came over to take her hands. "Stand on the shore and look to the south. If you feel the faintest breeze, call out to it."

Tova caught sight of the clock on the mantel and made a face. "I'd best get back. The princess might send for me."

She hugged them both and Rollo. Then Rollo, too, excused himself to go and lie by the fire in the sitting room. With one hind leg, he kicked the bedchamber door closed behind him.

"He always did enjoy the sitting room fire," the prince said.

"Yes, he's very lazy," the lass agreed, looking down at her hands awkwardly. They were alone together, in a bedchamber, and there was no enchanted sleep to overcome them now.

"You're very—"

"I just realized—"

They both laughed. "You go first," the prince said. He sat down on the edge of the bed and scuffed his feet on the rug nervously.

"I just realized," the lass repeated, "that I don't even know your name."

"Oh." He screwed up his face and laughed. "Sorry. It's a bit embarrassing, actually. My mother, rather like yours, was fond of old stories. I'm a prince, but I'm not the first son. I'm the third."

The lass groaned. "Don't say your name is Askeladden, please!"

"Close enough: it's Asher. My father thought Askeladden too foolish and romantic. And there was always the chance that something might happen to my brothers and I would be king. King Askeladden was just too much for him. Even for my mother, really.

"Of course, we should both be grateful for her silly stories, or we never would have met."

"What?" Feeling more comfortable, the lass sat beside him on the bed. "Why?"

"We heard tales, even in Christiania, of a girl in the forests who could speak to animals. Mother was all agog over them. That's why I sought you out. I thought that if I could talk to you as a bear, I would be able to tell you what was happening. I couldn't, but all the same I'm glad it was you I found."

"Me too." The lass put one hand over his. "Maybe now that my brother and mother live in Christiania, we'll be able to see each other again, once we get you home."

"What do you mean?" He drew back, frowning. "Of course we'll see each other, we'll—"

She shook her head, guessing what he was about to say. "You're a prince. A prince of my own country! I know what that means. You will marry a fine lady. And if I am lucky, I will marry a farmer or a woodcutter like my father. Askel has designs on marrying me to one of his wealthy city friends, but I'm not sure that I would care for that."

Now it was the prince's turn to shake his head. "No, no! I could never just let you go, after you'd saved me! And besides . . . I do love you." He put his arms around her and kissed her tenderly.

Tears leaked from the corners of the lass's eyes. This was beyond her imagining. Not the trolls, not the *isbjørner,* for all that it was the stuff of fairy tales come true. But that someone—a prince!—could love a woodcutter's daughter whose mother hadn't even loved her enough to give her a name.

"Would you—would you like to know my name?"

He pulled back and gazed at her in astonishment. "I thought that you didn't have one." Then he blushed. "Of course, you *should* have one."

"I can speak with animals because I caught the white reindeer. It gave me a name, but I have never told anyone what it is."

Asher raised both her hands and kissed them. "I

would be honored," he said, his voice little more than a whisper.

Leaning in close, she breathed her name in his ear.

"That's the most beautiful name I have ever heard," he told her, holding her tight to his chest. "Thank you, Bellalyse."

Chapter 32

O f course, the lass thought the next morning, since trolls can only destroy, they should have known that the princess would ruin their plans. There was a bitter taste in her mouth, and she wanted to spit. It wouldn't be fair to make the poor, captive servants clean up after her, so she just grimaced instead.

"Now, now," Princess Indæll clucked at her, waving a beringed hand, "no need to look so sour. You'll spoil the effect!" She stepped back to survey her handiwork.

The lass and Tova stood side by side in the princess's dressing room. When she had arrived at Asher's rooms that morning, the troll princess had not allowed the lass to leave. Instead Indæll had insisted, with an icy smile, that the lass attend her at the wedding. Now the lass was clad in a gown of green satin, and Tova in a gown of blue. Rollo had even been forced, protesting, into a tub. His gray fur had been brushed out and there was a green ribbon around his neck, tied in a huge bow behind his head.

"I have never had human bridesmaids before," the troll

princess said. "I shall be the envy of every lady of the court!"

"I'm sure that your highness is already the envy of all who see her," Tova said, bobbing a curtsy.

The lass gave her a look.

"Habit," Tova whispered out of the side of her mouth.

Now the princess looked at the lass, who gritted her teeth, curtsied, and murmured something she hoped sounded like a compliment. It seemed to satisfy Indæll, and she went back to admiring herself in the huge mirror that covered the far wall.

For her wedding, the troll princess was attired in a gown of white satin. The shift underneath it was cloth of gold, and the bodice of the gown was thick with rubies and pearls. Her red hair was pomaded and curled and arranged to show off the heavy ruby-encrusted crown she wore. There was rouge on her cheeks, clashing oddly with her greenish gray skin, and her purple tongue kept peeping out to lick at the pink color slathered on her lips.

"I think I might be sick," the lass whispered to Tova.

"I heard that," the princess snapped, whirling. "If either of you do anything to ruin my wedding, I will hang you both by your thumbs from the highest tower!"

"Yes, Your Highness." Tova curtsied.

"Yes, Your Highness." The lass followed suit.

"Good."

There was a soft tap on the door. "If Your Highness is ready, the court is waiting below," a faun footman said.

"Is my prince ready?"

"He is, my princess."

Indæll smirked at the lass. "Oh, good."

Tova sidled closer to the lass. Using their full skirts as concealment, she took the younger woman's hand in her own. The lass squeezed Tova's hand. It was all she could do to keep herself from lunging at the troll princess and strangling her with one of the ropes of pearls the vain creature wore.

Princess Indæll's smile widened, as though she guessed the lass's thoughts. She stood and snapped her fingers. The pixies who had dressed her flew forward, bearing a heavy cloak. It was scarlet satin, lined with *isbjørn* fur. The lass clenched her jaw at the sight, wondering if the cloak was made from one of the princess's former husbands. Seeing her look, the princess stroked the fur before gesturing for the pixies to drape it across her broad shoulders.

Indæll swept out of her dressing room with the pixies trailing her to hold up the edges of the cloak. The lass and Tova followed, and after them came various female creatures in livery. In the corridor they were joined by a dozen hideous troll maidens dressed in extravagant silks and velvets, draped with jewels and all atwitter over the wedding. They paraded through the palace to the grand ballroom for the marriage of the troll princess to her human prince.

The ballroom was hung with long banners bearing the *isbjørn* and jagged sword symbol of the trolls. Musicians played their strange music in a high gallery opposite the dais. On the dais stood the troll queen, her yellow curls shining, dressed in a blue gown trimmed with *isbjørn* fur and embellished with diamonds and silver embroidery. She held out her arms to her daughter, who strode through the crowd and embraced her mother. The lass and Tova took up positions on one side of the dais, and all turned to wait for the prince.

He marched in with a dozen young male trolls. It wasn't clear whether they were his attendants or his guards; probably both. He wore a white tunic and scarlet cloak, and on his head was a circlet of gold.

Prince Asher took his place beside the troll princess on the dais, not looking at the lass or Tova. The lass's heart squeezed at the nearness of him, and his apparent indifference, but she told herself that it was only an act. The bridal pair clasped hands and turned to face the queen. They made a ridiculous couple: the troll with her long nose and bulging eyes, standing head and shoulders above her young, handsome bridegroom.

The troll queen raised her arms. "Our people, rejoice! After languishing alone for a dozen years, our beloved princess, the beauteous Indæll, has at last found a prince worthy of her!"

Monstrous howls rose from the troll court. They

stamped and slapped their huge hands together in awful cacophony. Or at least, most of them did. The lass noticed that those trolls who were clad in skins and moss only scowled.

"And now, in the sight of those assembled, the most magnificent of our magnificent race, I shall join these two together." The troll queen placed her hands atop the clasped hands of the prince and princess. "In the manner of our people you shall be joined together until one of you shall pass into the darkness below," she intoned. "Until that dark day, Prince Asher of the humans, what do you offer Princess Indæll?"

"I offer all that I can offer: myself, until the day I pass into the darkness below," the prince said in a monotone. "I shall protect her honor where it is challenged. I shall love her, and worship her, and submit to her until the end of my days." It was plain that he was reciting a memorized speech.

There were more howls from the trolls, though the lass noticed that these were not as hearty. A few appeared bored, and the grim, old-fashioned trolls scowled even worse. Perhaps this was the speech required of all the princess's husbands over the years.

"And now, Princess Indæll of the lands of ice and snow, what do you offer to Prince Asher?"

"I shall be a good wife, and shall love and cherish him all his days," she simpered.

The lass shuddered, hearing the emphasis on "*his*

days." The princess, and everyone here, knew that she would long outlive Asher, but it bothered none of them. Well, none of the trolls, at least. The prince's jaw tightened, and Tova clasped the lass's hand again.

"But as an assurance of her wifely skills," Asher said, "I wish for my bride to perform a task for me."

The whole room froze. The lass felt cold sweat trickling down her spine beneath her satin gown. Then the trolls began to babble in low voices. It seemed that this had never happened before.

The prince lifted his hand and a centaur pushed through the crowd of watching trolls. It was the same centaur who had carried Asher to bed. He held a copper washtub full of water, and there was a small basket hanging from one elbow. With a flourish and a bow, he set his burdens down on the dais.

"Even when there are servants to do such work, a good wife should be able to wash her husband's shirts as a gesture of fidelity," the prince announced. "Or so it is said among my people."

Tova snorted softly, and the lass gave her hand a little squeeze in reply. If this "saying" had been true, there were many wives who would have been judged poorly by their neighbors.

"He's ruining the ceremony," a large troll in a pink satin waistcoat shouted. There were murmurs of agreement.

"It *is* tradition, or have you forgotten that too?" one of the fur-bedecked trolls shouted back. "Go on, human!"

Asher continued: "I have here a fine nightshirt of which I am quite fond. Tallow has been spilled on the shoulder. If Her Highness would be so kind as to scrub it clean for me, without magic, it will prove to me that she is a good wife."

"But I have never done such a *common* task," Princess Indæll protested. "Surely there is some other boon you will ask? I would be pleased to perform magic for you." She gestured, and a diamond ring appeared in her hands. She proudly held it out to the prince.

He took it and slipped it on one finger as if it was of no great consequence. Turning to the old-fashioned troll who had shouted for him to "go on," Asher said, "Is it not your custom to grant the *first* request made?"

"Aye," the troll agreed. He had only one good eye; the other was covered in a patch that looked like a whole rabbit skin. "Each shall request and grant one boon. She must wash the shirt. Without magic."

"And if she doesn't, the marriage is void?" The prince's voice was blank, as though it didn't matter to him one way or the other.

"Aye."

"Thank you, Lord Chamberlain."

"I think I might faint," Tova whispered without moving her lips.

"*You* might?" was the lass's tense reply.

Tossing her head, Princess Indæll strode over to the washtub. A snap of her fingers, and a chair was brought to raise the tub up for her convenience. From the basket she pulled the nightshirt and a bar of soap and dipped them both in the washtub with clumsy hands. Seeing the fearful look on the troll princess's face, the lass could almost feel sympathy for her.

Almost, but not quite. She thought of Hans Peter and Asher, and all the others who had gone before. She thought of Erasmus, Fiona, and Mrs. Grey, swept away in the night. She remembered the three *mosters* and the endless cold that the trolls had brought to her homeland. Clutching Tova's hand—Tova, who must remain behind while Asher escaped—the lass leaned forward to watch.

The stain on the white shirt did not wash away. Instead it turned black and began to spread across the linen. The harder the princess scrubbed, the darker and larger the stain grew. The princess's face turned an ugly puce color that rivaled her rouge. Some of her curls straggled down from her coiffure and she tossed them angrily over one shoulder. The rings on her fingers snagged the soft fabric, so she ripped them off and threw them aside.

Rollo bent down and picked up two in his mouth, pressing them into the lass's free hand. The lass looked over and saw the centaur putting several in the pocket of his tunic. He gave a ghost of a smile when he saw her watching.

Princess Indæll threw back her head and howled. As she did, her crown fell off her head, taking her hair with it. The red curls were nothing but a wig, and underneath, her scalp was sparsely stubbled with coarse gray hairs. The lass couldn't suppress a gasp of surprise, loud enough that the princess looked up at her.

"You!" She pointed one long, dripping finger at the lass. "This is your fault, I know it! You horrible thing, why did you have to come here? You've ruined everything!" She lunged at the lass.

Rollo leaped in front of his mistress, hackles raised and teeth bared. Tova pulled a small knife from her own belt and took a step forward. The lass, for her part, stood her ground, clenching her fists and raising her chin.

"How is it my fault that you cannot perform a simple *womanly* task?"

With a shriek, the princess reached out her clawed hands for the lass. Rollo snarled and snapped at Indæll, catching a fold of her skirt in his fangs and tearing it free.

"Daughter, control yourself!" The queen's voice was a whipcrack. "There is no need for all this unpleasantness." She put a soothing arm around her daughter's shoulders. "The humans will be dealt with in good time, each in their own way." She bestowed an oily smile on Asher, and then a more menacing one on both the lass and Tova. "But for now, let us try again."

Both mother and daughter plunged their hands into

the soapy water. Each grabbed half of the blackened shirt and scrubbed it as hard as they could against the washboard. Within seconds the nightshirt was black as pitch all over. The queen scrubbed so hard that she knocked her own wig askew, revealing bristling white hair. Her nose ran with the effort, dripping into the wash water and befouling it further.

"Stop!" The prince raised his hands. "It's as plain as the nose on your face that you cannot do even this one simple task," he told Indæll. "By the laws of your own people, this marriage is invalid. I will have no wife but the one who can clean this shirt for me." Over the roars and howls of the troll court, he turned and beckoned to the lass. "Why don't you try?"

The lass gulped. This had not been part of their arrangement. The shirt looked ruined to her eyes, and she wondered if this was the prince's way of getting rid of any obligation to her as well.

Tova nudged her, and she stumbled forward. Princess Indæll was threatening to make a pair of boots out of the prince, and a belt out of what would be left of the lass when she got through with her. The queen glared at the lass and growled, but then her sickening smile returned. She nodded agreement, clearly certain that the lass would not be able to undo the damage the trolls had done to the shirt.

"Please bring me fresh water and more soap," the lass asked the centaur.

He trotted away and came back a moment later, smiling broadly. Another chair was brought, and the washtub settled on it. The lass asked Tova for her belt knife, then plucked the stained nightshirt out of the foul water and laid it gently in the clean. Locating the original spot of hardened tallow on the shoulder, she used the knife to carefully scrape it away, as Jorunn had taught her. She handed back the knife, rubbed the soap across the shirt, and then dunked it in the water. Drawing it up against the board, she scrubbed it with the firm but gentle pressure that she had learned as a child, and then dunked it again to rinse.

Through the dingy, foamy water, the lass could see that the shirt was growing whiter. And so could Princess Indæll.

"He's mine," the troll princess screamed, and pointed a knobby finger at the shirt. There was a crash of thunder as the power Indæll directed at the shirt, in defiance of her promise, backfired and struck her in the face.

The troll princess crumpled to the ground, dead.

"No!" the queen screeched and lunged at the lass, who held up the now-snow-white shirt like a shield. When the queen's hands tore at the shirt, she screamed even louder. "It burns!" She sank to the floor, clutching her daughter's twisted body in her burned hands and howling, quite mad.

"My daughter, my beautiful daughter," the troll queen moaned. Her face was so pale that the lass could see the blood pulsing in it. "My daughter, my daughter." A long string of green drool trailed from her chin.

Nauseous with horror, the lass had to cover her ears. The trolls howled and stamped their feet and rushed the dais. Someone crouched beside the lass and wrapped his arms around her: Asher. Then she felt Rollo pressing against her, and another pair of arms joined the embrace.

"What will we do?" Tova whispered.

"Stay still," Asher said in reply. "Let's try to slip away as soon as they——"

"Kill the humans!" shouted one troll, and the others began to take up the cry. "Kill them, kill the humans!"

They all let go of one another and jumped to their feet. Rollo bared his teeth, and both Tova and the prince produced knives now. The lass had nothing but her fists, and she slipped the princess's rings onto two fingers to make her punch more painful, a trick learned from Askel.

"No!" The one-eyed chamberlain pushed his way onto the dais. "It isn't because of the humans that we have come to this; it is our own vanity!" He glared around the room with his one eye. "The fine clothes! The jewels! Keeping servants and living in palaces! And even worse: taking human consorts! For three thousand years our queen has reigned in the far north, and now because of her daughter's perverted tastes she has lost her reason!"

The younger trolls took exception to this, and attacked

the chamberlain. His followers, dressed in moss and skins as he was, defended him. Not that he needed defending: the lass saw him reach out and rip the head off a young troll bravo in lavender silk without any sign of strain. Some of the trolls in human clothes ripped off their coats and gowns and joined the chamberlain, until the whole ballroom was a mass of howling, biting, snarling, wrestling trolls.

"Come on!" Asher had to shout to be heard over the din.

Ducking down, he took the lass by one arm and Tova by the other, hurrying them to one of the long windows. The centaur was already there. Turning, he kicked out with his hindquarters and shattered the panes of glass, since the latch was at troll height and none of them could have reached it.

They climbed through, the centaur waiting until Rollo had leaped out after the three humans to jump himself. Other servants were fleeing as well: a steady stream of blue-clad fauns, centaurs, pixies, and other creatures were making their way out of the golden palace and toward the southern shore of the icy island.

"What will we do about the ribbons?" The lass's voice came in a gasp as they ran over the sharp hillocks of packed snow.

"The power is weakening," the centaur explained. "I felt it when the queen went mad."

With a scream, Tova collapsed. She had tripped on a protruding spur of ice. The lass knelt beside her and raised

Tova's skirt. There was a long gash in her stocking, and her shin was raw and bloody beneath it.

"And I think my ankle's sprained," Tova said. Then she gave a gasp and her face darkened with blood. She clawed at the ribbon around her neck.

"Cut it off!" the lass shrieked to Asher, horrified. All around them, the servants were falling to the ground, choking. The centaur went to his knees, coughing.

"It will be better to die," he gasped.

Asher drew his belt knife and cautiously slit the ribbon around Tova's neck. Instantly, she sat up, breathing freely. She tossed the thing aside and shouted for joy.

The lass snatched Tova's knife and freed the centaur, then the faun who lay nearby. He in turn freed others, until all the servants were once more running for the shore, exulting.

Behind them, the mayhem of the troll palace increased. Tova shook her head. "Just leave me," she said. "I can make my way later."

"I can carry you," the centaur said. He reached down and grabbed her, twisting to seat her on his broad horse back. "We need to get clear before the rest of the queen's magic fades."

"Why, what will happen?" the lass asked.

It was Asher who answered her. "The palace was made by magic. So was this island. As the queen's magic fades . . ."

He didn't need to finish. Hand in hand, the lass and her prince ran over the slick, sharp hills and hollows. Rollo was right beside them, with the centaur and Tova keeping pace.

"Ouch!" Now it was the lass's turn to stop and cry out in pain. But it wasn't her legs, it was her fingers. The princess's rings were white hot. Before she could take them off the gold melted and trickled between her fingers and the gems turned to dust. There were red burns in the shape of the rings on her fingers, but they were not severe. Asher scraped up some snow to soothe the burns. The lass clutched it in her fists as they continued to run.

They did not look back until they reached the shore. By that time, the trolls' shouts had turned to cries of pain and fear. The gold palace was melting just as the lass's rings had. Turning red and then white with heat in the light of the pale northern sun, the magnificent palace slumped and ran like tallow.

On the shore, standing in a cluster of blue-liveried servants with her eldest brother's true love and her own true love on either side of her, the lass watched the fall of the great troll kingdom. When it was over, all she could think was that she was cold, and there was no way for them to get home. Already, long cracks were appearing in the island: it would not last another day.

A young male faun approached the lass with a shy smile. He swung her unwieldy pack from his own back, and offered it to her. Tied to the top was Hans Peter's parka.

"I found this when I was cleaning the prince's chambers this morning, my lady," he said in a soft voice.

"Oh, thank you!" The lass started to put it on, then stopped. "But really, it's yours if it's anyone's," she said to Tova, offering her the parka.

"And you can wear mine," Asher said. Another faun had come up to them, holding up a brilliantly white parka with red bands of troll embroidery on it. "I doubt that it will turn you into a bear."

"Perhaps, though, if you wouldn't mind," the lass said, hesitant.

"Yes?" He took her hand.

"Perhaps you should put it on and carry us away from here."

The prince's jaw tightened at the idea, but finally he nodded. He pulled on the parka, then the boots that another servant—a brownie—brought him.

Nothing happened.

"The spell is broken," he said. He took off the parka and wrapped it tenderly around the lass. "We'll have to find another way. If we swim to the nearest ice floe, then warm ourselves as much as possible—"

"You'll all freeze to death," said a voice that came swirling around them.

"North wind!" The lass clapped her hands and then winced as the clapping hurt her burns. "You came back!"

He took on his human form, standing before them

white and silver and proud. "I felt the troll queen's hold loosen, and had to come and see what had happened." He smiled. "Truth be known: I wasn't far off. I hoped that you would succeed in defeating her."

"And she did," Asher said, smiling at the lass with pride.

"I can carry you south," the north wind said. "Not all of you, though."

Frowning, the lass looked at the creatures assembled around them. They all stared back, faces screwed up with various emotions, from hope to dismay to grim resignation. She shook her head.

"How many of us could you take at a time? I won't go if even one of these poor creatures has to stay."

"I agree," Asher said.

"And I," said Tova.

The north wind whistled thoughtfully. Tendrils of air curled around the servants, lifting a few of them off the ground as if to test their weight. Then he surveyed the ice floes floating in the frigid water off the shore.

"I'll lift you all onto the ice floes and blow you south. I don't know how long it will take, but I'm sure I can get you to civilized lands. You're on your own from there, unless one of my brothers will carry you farther."

"Thank you!"

A great gust of frigid air picked up the lass, her prince, Tova, Rollo, and the centaur. Some five others that were near them shrieked as they were gathered up as well. Without another word, the north wind commenced dropping them onto ice rafts for the long journey away from the island of ice that lay east of the sun and west of the moon.

EPILOGUE
Princess of the Palace of Golden Stone

By the time the lass reached her old home in the forests and valleys of the North, the troll queen's winter had broken. Everywhere there was green; flowers bloomed beneath the fir trees and birds sang in their branches. Their companions had dwindled, going off to their own homes until only the lass, Rollo, Tova, and Asher remained. As they came around the side of the mountain where once Askel and the villagers had hunted the white reindeer, Tova stopped.

"I can't," she said. Her face was white and still. She put her hands up to her cheeks. "I can't."

The lass went to her and put her arms around the other woman. "Of course you can!"

"It's been too long. For the past ten years, I've lived among trolls and talking bears and centaurs and—"

"And what wonderful stories you shall have to tell your children," the lass said, interrupting her increasingly hysterical rant.

"He won't want me," Tova wailed. "Look at me!"

They looked. Even Rollo stopped chasing butterflies to study her. Her cheeks were rosy as ever, albeit a bit chapped from the winds. Her hair was coming loose from its braid, and the blue livery she wore was sadly tattered and stained.

Asher began to laugh. He held out his arms, displaying

the rents and stains that marred his white wedding finery. He gestured at the lass, who looked just as bad. Rollo shook himself, and dust and fir needles flew out of his coat.

"We're all a sorry sight," Asher said. "There's nothing we can do about it."

"That's not true," the lass said. She was looking down the side of the mountain, where she could see a large black boulder and a fast-flowing stream.

"What is it?"

"You stay here, and don't you dare look," she said to Asher. Then, taking Tova by the hand, the lass led her to the stream. "In my pack I have soap and a comb. And in your pack, there are two beautiful *bunader*."

While Asher and Rollo tidied themselves as best they could, the two young women laughed and splashed and washed off the dirt of travel in the cold stream. They combed and braided each other's hair, and then the lass put on Tova's old everyday clothes, while Tova dressed herself in the wedding *bunad*.

"Are you sure?" Tova's voice was barely a whisper as they made their way back up the path to the prince. "Are you sure?"

The lass hugged her again. "Oh, yes. He's been waiting for you."

They rejoined Asher and Rollo. Farther down the path they could see a lazy swirl of smoke that came from Jarl Oskarson's cottage.

"But I don't have a dowry," Tova said. "All those years living in a palace of gold and I don't have a coin to my name."

"Do you really think that it will matter to Hans Peter?" The lass clucked her tongue. "But if it will reassure you . . ." From her bodice she pulled the string of puce satin pockets. It was so worn that the belt had frayed beyond repair when she took it off to wash. "Not all of the troll's jewels were illusion."

Taking one of Tova's hands, she poured out a king's ransom in rubies. "Do you hear that whistling? That's Hans Peter, up on the roof mending the shingles." She took Tova's other hand and filled it with pearls. "Take your dowry, and go."

Tova paused only a moment. Then she pecked the lass on the cheek and raced down the path. The others watched from the top of a small rise as she ran into the clearing in front of the cottage.

Up on the roof, Hans Peter had stopped to peer down at the woman who had just come barreling into the yard. His white hair gleamed in the sun, and his face was ruddy with work.

"*Isbjørn,* my *isbjørn,* is that you?" A trickle of rubies ran from between Tova's fingers and rained down on the packed dirt beside the well. A patter of pearls joined the rubies as she stretched out her hands to him.

With a loud cry Hans Peter slithered off the roof. He

was running as soon as his feet hit the ground, and in seconds he had swept Tova up in his arms.

"Oh, I'm so glad," the lass said, tears running down
her face. "He's finally going to be happy."

"And what about you?" Asher took her in his arms.
"Are you finally going to be happy?"

"I don't know." She looked up at him from under her
damp lashes. "Am I?"

"Well, I *am* the lucky third son. So I thought I would
take you home, my Princess Bellalyse who can talk to animals, and care for you in fine style in my family's palace.
It's not made of gold, but it is made of golden stone, and
when the sun shines on it, I think it's beautiful."

"Anywhere where I can be with my very own *isbjørn* is
good enough for me," the lass replied.

And the prince who had once been a bear pulled close
the girl who had once had no name, and kissed her. Then,
arm in arm, they strolled down the path to celebrate with
her brother, who had been enchanted himself, and their
friend, who had served for ten years in the royal palace of
the trolls.

Leaning on a cane, the woodcutter Jarl Oskarson came
out of his cottage to see what all the commotion was about.
His face glowed with delight to see his eldest son embrac-
ing his lost love and his youngest daughter hand in hand
with her brave prince. The lass tossed aside her father's
cane and took one arm while Asher took the other. Tova

and Hans Peter completed the circle, and they danced around the yard while Rollo yipped and leaped into the air with glee.

And so they lived for many a long year, as happy and lighthearted as the birds in the trees and the flowers on the hill in spring.

GLOSSARY

Most of the names and words used are Norwegian, but some are Old Norse (ON), the root language of Icelandic, Norwegian, Swedish, and Danish.

Annifrid (Ah-nee-freed): one of the lass's sisters.

Askeladden (*Ahs*-keh-lah-den): traditionally the name of the third, lucky son in Norse fairy tales, the "Ashlad" or male Cinderella, here the third son of Jarl and Frida.

Banahøgg (bah-nah-hoyg): ON, literally "death-blow," the name of a troll.

Bunad (*boo*-nahd): a traditional woman's outfit, consisting of a white blouse worn under a dark wool skirt and vest. The hem of the skirt and the edges of the vest are heavily embroidered in red, blue, and yellow. The vest fits tightly, the skirt is bell shaped. Plural: *bunader*.

Edda (ed-duh): the ancient poetry of Scandinavia, most eddas are sagas, meaning that they tell a story, whether tragic, comic, or romantic.

Einar (*ay*-nahr): the lass's next oldest brother.

Erasmus (er-az-*mus*): the faun who serves in the *isbjørn's* palace.

Falskur (*fahl*-skuhr): ON, faithless, false, the second *moster*'s horse.

Frankrike, Fransk (*frahnk*-ree-kuh, frahnsk): France, French.

Frida (*free*-dah): the lass's mother.

God dag (goo dahg): "Good day," a greeting.

Hans Peter (hahns pay-ter): the lass's eldest, and favorite, brother.

Hjartán (*hyahr*-town): ON, heartless, the first *moster*'s horse.

Indæll (in-*day*-tl): ON, delightful, the troll princess.

Isbjørn (*ees*-byurn): polar bear (literally, ice bear). Plural: *isbjørner*.

Ja (yah): yes.

Jarl (yahrl): the lass's father.

Jorunn (*yoh*-ruhn): the lass's eldest sister.

Katla (*kaht*-lah): one of the lass's sisters.

Lefse (*lehf*-suh): a thin crepe made with potato flour.

Morn'a (*morn*-ah): good morning.

Moster (moss-ter): auntie, a polite term for an older woman (literally a contraction of *"mor's søster,"* or "mother's sister").

Pika (*pee*-kah): girl.

Skarp-heðin (skahrp-heth-in): ON, spear-head, a troll sentry.

Skrælings (skray-lings): ON, the Viking name for the natives encountered on their eleventh-century journey to North America.

Tordis (tohr-dihs): the lass's second oldest sister.

Torst (tohrst): the lass's second oldest brother.

Tova (toh-vah): Hans Peter's lost love.

Tysk (toosk): German.

Vaktmann (*vahkt*-mahn): guard.

Vongóður (fahn-goh-thur): ON, hopeful, the third *moster*'s horse.

SELECT BIBLIOGRAPHY

Here is a selection of books that inspired, influenced, and aided in the writing of *Sun and Moon, Ice and Snow*.

Asbjørnsen, Peter Christen, and Jørgen Moe. *Norwegian Folk Tales*. New York: Pantheon Books, 1960.

Booss, Claire. *Scandinavian Folk and Fairy Tales*. New York: Gramercy Books, 1984.

Gordon, E. V. *An Introduction to Old Norse*. 2nd ed. Oxford: Oxford University Press.

Ibsen, Henrik. *Peer Gynt*. London: Penguin Books, 1966.

Lynch, P. J., Illustrator, and Sir George Webbe Dasent, translator. *East o' the Sun and West o' the Moon*. Cambridge, MA: Candlewick Press, 1991.

Magnusson, Magnus, and Hermann Palsson, translators. *Njal's Saga*. London: Penguin Books, 1960.

Terry, Patricia, translator. *Poems of the Elder Edda*. Rev. ed. Pennsylvania: University of Pennsylvania Press, 1990.

Theodor Kittelsen, a nineteenth-century Norwegian artist, is considered the definitive "troll painter." His work may be viewed online at http://kittelsen.efenstor.net.

ACKNOWLEDGMENTS

This book was made possible by the letter "ø."

Also the letter "æ."

The first time I saw them, I fell in love and just had to learn the language they belonged to. That language turned out to be Norwegian, with its rich history of folk tales about trolls and polar bears and clever young lads and lasses out to make their fortune. I only hope that I didn't offend my Danish blacksmith forbears by choosing to study Norwegian instead of Danish in college.

On that note, I would like to thank my Norwegian teachers: Professor Sandra Straubhaar, Henrietta Christofferson (a fellow Norwegian-speaking Dane), and Justin Galloway. I also wish to thank Professor George Tate, who taught me Old Norse and introduced me to such amazing figures as Egil, Njal, and the real Skarp-Heðin. My fascination with those exotic letters, and with the amazing stories of the North, has not only led me to some strange places but also endlessly entertained me, and I have nothing but the most profound love and respect for everyone who guided me along the way.

A big shout-out also goes to my stellar agent, Amy, and my wonderful editor, Melanie, for pummeling the manuscript into shape and reining in my tendency to include long, pointless descriptions of people carding wool or peeling apples. This story also passed under the scrutiny of my writers' group, SLAG, to whom I owe many thanks indeed.

My sister was a bit put out that *Dragon Slippers* was not dedicated to her. This book is also not dedicated to her, because there is a very special book with her name on it waiting to be published and I refuse to dull the impact by dedicating other books to her, even though she is both my best friend and fashion consultant. My husband, son, and the rest of my crazy family were also influential in the writing of this book, which sadly is also not dedicated to them.

But it is dedicated, with much love, to my dear, dear parents. They may have rolled their eyes when I switched my minor from Theater to Scandinavian Studies, but they continued to give me their support (and pay my tuition!). And, what do you know: Scandinavian Studies really did turn out to be more useful in the long run. For many years they put up with my passion for all things Norwegian, and I hope that in some small way this book helps to repay the debt I owe them.

Author's Note

*L*ong ago and far away, as the stories say, I fell in love—not with a person but with a place. I fell in love with Norway, with its massive craggy cliffs and dark, rich forests. I fell in love with a language that sounded like a song and a storytelling tradition that was alternately humorous, thrilling, and terrifying. I soon discovered "East o' the Sun, West o' the Moon," that wonderful old tale of a noble polar bear, a courageous young maiden, and some very wicked trolls. It had everything the heart could desire: romance; danger; magic; treasure; complicated shirt-laundering; and marvelous, horrifying, fascinating trolls. I told myself that one day I would take that story and turn it into a novel so that I could share this tale with a new audience, as well as explore all the questions that weren't answered in the original—like what the young girl's name was and why her parents gave her up to the polar bear so easily.

Over the years I kept these goals in mind: I wanted to be a writer, and I wanted one of my books to be a retelling of this story. I took Norwegian and Old Norse as part of my Humanities/Comparative Literature major and I minored in Scandinavian Studies, but it was years before I felt like I was ready to write this book. Once or twice I had little moments of inspiration: I found myself jotting down notes in church on the back of a newsletter one Sunday and hid it away in a drawer for several more years. During a physics class I wrote the first few pages in a notebook that I can no longer find, and the pages weren't very good anyway. Then, shortly after writing *Dragon Slippers*, I was sitting at my computer and thought, "It's time." My palms started to sweat, and I needed to eat some chocolate to soothe myself first, but it was definitely time.

Time to tell the story of an unwanted, unnamed daughter who is kissed by a white reindeer, is sought by a polar bear, and encounters fabulous palaces, strange creatures, magic, kindness, cruelty, and love. Time to soar across the world on the backs of the four winds, to meet mysterious old women who give strange advice and even stranger gifts, to befriend wolves and gargoyles, to bargain with trolls.

Time to travel to a palace of gold that lies east o' the sun and west o' the moon.

Jessica

Don't miss Jessica Day George's retelling of

The Twelve Dancing Princesses

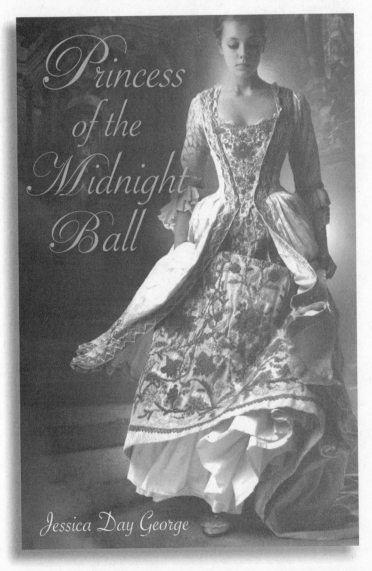

Princess of the Midnight Ball

Jessica Day George

Read on for a sneak peek . . .

Twigs

As soon as Rose's head passed down into the floor and out of sight, Galen leaped to his feet, yanked the purple cape out of his satchel, and threw it around his shoulders. Hugging the satchel close to his chest, he hurried after her. The portal in the floor brushed his close-cropped hair as it closed, and he bit back a curse.

He had feigned sleep, even though he was so keyed up that he couldn't imagine closing his eyes. He'd worried that the snoring was a bit much but knew that he couldn't stop once he'd started, and it seemed to convince the princesses.

Except for Rose. Rose was far too clever.

When she came up to touch his shoulder, he was terrified that she would see him peeking at them from under his lashes. In his relief when she turned away, he had almost forgotten to continue snoring. And then, incredibly, the rug had turned into a staircase leading down into the floor.

Rose stopped suddenly, and Galen nearly ran into her.

"What was that?" Her voice was breathless with fright. She spun around and Galen tensed, but she peered right through him.

"What's the matter?" Lily called from the front of the line.

"I thought I heard footsteps. Heavy footsteps," Rose said. "I feel like someone is following me."

Lily held her lamp higher. "There's no one there, Rose. How could there be?" She continued on down the steps, and the other princesses followed her.

"Just a draft, I suppose." Rose sighed.

Galen did his best to creep silently down the stairs after that, breathing into the collar of his cape so that he wouldn't blow on Rose's neck. At last they came to the foot of the golden staircase, and Galen gaped at what lay before them.

All around was darkness, darkness that their lamp only dimly illuminated. But directly in front of them was a tall gate made of silver and set with pearls the size of pigeon's eggs. There was no fence, only a gate, and beyond it a forest of strange pale trees.

Lily swung open the gate and the princesses passed through, with Galen at Rose's heels. He dodged to the side as she turned and shut the gate behind them, closing the pearl-inlaid latch, and then they went forward into the forest.

To find a forest in this strange underground world was odd enough, but this was no ordinary forest. The trees were of shining silver, their branches spreading high into the blackness above them and glowing with their own light. The leaves rattled and chimed together, moved by a breeze that somehow did not touch the humans: Galen's cape was not stirred by any wind and the princesses' hair was not ruffled.

Galen stared around in amazement at the forest, but the princesses passed through without comment. He realized that they must see this every night, and it no longer amazed them, if it ever had. The forest, then, was not their reason for coming.

The silver trees thinned and then stopped, and they were on the shore of a great lake. Beneath their feet coarse black sand glittered, and the water that lapped the shores was black and violet and deepest blue. Twelve golden boats with a single lantern hanging from each bow were drawn up on the sand, tethered to twelve tall statues.

Then one of the statues moved, and again Galen found himself hard-pressed not to curse aloud. They weren't stone, but living beings: tall young men, stern of face and black of hair, dressed in ebony-hued evening clothes. Galen hesitated to call them human, however. There was something amiss in their bearing, in their pallor and the coldness of their expressions. With a start Galen recognized one of the figures as the creature the girls had referred to as Rionin, who had tried to climb into the princesses' rooms weeks ago.

Surely nothing human could live in this sunless world, Galen thought. Whatever Rionin and his companions were, they were not mortal.

One by one the princesses took the proffered hands and were helped into a golden boat. Galen waited until Rose's dark-haired suitor had seated her in the bow and was about to push off into the strangely colored lake. Then Galen stepped into the boat and sat on the empty stern seat.

Each of the silent escorts sat in the middle seat and took up the golden oars. In perfect synchronicity, the twelve boats set out across the lake, the suitors rowing silently as one.

Their precision was somewhat ruined by Rose's rower, however. Halfway across the lake he slowed, and Galen heard him pant a little.

"Is something wrong?" Rose had been gazing forward, but now she looked back at her escort.

"The boat seems a little heavier this time," the rower said. His voice was deep and smooth.

Rose blushed. "Sorry," she muttered. Galen stifled a laugh.

Ahead of them Galen now saw lights glimmering in the blackness. They did little to illuminate the lake, but the purplish flickers ahead showed that they were rapidly approaching . . . something.

The golden boats scraped on more gritty black sand, and at last Galen could see the source of the strange light. It was a great palace of slick black rock. The candlelight that flickered in the windows gleamed purple because the panes too were black.

One by one the princesses were helped out of the boats, and one by one they passed through the great arched doors and into the black palace. Hard on Rose's heels, Galen followed. His palms were wet with sweat, but he focused on her slim back and reminded himself that he was invisible to the cold eyes of her escort.

Within the palace, the colors were much the same as the

water of the underground lake. Purple and blue and gray and black tapestries covered the walls. The floor and ceiling were gleaming black, and the furniture was made of silver, cushioned with silk in the same solemn colors as the tapestries.

They passed through a long hall and into a ballroom where amethyst chandeliers hung over a floor inlaid with silver and lapis lazuli. Musicians played in a gallery so high above their heads that Galen could barely make out their forms, and servants in black livery passed among the guests with trays bearing silver goblets of wine. When the princesses arrived, the guests all stopped dancing and talking and applauded them. The grim suitors bowed, the princesses curtsied, and the musicians struck up a lively tune. Rose and her sisters were whirled away, leaving Galen alone and unseen to watch.

Glad that no one could see him gaping like a half-wit, Galen wandered through the ballroom. It was a wonder that the sisters had seemed so reluctant to come here, their faces strained and Pansy frankly in tears. What young girl wouldn't love to dance away her nights in this splendid castle, in the arms of a handsome suitor?

But as he roamed the edge of the dance floor, Galen started to think that it was not as beautiful here as he had first thought. The other people at the ball all smiled and sipped their wine and danced, but their smiles were not ... quite ... right. Their lips stretched too wide, and they seemed to have too many teeth. Their eyes glittered like the jewels they wore, and their skin was too white and smooth.

And then still there were the princesses. They danced. They ate delicate pastries and strange fruits.

But they did not smile.

Hyacinth wept, the tears running silently down her cheeks as she whirled around the floor in the arms of her tall partner. Pansy sobbed noisily, and occasionally stopped dancing to stomp on her partner's feet. He wore a look of long-suffering, and after a few dances he simply picked her up and carried her around the floor, swaying in time to the music.

"Do they *have* to dance?" Galen said aloud without thinking. The white-faced woman standing near him narrowed her eyes and stared right at the spot where Galen stood. Holding his breath, he backed away.

Galen remembered how Pansy had burst into tears earlier when he had offered her a "ball." He thought about Rose's illness, and how it had continued for months while her slippers were worn out night after night. Surely she would not have come here to dance in the extremity of her illness unless she had no other choice. The one night they hadn't danced, Rionin and his brethren had invaded the garden.

But why? Who was forcing them to come here?

An hour later, this question was answered. The music stopped, and the dancers all turned to look expectantly at a tall door at the far end of the room. The musicians played a long fanfare, and the door opened to reveal a tall man wearing a long black robe and a crown tarnished blue-black.

"All hail the King Under Stone," one of the footmen

shouted. He banged a silver staff on the floor three times. "All hail the king!"

"All hail the king!" the guests chanted in reply.

As the man stepped into the room, Galen swallowed thickly. If the smiles and eyes of the courtiers had made Galen nervous, the appearance of their king made him break out in a cold sweat.

Skin as white as paper, taller and thinner than anyone Galen had ever seen, the king of the underground palace surveyed his court with eyes like chips of obsidian. His thin lips peeled back from sharp white teeth in a hideous parody of a smile.

"So nice to see that my sons' brides-to-be have at last recovered their strength," the king said in a wintry voice. "It is always so refreshing to see our royal flowers in bloom." His cold eyes rested on Rose. "Our dear Rose, especially."

Without thinking, Galen's hand went to his hip where once he had worn a pistol. He bit his tongue, though, and forced himself to relax so that he would not give away his presence.

The King Under Stone. Rose and her sisters were prisoners of the King Under Stone. Galen's knees almost buckled. There wasn't a mother in Ionia who hadn't frightened her children into obedience by using that name, or who hadn't prayed over the same child so they might never encounter that evil being.

He was the stuff of nightmares, the stuff of campfire tales. A magician so steeped in evil that he had ceased to be human, transforming himself and his most devout followers into something *other*: immortal and monstrous. According to legend, centuries ago every country on the continent of Ionia had risen up against him and cast him into an underground prison. He was too powerful to be destroyed completely, and trapping him in a sunless realm with only his followers to rule over had been the only solution. An army of white witches had been gathered to do the deed, and the effort had cost many of them their lives. It was a legend everyone knew.

And now it appeared that the legend was true.

The King Under Stone glided across the floor to the dais and sat in his tall throne. "Please, continue dancing. You know how much I enjoy the dancing."

The court tittered at this, and the king clapped his long, thin hands. The musicians began a jig, and Under Stone sat, immobile, his long silver hair hanging down either side of his skeletal face, and watched the princesses.

Pansy's partner had at last given in and allowed her to sit in a chair to one side of the room, asking one of the hard-faced court women to dance instead. Galen sidled across the room and sat in the empty chair beside the young princess.

"Paaaaansy," he whispered in a hollow voice. "Don't moooove. I am a goooood spirit!"

Pansy sat up straight and whimpered, her eyes flickering around as she searched for the source of the voice. "Who's there?"

"I'm a good spirit," Galen repeated. "I want to help yooooou."

She bit her lip, tears leaking from the corners of her reddened eyes. Galen's heart went out to her. This poor child was clearly beyond the edge of her endurance, but he didn't dare to put his arm around her. For one thing, good spirits did not wear heavy wool suits, and for another, he didn't want anyone to see Pansy's shoulders turn invisible.

"Why do you come here?" Galen asked.

Pansy wrinkled her nose. "We have to," she said in a matter-of-fact voice. She blinked, looking around again for the good spirit.

"But why?"

"Because of Mother, I guess."

"What did your mother dooooo?" Galen pressed.

"Pansy, get up!" Poppy had appeared in front of them. She had an anxious look on her face. She grabbed her little sister's hands and pulled Pansy off the chair. Poppy glanced nervously over her shoulder to where her partner stood in conversation with Pansy's. "You have to dance again!"

"I'm tired," Pansy whined.

"We're all tired," Poppy snapped. "But we still have to dance."

"But Telinros said—"

"Telinros doesn't matter," Poppy said. "Look at the king!" She jerked her head at the king, who was frowning in their direction. "You've sat out one dance; that's the most any of us get. Come along." And she led the drooping Pansy back to her partner.

From his chair, Galen watched Poppy and Pansy enter the dance once more. Rose whirled by with her suitor, and Galen briefly considered sticking out one of his boots and tripping the dark prince. He decided against it, though, since Rose might fall and hurt herself.

Galen sat back and observed. As the glittering court went around and around the dance floor, his eyes were drawn to the king. The King Under Stone sat even straighter on his throne. His eyes were shining and his white hair and skin had become silvery. As his courtiers and the princesses faded with exhaustion, the king appeared to become stronger, his skin almost glowing.

"He's feeding off their energy," Galen murmured, sickened. How had Queen Maude become embroiled in this? Had she been one of the courtiers? And why had her daughters become enslaved to the King Under Stone?

He found that he couldn't watch the king, or even the dancers, too closely. The whole spectacle sickened him. He let his eyelids slip halfway down and watched the feet of the dancers as they whirled by.

The striking of a great gong woke Galen some time later, and he realized that he had dozed off. Looking around frantically, he spotted Rose, and then quickly counted to make sure that the other princesses were there as well. The king had risen from his throne, rejuvenated, and the courtiers were assembling before him. The princesses with their partners came to stand in a space cleared for them in front of the dais.

"Another night has passed away," the pale king intoned. "Far above us in the mortal world dawn arrives in the kingdom of Westfalin. Two favors did I grant Queen Maude in return for four and twenty years dancing in my court. She gave me fourteen years before her death, five years and fifty-three days of payment remain. And then, my sons, you shall wed your princesses and keep them here to delight us forever."

The court clapped their pale hands and laughed their shivery laughs. The king's dark sons smiled down at the princesses with a proprietary air but the princesses merely stood, exhausted and silent. Galen edged around the crowd and stood behind Rose. Her head turned slightly, as though she heard him approach, but she said nothing.

The dark suitors led the princesses away then, through the long hallway and out the tall doors, to crunch down the black sand to the golden boats. Once more Galen hopped into the boat after Rose, and once more her suitor lagged behind the others, a disgruntled expression on his face.

At the far shore of the lake, the suitors helped the princesses out of the rowboats but would not take one step farther toward the forest. The princesses continued on alone, without looking back, into the silver trees.

Trailing behind Rose, Galen thought about what he would tell King Gregor. How to explain where the princesses went every night? How to tell the king that his late, lamented wife had made some sort of bargain with the strange, cold king of this underground realm? The princesses could not speak to support his story, and it was very likely that the king would not believe him.

As they passed beneath the gleaming, otherworldly trees, Galen reached up and snapped off a pair of twigs. The sharp cracking noise made Rose stop dead in her tracks, and she turned around, wildly searching for whatever had made the sound.

"What was that?"

"Rose?" Up ahead, lamp once more in hand, Lily turned and looked down the line of girls. "Are you all right?"

Galen stood very still, holding the twigs beneath his cape. They were cold, and very slick and hard. If he didn't know better, he would say that they really *were* silver, and not the product of a tree at all.

"Didn't you hear it?" Rose squinted at the trees. "There was a loud cracking sound!"

"I didn't hear anything," Lily said, her usually gentle voice impatient. "Let's go! The maids and your gardener will wake soon."

"I heard it too," Orchid said. She was standing just in front of Rose. "Maybe one of the branches broke."

The sisters all looked at the black ground around the trees, but no glint of silver from a broken branch or even a fallen leaf could be seen. Petunia got down on her hands and knees and crawled around the base of the nearest tree.

"Petunia, stop that!" Iris hauled the youngest sister to her feet. "You're getting filthy!"

Black mud that sparkled faintly in the light from Lily's lamp covered Petunia's skirt and the toes of her ruined dancing slippers.

Daisy was hopping from foot to foot. "We have to go," she said. "We've never been this late: the staircase is already there. What if it goes away again before we set home?"

Slipping the twigs into the pouch hanging from his belt, Galen strode after the princesses as they trotted through the woods and passed under the pearl-studded arch. Rose shut the gates behind them, nearly catching the tail of Galen's cape as he slid through. With a jolt Galen realized that they would expect to see him sleeping in the chair before the fire when they came up through the floor. He sprinted past the princesses, making Lily's lamp flicker as he passed, and took the golden stairs two at a time, trying his best not to make too much noise even as he raced ahead of them.

"What was that?" he heard one of them cry out as he passed.

Galen yanked off the cape and shoved it into his satchel as he dropped into the chair. He fought to turn his panting breath into snores even as, from beneath his lashes, he saw Lily's head rise up out of the black square in the floor. She came at once to his side and peered down at him, checking to see if he was still asleep. As the lamplight fell on his face, he snorted and shifted in his chair but didn't open his eyes.

"Is he still asleep?" Rose whispered.

"Yes," Lily whispered back.

Galen listened as they rustled about, helping each other undress and go into their separate bedrooms to catch a few precious hours of sleep. When they had left the sitting room, he took out his cape and refolded it so that it fit into the satchel better. Then he stretched and found a more comfortable position in the chair, to sleep a little bit himself. He had a lot to think about, but he was far too tired to reason it out now.

"I don't know how they can do it night after night," he mumbled as he drifted off. "Poor Rose. . . ."